RETURN TO THE WILD

SEEKERS

THE BURNING
HORIZON

SEEKERS

RETURN TO THE WILD

MANGA

Also by Erin Hunter

WARRIORS

EXPLORE THE
WARRIORS
WORLD

RETURN TO THE WILD

SEEKERS

THE BURNING
HORIZON

ERIN
HUNTER

HARPER

AN IMPRINT OF HARPERCOLLINS*PUBLISHERS*

Library of Congress Cataloging-in-Publication Data
Hunter, Erin.
    The burning horizon / Erin Hunter. — First edition.
        pages   cm. — (Seekers, return to the wild ; book 5)
    Summary: "The four bears are determined to reach Great Bear Lake
before the longest day gathering, but when Lusa is separated from the others,
she faces difficult questions about her future"— Provided by publisher.
    ISBN 978-0-06-199646-7 (trade bdg.)
    ISBN 978-0-06-199647-4 (lib. bdg.)
    [1. Bears—Fiction. 2. Voyages and travels—Fiction. 3. Fate and
fatalism—Fiction. 4. Fantasy.] I. Title.
PZ7.H916625Bu 2015   2014026691
[Fic]—dc23   CIP
                                                                 AC

                Typography by Hilary Zarycky
14 15 16 17 18   CG/RRDH   10 9 8 7 6 5 4 3 2 1
                            ❖
                      First Edition

Special thanks to Cherith Baldry

The Bears' Journey: Bear View

Lusa — — —
Kallik and Yakone –·–·–·–
Toklo ···············

Rock

BAFFIN ISLAND

The Melting Sea

BURN-SKY
GATHERING
PLACE

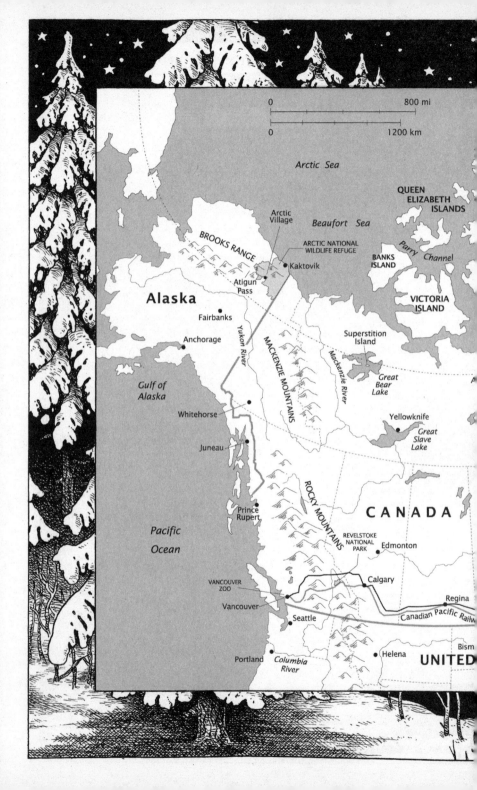

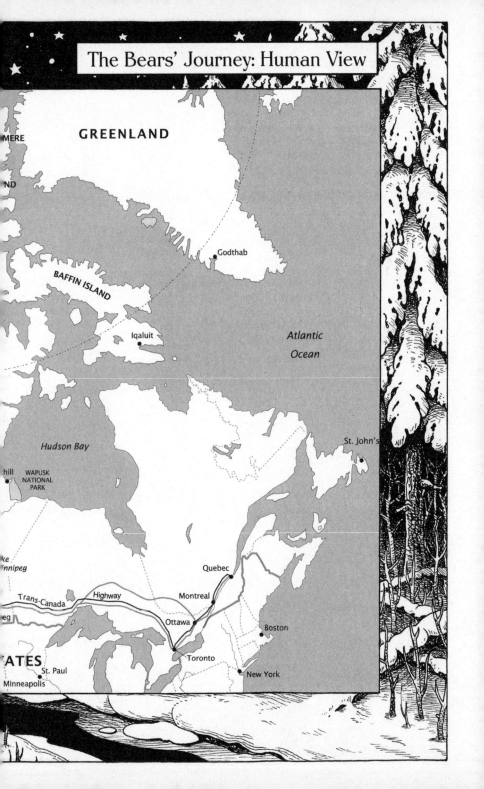

The Bears' Journey: Human View

GREENLAND

MERE

ND

BAFFIN ISLAND

Godthab

Iqaluit

Atlantic
Ocean

Hudson Bay

St. John's

hill

WAPUSK
NATIONAL
PARK

ke
nnipeg

Quebec

Trans-Canada   Highway   Montreal

eg   Ottawa   Boston

ATES   Toronto

St. Paul   New York

Minneapolis

CHAPTER ONE

Toklo

Toklo padded through the trees at the edge of the forest, with Lusa, Kallik, and Yakone a little way behind him. On one side of them the trees crowded closely together, while on the other the sheer wall of the Sky Ridge stretched up to the cloudless blue sky. The trees were in full leaf, but the shade gave only a little relief from the scorching sun. Toklo let out a grunt of discomfort, longing for the cool of evening and the chance to rest.

Each pawstep he took was more difficult than the one before, not only because of the heat and exhaustion, but also because each one took him farther from his own territory. Toklo could still feel the aches and cuts from his punishing battle with his father, Chogan, the old bear who had once driven him away with his mother Oka and his brother Tobi. In his mind he could still hear Chogan's threatening roars, smell the hot reek of blood, and feel fierce satisfaction as his claws slashed through his father's pelt. It was from Chogan that he had won his territory.

Chogan had better enjoy the rest of his time there, Toklo thought grimly. *Because it won't last long. He knows he only gets to stay for now because I promised to go with Lusa to Great Bear Lake.* Toklo felt strength and power flow through his body at the memory of his victory, but at the same time there were doubts in his mind. *Am I really old enough to have my own territory? Am I ready to be on my own?*

Toklo worried, too, that while he was away another strong brown bear might come and drive out Chogan from the territory he had just claimed.

But it's mine. He let out a soft growl. *Every pawstep of that ground holds memories for me, and I'll fight for it again if I have to.*

For a few moments Toklo concentrated on finding a clear path among the rocks strewn over the ground, and listened to the chatter of his friends behind him. Kallik and Lusa were discussing the journey to Great Bear Lake and telling Yakone how so many bears traveled there for the Longest Day Gathering.

"*Thousands* of bears!" Lusa exclaimed. "More bears than there are stars in the sky!"

Toklo let out a snort of amusement at the little black bear's excitement, but his thoughts soon drifted back to his territory. It felt strange to be leaving his brother Tobi's grave site behind, when he had only just found it. He pictured the small mound of earth beneath the overhanging rock with the berry bushes clustering around it, and his pawsteps grew heavier still. Suddenly it felt like he was tearing himself away from his brother. But he trusted the brown she-bear, Aiyanna, to look after the burial mound until he returned.

And I will return—to her. . . .

Feeling a curious pang pierce his chest, Toklo stopped and turned his head toward the Sky Ridge. *Is all this hesitation because of Aiyanna?*

He shook his head impatiently. *No, that can't be it. It's just my grief for Tobi and worry about my territory, that's all.*

"Toklo, are you okay?" Lusa scrambled over the rocky ground, her pelt brushing by arching fronds of fern, until she caught up with him. "Are you *sure* you want to keep traveling? The whole point of our journey now is to find homes for ourselves," she continued when Toklo didn't reply at once. "I know how hard it must be for you to leave the home you've just found." She butted his shoulder gently with her muzzle. "I'll understand if you think your part is over."

Toklo turned to look at Kallik and Yakone making their way toward him. They had left the Melting Sea to help him and Lusa find their homes, when they could have stayed with Kallik's brother Taqqiq and the other white bears.

I'm not the only one to leave something important behind, he thought, his resolve strengthening. *Because this matters more. All four of us should be together when we reach the end of our journey.* Grief prickled deep in his belly as he recalled how Ujurak had died on Star Island, protecting them from an avalanche. *We should be five. . . .*

From the corner of his eye Toklo spotted a frosty glint of light, as if a star had awoken beyond the branches of the forest trees. When he turned his head it was gone, but comfort flowed over him like a warm tide.

We are still five. Ujurak is watching over us.

"Thanks, Lusa, but I'm fine," Toklo said, touching her head with his muzzle. "We all need to reach the end of our journey before it's over, and that hasn't happened yet. I made you all a promise, and I'm keeping it."

"Great spirits, it's hot!" Kallik gasped, when she and Yakone had struggled up to join Toklo and Lusa. "I can't wait for burn-sky to end."

"By then we'll be back on the Endless Ice," Yakone reminded her as he gave her ear a friendly nuzzle. "We'll have our own home there. No more earth beneath our paws!"

The white male's words reminded Toklo once again of the sacrifice Yakone and Kallik were making by staying so long among forests and mountains. He noticed that Yakone was limping again, a few trickles of blood oozing from his injured paw.

It starts to heal, and then he stubs his toes on a rock, or trips over a branch, and it opens up again, Toklo thought. *He needs time to rest, but it's time we don't have. Not if we're going to reach the lake by the Longest Day.*

"Great Bear Lake, here we come!" he announced.

Lusa gave an excited little bounce. "I hope I meet Miki and the other black bears at the lake," she said to Toklo. "They taught me so much about living as a wild bear. I know they'll let me stay with them."

"Let's hope they're at the gathering again," Toklo responded to Lusa as they padded through the trees. "We rescued Miki from those spirit-cursed white bears, so his family owes you something. And I'll stay with you until we find them, or some other black bears you can live with."

Lusa blinked up at him affectionately. "Thanks, Toklo." She turned and stared up in dismay at a rocky shelf that blocked their path a few bearlengths ahead. A steep, tumbled slope stretched way above her head, with trailing plants and spindly bushes growing from the cracks. A fallen tree was wedged diagonally across the shelf, and the bears would have to push their way through its branches before they could even start the difficult climb up the rock.

"Great spirits, how are we going to get up there?" Kallik asked tiredly.

Toklo stopped for a moment, considering. The forest around them was silent except for the piping of a single distant bird. The sun shone warm on his fur; the air was still and stifling, without even the whisper of a breeze.

Kallik and Yakone must find the heat even harder to cope with than I do, Toklo thought.

Lusa had trekked along the bottom of the shelf, looking for a path. "Come over here!" she called. "It's easier once we get past that tree."

Following her, Toklo saw that she was right. Farther into the forest the rock wall was lower, the stones broken up with more vegetation in the gaps.

"Get on my back," he said to Lusa. "I'll boost you up the side of the cliff."

He could feel Lusa's claws digging into his fur as she scrambled up, then took a leap from his back and clung to the rock face. Earth and small stones showered down on Toklo as she climbed; a moment later he could see her bright face gazing down at him from the middle of a clump of ferns.

"There are plenty of pawholds," she told the others. "The climb isn't too bad."

Toklo wasn't sure about that. Kallik and Yakone weren't such agile climbers, especially now when they were tired. "What do you think?" he asked the two white bears as they plodded up to him.

"We don't seem to have much choice," Kallik replied. "We have to go this way. If we head farther into the forest, we'll be traveling in the wrong direction, and we don't know how far these rocks stretch." She gave Yakone a doubtful look. "Will you be okay?"

Yakone set his mouth determinedly. Toklo could see that he wasn't going to let his wounded paw hold him back.

"Don't fuss. I'll be fine," he growled.

Kallik opened her jaws as if she was about to protest, then closed them again without speaking, though she still looked uneasy.

To prove his words, Yakone dug his forepaws into cracks in the rock and scrabbled with his hindpaws to push himself upward. Kallik gave him a shove from behind to help him on his way, then followed. Once Toklo was sure they could manage, he began hauling himself up the cliff, tearing at the vegetation as he struggled to find pawholds. His claws were clogged with mashed-up leaves and his fur felt full of grit by the time he stood beside his friends at the top.

"Made it!" he grunted with satisfaction.

From the top of the cliff the ground fell away in a much shallower slope, covered with grass. At the bottom Toklo could see a lush growth of ferns, and he caught glimpses of a narrow stream winding its way among the clumps.

"Water!" he exclaimed, realizing for the first time how thirsty he was. "Come on!"

Lusa outran him as he galloped toward the stream, but the small black bear was so eager to reach the water that she tripped and went rolling head over paws down the slope. At the bottom she bounced up, pieces of leaf and twig clinging to her fur, and plunged her snout into the stream.

Toklo joined her, followed a few moments later by Kallik and Yakone. Kallik was matching her pace to Yakone's, whose limp seemed worse after the scramble up the rocks. Toklo knew that the white male's injured paw must be painful. The wound looked red and swollen, and blood was still trickling out, but neither of the white bears complained, just bent over the stream and drank thirstily.

"Yakone, are you okay?" Toklo asked. "Do you need to rest your paw?"

Yakone looked up, droplets of water spinning away from his muzzle. "My paw is fine," he said.

Toklo knew he was just being brave. *I know he worries about holding us back.* But Yakone clearly didn't want sympathy, so he said no more.

Lusa finished drinking and glanced around at her three friends. "You know, there aren't any other bears like us," she said.

Toklo gave her an affectionate nudge. "So you've met all the other bears in the world?" he teased her. "When did that happen?"

Lusa batted at him with one paw. "No, listen. Toklo, I know that what you really want is to stay here in the mountains on your own territory, and yet you drag yourself away from it for your friends. Kallik and Yakone left the Melting Sea for us. We've had help from flat-faces, like when Ujurak swallowed that fishhook, and we've traveled on a firesnake. How many other bears could say that?"

Toklo nodded reluctantly. He understood Lusa's point, but he wasn't sure that their choices had been the right ones. The two white bears looked grubby and exhausted, and Lusa was thinner and smaller than the other black bears they had met on their way. *Is it because she's been traveling for so long?*

As he was wondering whether they could afford a short rest, Toklo picked up a new scent on the air. His neck fur rose in apprehension as he lifted his snout for a good long sniff.

It smells like wolves . . . but not quite the same. Are we in danger?

"Keep still," he ordered in a low voice.

He sank down into the vegetation with the others beside him, all of them sniffing now. Toklo could make out only one scent, and after a few moments he spotted an animal slinking along the line of trees.

Not a wolf—a coyote!

Lusa let out a gasp of alarm, while Kallik and Yakone stiffened, their fur bristling. The creature seemed unaware of them. It was prowling along at a deliberate pace, its nose down and its gaze fixed on the ground, making Toklo think it was on its own hunt. Memories of how they had been tracked by the pack of fierce coyotes flashed back into his mind, but he squashed his fears down.

This coyote is alone, and it doesn't look like it's after us. It's hunting something else.

Thinking about hunting made Toklo realize how hungry he was. *I'd love to know what the coyote found,* he thought. *I haven't caught a sniff of prey all day.* "It might lead us to some food," he whispered to Kallik, who was closest to him. "Just one coyote and four of us—it should be easy!"

"Maybe." A gleam of humor woke in Kallik's eyes.

"So what's the plan?" Lusa asked.

"I think we should follow it," Yakone suggested. "Let it make the catch, and then we snatch the prey."

Kallik nodded. "Good idea."

"Okay, so we spread out," Toklo said. "That way if it runs off with its prey, one of us will be there to grab it."

The four bears rose to their paws and padded through the trees as quietly as they could, forming a wide ring around the coyote.

The stupid thing doesn't even know we're here, Toklo thought. *It's totally focused on its hunt.*

Watching Yakone limp through the undergrowth, a dark memory assailed Toklo of how the coyote pack had followed the trail of blood from his injured paw, relentlessly tracking them down. *This coyote could do just the same, given half a chance. But he's alone,* he reminded himself. *We'll be okay.*

By now Toklo had spotted the coyote's prey: a pika, a furry creature a little smaller than a rabbit. He signaled to the others to keep well back so as not to spook the little animal, and concentrate on tracking the coyote. He was enjoying the practice of putting his paws down silently, making sure that he didn't brush against the undergrowth.

He spotted Kallik maneuvering so that she stayed upwind of the coyote and crouching down to slide underneath a low branch. He could see from the glimmer in her eyes that she was enjoying this, too.

Wry amusement bubbled up inside Toklo as he watched the coyote snuffling along the pika's scent trail. All its attention was still focused on its prey. As it drew closer to the pika, Toklo signaled to his friends again, jerking his head for them to move inward, tightening the circle.

We don't want to lose it now.

The pika stopped to nibble something on the ground underneath a juniper bush, and that was when the coyote sprang, snapping its jaws shut on the pika's neck.

Before the coyote could take a mouthful of its prey, the bears leaped forward. Toklo let out a roar, hoping to scare it off. The coyote looked up, wide-eyed with alarm, then snatched up the pika and tried to dart away.

Kallik plunged forward and raked her claws along the coyote's side. "Drop it, mangefur!" she snarled.

The coyote let out a yelp of terror. For a moment it froze, expecting Kallik to deal it a killing blow. But she stepped aside and the coyote fled, leaving the pika behind.

Toklo padded up and gave the pika a sniff. "It's not much for four hungry bears."

"Three," Lusa said, beginning to grub happily in the ground among the ferns. "There are plenty of roots here for me."

Even divided among three, the pika did no more than take the edge off their hunger.

"Should we hunt some more?" Kallik suggested.

Toklo shook his head. "Look through the trees," he said. "There's another cliff ahead. And there'll be fallen trees, ravines, rocks. . . . We need to keep walking while it's still daylight."

Kallik gave Yakone a glance. "Are you worried Yakone will have trouble with the terrain?" she asked Toklo. "He'll be fine."

Yakone nodded. "You don't need to worry about me."

"I'm not," Toklo told him, not sure he was being entirely truthful. "But we'll walk at your pace, no faster. Let's go."

Another hard scramble brought the bears to the top of the next cliff and into a stretch of land where the trees were interspersed with wide-open spaces covered in long grass. With little shade, it was harder than ever to keep going. Toklo could see that the white bears were beginning to stagger, their chests heaving with each breath.

But we have to keep moving, or we'll never get to Great Bear Lake in time.

His belly still rumbling after his share of the pika, Toklo kept sniffing the air as he padded along. He had just picked up a warm prey-scent when he heard a startled yelp from Kallik.

A hare had jumped up from the grass right under her paws. Instinctively Kallik lashed out, and the hare dropped limply to the ground.

"Great catch!" Yakone praised her.

"I didn't do anything," Kallik said, looking dazed. "It was right there. How could I have missed it?"

"Maybe Ujurak sent it," Lusa suggested.

"Maybe," Toklo agreed. "Thank you, spirits, whoever you are."

Kallik picked up her prey and headed for the next clump of trees, which cast a welcome patch of shade. Gathering around, they all shared the hare.

When he had filled his belly, Toklo felt sleepy. The shadows were lengthening as the sun slid down the sky, and he was tempted to stay where they were for the night. He knew that none of the others would argue if he suggested it.

No, he thought, stifling a yawn. *We can manage another skylength before nightfall.*

They kept walking even after the sun had gone down, though light still lingered in the sky, until Toklo realized that none of them could go another pawstep. He halted at the edge of a hollow among the roots of a pine tree, with bushes overhanging it.

"Let's rest," he said. "This will make a good den."

Lusa puffed out a breath. "Thank Arcturus! My paws are falling off."

She slid down into the hollow. Kallik and Yakone followed,

careful not to squash her. Toklo hesitated for a moment, wondering if he ought to keep watch.

But I'm so exhausted, if anything crept up on us, I wouldn't have the strength to fight.

He clambered down into the den to join the others, wriggling to make space for himself. In the dim light he could see Lusa with her paws wrapped over her nose, and Kallik and Yakone lying close together, already snoring. With a sigh of relief, Toklo let himself slide into sleep.

Toklo woke and stirred in the temporary den, then stretched his jaws in a vast yawn. Poking his head out from under the bushes, he saw that the sky was paling toward dawn. Dew glimmered on the grass, and shreds of mist drifted among the trees. The air smelled clear and fresh.

His three companions were still sleeping, their bellies still comfortably rounded from Kallik's hare. This would be the third sunrise since the bears had set out from the Sky Ridge, and there had been more prey after that.

Leaving the others undisturbed, Toklo heaved himself out of the den and padded toward the edge of the trees to look out across the open grassland. All around him mountains rolled endlessly away, wooded slopes giving way to bare rock. Some of the summits shone white where snow still lay unmelted.

It's like we're the only living things in the whole world!

The thought had barely crossed Toklo's mind when a flock of birds flapped noisily out of the trees above his head, and immediately after a long screech ripped through the air, followed by a harsh rumble that throbbed in Toklo's ears.

Toklo's shoulder fur began to rise, though he knew the sound was only a firesnake racing through the trees along an unseen SilverPath. "I know it can't reach us up here," he grumbled aloud, "but it doesn't belong here, and I don't like it!" He shuddered at the memory of their journey on the firesnake, the speed and noise and the reek of flat-face stuff.

He turned his focus back to the mountains. Somewhere far ahead, beyond the rolling hills, was Great Bear Lake, where all the other bears would be traveling for the Longest Day. Toklo had made the journey before, but everything was different now.

I was so young then, so lost and angry and frightened. I didn't even know where I was going; I just knew that I had to leave the place where Oka lived because of her grief and her rage. Meeting Lusa and Ujurak was the best thing that could have happened to me. I wasn't lonely anymore, and they gave me something to live for.

A pang of grief pierced Toklo as he thought about Ujurak. *Is he watching me right now?* Looking up, he could see one or two stars still glimmering in the dawn sky, but he couldn't make out his friend's star-shape.

Toklo asked himself whether Ujurak would have told him to stay in his newly won territory. Lusa probably would have been fine traveling to the Longest Day Gathering with Kallik and Yakone, and they could have helped her to find a new home before heading off to find their own. And Kallik and

Yakone would always have each other, so no bear would be left alone.

There'll come a time when I have to make the long journey back here by myself.

Toklo's belly churned as he realized that by choosing to travel once again with his companions, he was putting off the inevitable separation.

A familiar voice echoed in his mind. "Perhaps it's fitting that the final part of your journey, to claim your own territory, should be alone, like a true brown bear?"

Toklo caught his breath. Turning, he saw a small, dark-furred bear standing beside him. "Ujurak!" he exclaimed.

"After all," Ujurak continued, as if they were in the middle of a conversation, "won't you get more respect at the Sky Ridge if the other bears know you as 'the wanderer'? The bear of all territories, the bear who has seen more of the world than any of them will be able to imagine?"

"Maybe . . ." Toklo murmured.

"Other brown bears will look upon you as fierce *and* wise," Ujurak said, "but only if you make it to Great Bear Lake, to the gathering. Nothing is more important than that right now. For Lusa, and for you."

Toklo put his head on one side. "What do you mean? Is something going to happen to me at the lake?"

"I can't say," Ujurak replied. "It's something you must discover for yourself. But trust me, it's vital for you to get there."

A rustling sound behind Toklo made him turn his head,

and when he looked back, Ujurak was gone. Lusa appeared through the trees, blinking and stretching as she stumbled up to Toklo.

"Why are you out here by yourself?" she asked through a massive yawn.

"I wasn't by myself," Toklo replied. "Ujurak was here."

Lusa's eyes sparkled with excitement, the last of her drowsiness vanishing. "Oh, I wish I'd seen him!" she exclaimed. "What did he say to you?"

Toklo decided not to tell her that Ujurak had said the gathering would be of huge importance to him. *It's all too mysterious,* he decided, wanting to think about it more by himself.

"Not much," he replied. "Or not much that I understood."

"Does he think it's right for you to go to the lake?" Lusa asked anxiously.

Toklo nodded. "Yes, he does."

"I'm so glad." Lusa let out a sigh. "It feels good having you with us."

The glittering edge of the sun was just appearing between two mountain peaks. Toklo glanced down at Lusa, seeing a deep sadness in her eyes as she watched. He moved closer to her so that their pelts were brushing.

"The four of us won't have many more times like this, will we?" Lusa murmured, leaning against his shoulder. "I know our journey together has been full of danger, but even so—I'll miss it."

"Me too," Toklo agreed. "It'll seem really strange, settling down in one place instead of moving on all the time."

"And no more adventures," Lusa said wistfully.

"I know," Toklo responded. "But it's time, Lusa—time to find a territory that truly belongs to us." He tried to sound cheerful.

"But we've made a territory for ourselves with every step of our journey, haven't we?" Lusa asked, turning her head to look at him with berry-bright eyes. "That territory will stay in our hearts through the memories we have."

Toklo had never thought of it like that. "You're right, Lusa," he said. "A territory in our hearts."

CHAPTER TWO

Lusa

Lusa swallowed her last mouthful of elk and swiped her tongue around her jaws. "That was great," she sighed. "We must be the best hunters in the whole wild."

"I'm stuffed," Toklo said, shuffling back from the carcass. "I feel as if I could sleep for a whole suncircle."

The four bears were sharing the prey near their temporary den, the hole underneath the pine tree. Sunlight glanced through the branches, and the air was full of warm scents. Lusa was struggling with drowsiness, too.

"It was a good idea to stay here an extra day and hunt, Toklo," she said. "We needed to build up our strength."

Toklo shrugged. "It just seemed sensible."

Lusa butted Toklo's shoulder gently with her head, knowing that he didn't want to act like he was in charge. "We all appreciated it."

But looking at her friends, Lusa was still worried. They all looked so tired, and their pelts seemed to be hanging from their bones, even though they had eaten well since they left the Sky Ridge. *Have we traveled too far?*

Still, it was good to see Kallik and Yakone contentedly sprawled out side by side, and the extra day's rest had helped Yakone's paw start to heal again.

"I know why you love the mountains so much," Kallik said to Toklo. "You hunt best among rocks and trees."

Toklo gave a pleased grunt. "True. But it's time to move on now."

He took the lead as they set out across the open grassland and then down a steep slope that led into denser forest. But as they plunged back into the shade of the trees, Lusa heard high-pitched yelping sounds, and the thump of heavy paw-steps, drifting up from somewhere below.

"Flat-faces!" Toklo exclaimed, halting.

He jerked his head, signaling to the others to scramble back to higher ground. Kallik and Yakone dove into the cover of a rocky outcrop, while Lusa joined Toklo behind a huge boulder a couple of bearlengths away.

The sounds of flat-face voices and the clump of their clumsy paws grew louder. Peering cautiously from behind the boulder, Lusa saw a ragged line of flat-faces heading diagonally across the slope. They all had huge black eyes that seemed to poke out of their faces, and brightly colored pelts. They moved slowly, looking around them, but Lusa didn't think they were hunting. They weren't concentrating enough for that.

"What are they doing?" Lusa whispered to Toklo. "They

didn't touch the berries on that bush, and they stomped right over those deer tracks. What do they want?"

The brown bear shrugged. "Who knows? We'll just wait here until they've gone, and then move on again."

But the flat-faces didn't pass by. Instead, they stopped, removed bundles tightly wrapped in pelts from their backs, and sat down. Yapping cheerfully to one another, they began pulling packages from their bundles. Even though she had eaten well, Lusa's belly began to rumble as she picked up the scent of food, and her jaws watered as the flat-faces opened the packages and began to pass the food around.

"Oh, spirits!" Toklo groaned. "If they're stopping to eat, they could be here for a while."

Looking around, Lusa spotted another path that curved upward, away from the slope where the flat-faces were sitting. She nudged Toklo to point it out to him. "There might be a way around the flat-faces," she murmured. "But we'll have to climb a little higher."

"It's taking us in the wrong direction," Toklo grumbled, then shrugged and grunted agreement, signaling to Kallik and Yakone. Lusa took the lead as they headed up the new path. It was wide enough for all of them to pass, but narrower than the paths they had used so far, and it wound around the hillside with a sheer drop on one side. Lusa began to worry that if it shrank any further, one of them might fall.

Yakone, just behind Lusa, slipped and dislodged a stone from the edge of the path. "Seal rot!" he muttered, but he managed to keep his balance. The stone bounced down the side of the mountain with a rattle.

The flat-faces had heard the noise. All of them looked up and pointed their paws, making chuffing noises. Lusa didn't think they were afraid; they seemed delighted to see the bears, their voices growing shrill with excitement as they raised small black boxes.

Lusa flinched, afraid the things might somehow hurt them. But she soon realized they were harmless. Still, her fur prickled at being exposed to the flat-faces' gaze.

It's like being back in the Bear Bowl.

A powerful vision of her first home flashed into Lusa's mind. The expanse of earth in the Bear Bowl seemed so small to her now, with a single tree and flat-face walls all around her. She remembered how the flat-faces had crowded around the edge of the Bear Bowl, gazing down at her and chattering. The first time she had ventured out from her BirthDen, she had been terrified.

Be brave and keep playing, her mother, Ashia, had said. *They won't hurt you, little one.*

For a moment the soothing sound of her mother's voice filled Lusa's head, blocking out everything else. Ashia had rolled over with her paws in the air and let Lusa scramble all over her; then she'd given her a piece of fruit to eat, and soon Lusa had almost forgotten the flat-faces. She felt safe, cared for, and so tired that she could sleep forever. . . .

Yakone stumbled against Lusa, jolting her back to the

sun-scorched mountain and the stones sliding beneath her paws.

"Lusa!" Toklo hissed from behind her. "What's wrong with you? We have to get moving *now!*"

Lusa realized that they might have only moments before the flat-faces started to pursue them. *That was then; this is now,* she told herself, shaking off the memories like a troublesome fly. *I'm a wild bear now.*

She set off again, trying to quicken her pace, but there were more loose stones on the path, and she had to put her paws down carefully. Then she spotted a dense patch of scrub a few bearlengths farther up the path and headed for it, hoping it was big enough for all of them to hide in. Glancing over her shoulder, she tried to see if the flat-faces were following.

As they left the path and plunged into the scrub, Lusa relaxed slightly. *Nothing bad has happened,* she thought. *And not all flat-faces are hostile.* Even so, she kept going, thorns and brambles raking her pelt as she pushed through. Once they had gained some height she checked and looked back, peering through the foliage to see if she could spot the brightly colored pelts. To her relief there was no sign of the flat-faces, and their voices had grown fainter in the distance.

Toklo lumbered to her side, glaring at a chipmunk that was chattering at him from a branch just above his head. "Don't stop," he muttered to Lusa. "Even if we don't see them now, who knows what they might do?"

He took the lead as they continued, on and on until they had left the flat-faces far behind. The scrub gave way to dense undergrowth beneath close-growing pine trees. At least it was cool under the deep shade, but their progress was slow. Lusa noticed that Yakone was struggling to clear a path for himself without putting his injured paw to the ground. *It must be hurting him again.*

Lusa ducked and wriggled among the clinging vegetation, then turned back to tug aside vines and brambles so the larger bears could get through. "Over here," she said to Yakone, as the white male halted in front of a particularly dense bramble thicket. She pointed him toward a narrow gully with stones at the bottom, where he could slide down and stoop underneath the bramble tendrils.

Yakone blinked his gratitude and managed to thrust his way through, his body almost filling the gully.

All around them were the sounds and scents of small prey.

"I can't believe we're passing up the chance to catch something!" Lusa muttered to Kallik.

The white bear unhooked herself from a clinging bramble. "Right now I'm more worried about scratching my eyes out," she responded.

"That elk will keep us going for a while," Toklo grunted, ducking beneath a vine. "We need to put some distance between us and those flat-faces before we stop."

"But they're a long way behind us now," Lusa pointed out.

Toklo let out a snort. "You can never be too careful."

The bears kept going, pawstep by weary pawstep, though now they could see no more than a bearlength in any direction and had no idea where they were going. Though they knew they had to head along the side of the ridge, Lusa felt confused, trapped beneath the tree canopy, unable to check their direction.

"I'm going to climb a tree," she declared, frustrated by their slow progress. "That might help us to find a clearer path."

She scrambled up a blue spruce tree that looked like it might be taller than the others. Breaking out of the forest canopy, she caught sight of a stretch of ground farther up the slope where young trees grew more sparsely. But before she could examine it further or look for flat-faces, she heard a harsh screech. Looking up, she saw a large bird diving toward her. It swooped down and battered her head with its wings, while its talons clawed at her face.

Lusa raised one paw to swat the bird away and lost her grip on the branch. With a yelp of alarm she plummeted to the ground, feeling twigs break beneath her. She landed with a thump on something soft and furry. When she could catch her breath and look around her, she realized that Yakone had caught her on his mighty shoulders.

"Thanks!" she gasped, sliding to the ground. "A bird flew right at me. I must have gotten too close to its nest."

"You're welcome," Yakone grunted, flexing his shoulders with a hiss of pain. "Anytime."

"I've had enough of this," Toklo barked. "Birds attacking us . . . chipmunks chirping at us . . ." He swiped a paw at another of the little creatures chittering at them from a nearby branch, but it was too far away for the blow to connect. "Stuck here, wedged in the undergrowth . . ."

"There's a clearer patch farther up the slope," Lusa said, nodding in the direction she had seen. "Let's go that way."

She urged the others on through undergrowth that seemed even denser than before, their paws tangling in brambles and vines as they pushed their way through clumps of dogwood. Panting hard, they struggled upward, only to freeze at the sound of more flat-face voices coming from close by.

"Here! Hide!" Lusa pushed Toklo into a thicket of barberry bushes and followed him into shelter, wincing as the thorns tore into her fur. Kallik and Yakone thrust their way in as well and crouched at Lusa's side.

"Couldn't you have found us a nice clump of ferns to hide in?" Kallik asked irritably, licking at her paw where one of the thorns had scratched it.

"Shh!" said Lusa.

All four bears watched warily as the flat-faces came into view, stumbling through the undergrowth on huge, clumsy paws. They were different from the ones who had stopped to eat, though they wore the same kind of brightly colored pelts.

Lusa's heart pounded, and she concentrated on staying still and silent. Kallik was trying to balance on three legs to keep her scratched paw off the ground, while Toklo had ended up in a shallow stream that flowed through the thicket. Lusa choked back a snort as she spotted him sinking slowly into the peaty ground. But her amusement faded a moment later as a spider dropped down on a thread of gossamer and landed on her nose.

It tickles! I'm going to sneeze!

Suddenly the flat-faces broke out into excited yelping. Lusa gasped, afraid she and her friends had been spotted, but just then a bird erupted from a nearby juniper bush, and all the flat-faces cried out in delight. Some of them raised the little black boxes Lusa had seen before.

I wish I knew what they were, she thought curiously.

She concentrated on keeping still, feeling the spider crawling up her muzzle and through her head fur. Kallik had settled down and was licking her scratched paw, while Yakone peered between two branches to watch the flat-faces. Toklo had a disgusted expression on his face as he sank even farther into the soft ground.

To Lusa's relief, the bird flew off and the flat-faces moved on, following a narrow trail through the trees. The bears waited until the sound of their voices and their clumsy paw-steps had died away into the distance; then they scrambled out of the barberry thicket.

Lusa could feel the spider crawling through her fur, and it felt like her whole body was one huge itch. All the bears' pelts were covered with scraps of debris. Toklo was soaked to halfway up his legs, and he squished as he walked.

"What's wrong with this place?" he demanded. "Why is it crawling with flat-faces?"

"At least they don't have firesticks," Lusa pointed out.

"And they're not very observant!" Yakone snorted. "How could they miss four bears? Kallik and I are hardly blending in."

Lusa thought that Kallik and Yakone were probably grubby enough to hide among the brown tree trunks, but she said nothing.

The four bears pressed on up the slope, toward the clearer area that Lusa had seen from the tree. Before long they came upon a trail, stony and covered with the prints of flat-face paws. Flat-face scent hung about it.

"Should we follow it?" Lusa asked.

Toklo hesitated, then shook his head. "We never used paths like these the first time we went to the lake. I wish we could, but there's too big a chance of coming across more flat-faces. I know the ones we've seen so far haven't threatened us, but we can't take the risk."

Lusa sighed. "Okay."

Pushing through the undergrowth again, they passed some berry bushes, and Lusa spotted a few bunches of berries that were already ripe. She stripped them off the branches and gulped them down, relishing the sweet taste.

At last they emerged in the clearer area where the undergrowth thinned out between the spindly young trees. They were able to walk more easily without thorns snagging their fur or digging into their pads. Lusa and Toklo enjoyed the warmth of the sunshine on their fur, but Kallik and Yakone kept to the shade as much as they could, panting beneath the spreading branches of a pine tree.

Lusa realized that now that they were clear of the dense forest, they could see for long distances again. Heading to look out from a bare outcrop, she let out a bark when she spotted a huge flat-face denning place spread out in the valley below.

"Look!" she exclaimed. "I thought we were in the wilderness!"

Toklo came to stand beside her. "Well, now we know where all the flat-faces are coming from," he grunted.

Lusa stared down at the expanse of flat-face dens that seemed to huddle together in the midst of the forest and mountains that encircled them. Light glinted from the surface of a river that looped around the dens. "I hope we don't have to go any closer," she said.

Kallik left Yakone, who had flopped down under the tree to rest, his eyes closed, and padded over to join Lusa and Toklo. "It might not be so bad," she said, scanning the valley more closely. "Look, there are a few small BlackPaths, but only one main one leading into the denning place. We just need to cross that and the river, and then we can head toward the sunrise."

"Now I remember," Toklo huffed excitedly. "Ujurak and I came this way before, when the Pathway Star guided us to Great Bear Lake the first time. I think it should be okay."

"Thank the spirits," Lusa murmured, grateful that she could trust Toklo's memory. *I don't recognize this place at all,* she thought as she looked around. *Toklo and Ujurak must have traveled this way before I met them.*

Her optimism rose again as she gazed out across the wide

landscape. Their way stretched out in front of them. Even the denning area couldn't daunt her, now that she could see there was a way around it.

I think Toklo's right, she told herself. *We will make it to Great Bear Lake in time.*

CHAPTER THREE

Kallik

Kallik stood beside Lusa and Toklo on the outcrop as they examined the terrain ahead and began to plan their route.

"We can't go near those flat-face dens," Toklo growled. "And we'll have to stay alert to avoid the flat-faces wandering through the trees. I don't know why they can't just stay on the BlackPaths."

Kallik knew she should concentrate on what the others were planning, but she couldn't stop worrying about Yakone. She kept casting glances back at him where he was resting under the pine tree. His wounded paw had never really healed since the battle with the wolves.

"Are you okay to keep going?" she murmured, padding over to him. "That paw doesn't look too good."

"It's okay," Yakone replied.

Kallik grunted and bent her head to sniff at the wound. Her worries increased as she picked up the sweetish scent of infection.

"Toklo! Lusa!" she exclaimed. "Yakone's paw is infected

again. We have to find herbs to treat it."

"Honestly, it's fine," Yakone protested, but none of the bears paid any attention to him.

"I'll go find some," Lusa promised, and darted off into the bushes.

Toklo shifted his paws impatiently. Kallik guessed he didn't want to stay in one place for too long, but they all knew Yakone's health was more important.

A few moments later Lusa reappeared with a mouthful of leaves. Kallik chomped them up, enjoying the clean, bitter taste, and trickled the juices into Yakone's wound.

"Thanks," Yakone said. "I'm sorry for slowing you down."

Kallik nuzzled his shoulder briefly. "You're not," she responded. "The undergrowth is doing that all on its own."

As soon as the bears set out again, they had to head back into denser forest where once again the undergrowth hampered their pawsteps. Toklo fell in beside Kallik, an anxious expression in his eyes. "Is Yakone really okay to travel?" he asked in a low voice.

"I think so. As long as we don't overdo it," Kallik replied.

"No chance!" Toklo snorted, halting to tear away a trailing vine from around his neck.

They had gone only a few bearlengths when once again they heard the sound of flat-face voices, along with a clattering noise they hadn't heard before. Peering around a juniper bush, Kallik saw another stony trail stretching across their path. The clattering sound was made by hooves: a long string of horses, with flat-faces on their backs.

"Flat-faces are so lazy," Kallik muttered.

There was a large group of riders, and some of the horses had another animal tied to them with a long tendril. The second kind was smaller than the horses, but looked similar, though those animals had much longer ears and a long face.

"Are those horses, too?" Kallik asked.

No bear replied, though Kallik noticed that Toklo seemed to be thinking hard, with a distant look in his eyes.

"I saw animals like them once when Oka and I raided a flat-face den for corn," he murmured. "What did she call them?" He relapsed into deep thought for a moment; then his face lit up and he exclaimed, "Mules! They're mules!"

All four bears peered through the bushes as the horses and their flat-faces filed past. The mules had lumpy packages fastened to their backs, wrapped in pelts bare of fur. The creatures had small eyes, their expressions cross and stubborn.

"I don't think I'd like to get mixed up with one of *them*," Lusa declared.

As she spoke, one of the mules started to skitter sideways, dragging on the tendril that tied it to the horse ahead of it.

"Uh-oh! I think it's picked up our scent," Toklo muttered.

The flat-face on the horse leading the mule turned around to bark at it, and the mule fell into line once more. As the flat-face turned, Kallik spotted a long firestick slung over his shoulder, and her fur prickled.

"What do you think they're doing?" Yakone whispered.

"Who knows what flat-faces do?" Toklo responded irritably. "Who cares? All we have to do is stay away from them."

"Then they should stay away from us," Kallik said. "The woods are for us, not them!"

When the line of horses had disappeared into the trees, the bears hurried across the stony trail. Kallik bristled again at the strange scents that filled the air, but Toklo and Yakone both started sniffing appreciatively.

"I wonder what horse tastes like," Toklo said.

"Or mule," Yakone added. "There's a lot of meat on one of those."

"The flat-faces wouldn't like it if you started hunting their animals," Lusa warned them.

Toklo and Yakone glanced at each other, then shrugged. "They're only flat-faces," Toklo said.

"They have firesticks!" Kallik exclaimed, stepping forward to block the two males' path. "Have you two got cloudfluff between your ears, or what?"

Yakone sighed. "I guess you're right."

Kallik headed off with determined pawsteps, glad to hear that the others were following her. The ground in front of them fell away into a steep slope, and farther down she spotted the walls of a flat-face den. As she veered away, dogs started barking, sounding uncomfortably close. All the bears picked up the pace; Kallik's heart started to thump harder as she waited for the crack of a firestick.

But no flat-faces appeared, and as Kallik and her friends plunged into deeper undergrowth once again, the sound of barking faded into the distance.

By this time, they were getting used to traveling through

the dense forest. Yakone and Toklo would hold vines and brambles out of the way so that Lusa could wriggle through and begin making a path. Then Kallik would stamp down the surrounding branches.

"We've come a long way like this," Kallik commented at last, "but any creature passing this way would be able to see our trail."

"But nothing is tracking us," Toklo pointed out. "And there are so many flat-faces around here, I doubt there are any hunting packs of wolves or coyotes."

Kallik realized that Toklo was right. She looked at the other bears, noticing that their fur lay flat on their necks and they seemed relaxed, almost cheerful, in spite of the difficult ground. Though they didn't talk much because they wanted to travel quietly, they made their way with good humor.

"You expect me to get through there?" Kallik murmured as Lusa squeezed underneath some low-growing thorn branches. "Do you think I'm a mouse?"

"Yeah, a really big mouse!" Lusa responded, her eyes twinkling with amusement.

"Wriggle on your belly," Toklo suggested, managing to hold the branches a little higher to make room for Kallik. "And Yakone, watch out for that root. You don't want to bang your injured paw."

Yakone took the lead after they had negotiated the thornbushes. The slope was flattening out, and from somewhere ahead Kallik could hear the sound of running water.

Suddenly Yakone stopped. While Kallik glanced around for any signs of danger, he stalked forward again, then plunged into the lush vegetation that edged the stream. A moment later he stood up, holding a grouse in his jaws.

"Good catch!" Lusa exclaimed.

"Yeah, nicely done," Toklo added. "Let's rest for a bit and eat."

Before they settled down to share the grouse, all the bears took a drink from the stream. Standing beside Yakone, Kallik nudged his shoulder with her muzzle. "That was great," she said. "I'd never have known there was a grouse there."

"I got lucky," Yakone responded, though Kallik could hear the satisfaction in his voice. She was glad that he'd had a chance to provide food for them. *Now maybe he'll stop worrying that he's holding us back.*

Yakone tore the grouse apart, dividing it between himself, Kallik, and Toklo. Lusa was already digging up ferns and crunching the roots.

"Tell me more about the Longest Day Gathering," Yakone said through a mouthful of prey. "What happens there?"

"Like I said, lots and lots of bears meet together by a lake," Lusa explained. "Black bears, and brown and white. I've never seen so many bears in one place!"

"They exchange news and tell stories," Toklo said.

"Yes, and there's a ceremony," Kallik added. "At least, the white bears hold one. The oldest and wisest bear calls on the sun to leave so that the dark and cold can return. It's wonderful. . . . But it seems like such a long time ago that we were there," she finished with a sigh. "We've seen so much since then."

"And Ujurak was with us." Toklo looked sad for a few moments, then swallowed his last bite of grouse and sprang to his paws. "Let's get going!"

They crossed the stream and carried on over ground where the trees grew farther apart and they could make better progress. After a while Kallik heard the sound of running water again, this time a deep, slow surge. Flashes of astonishing blue appeared through the leaves, and a few pawsteps later they broke out into the open to see a river in front of them, lined on one side by a small BlackPath. "This must be the river we saw from the edge of the forest," Lusa said.

A shallow slope led down to the BlackPath and water, and on the other side of the river, a steeper slope climbed up to another ridge.

Toklo looked up to check the angle of the sun and the direction of the mountain slopes. "Yes, this is where we have to cross," he said with a confident nod.

Beyond the BlackPath the mighty current of the river rolled onward, the water reflecting the blue of the sky. Flecks of foam dotted the surface, and small waves broke against the rocks on the shore.

Kallik's paws tingled with excitement. She and the others waited at the edge of the BlackPath, crouched behind a bush for cover, while a firebeast crammed with flat-faces roared past. Then they raced across the BlackPath, scrambled over the rocks, and plunged into the water, heading for the far bank.

The cold shock of the water felt wonderful as Kallik struck out into the current. But it had been so long since they'd encountered deep water that she struggled a little until she found her rhythm. She glanced back to make sure her friends were coping.

Toklo was gasping and splashing but managing to stay afloat, and Yakone, beside him, was carving across the current with powerful strokes. Lusa had dropped back a little, so Kallik swam around in a circle back to her. As she reached Lusa's side, she noticed a small group of flat-faces bouncing toward them over the waves in some kind of broad, shallow thing that looked like a huge upturned leaf. Toklo and Yakone had already swum past it, but she and Lusa were right in its way.

"Great spirits, what's that?" Lusa gasped, staring at the flat-faces in terror.

The flat-faces had begun shouting and pointing at them and beating the water with wide-ended sticks. The upturned leaf carrying the flat-faces loomed up at them, springing off the waves until Kallik could see air beneath it. In another moment it would be on top of them.

Kallik looked around in desperation, but there were no rocks nearby, nowhere to hide, only the wide expanse of the churning torrent. Beside her Lusa was paddling frantically to stay afloat.

There's only one place to go. . . .

"Hold your breath!" Kallik barked to Lusa.

She grabbed the black bear by her scruff and dove down

below the surface of the water. The river crashed and foamed around them, rolling them over until Kallik lost all sense of direction. *This is nothing like swimming in the ocean!*

She kept striking out with her paws until the roaring in her ears faded and she reached deeper, stiller water. She still held Lusa's scruff in her jaws, willing the panicking black bear not to struggle.

A shadow fell over them, and Kallik looked up to see the huge shape of the flat-face leaf-thing passing above them. Blurred faces stared down at them, and the water was pierced by the flattened sticks.

Kallik dug her hind claws into the grit of the riverbed, crouching low over Lusa to protect her, as the current carried the flat-faces away. One of the sticks struck her back, and then was gone.

Getting a firmer grip on Lusa, Kallik dragged her back up to the surface. Both of them began gasping and choking as soon as their heads emerged. Farther downstream the flat-faces were twisting around to stare and shout at them, but there didn't seem to be any chance of them turning their leaf-thing back toward the bears. Kallik had to get Lusa to shore before her strength gave out. The small black bear was in no shape to swim on her own now.

With a stab of relief she spotted Toklo's head bobbing in the water beside her. Together they hauled Lusa to the shore, where the black bear lay limp on the pebbles, barely breathing. Yakone had run ahead to find cover and to keep a lookout for more flat-faces.

"Lusa!" Toklo nuzzled urgently at her shoulder. "Lusa, wake up! Lusa!"

With a jerk, Lusa coughed up a huge mouthful of water and shakily sat up.

"Are you okay?" Kallik pressed.

"Yes. I think so. Thanks, Kallik," she gasped. "But give me a bit more warning next time you want me to turn into a fish!"

"We can't stay here," Toklo urged. "Let's get under cover of the trees."

Yakone was already waiting under the branches, and when Lusa rose to her paws, they all headed into cover and began to climb again.

The smell of Kallik's fur wreathed around her with the tang of water and a faint trace of fish. For a moment she wished that they could stay by the river and hunt. *But those flat-faces might come back,* she told herself. *Better to get as far away as we can.*

The sun was going down, and Kallik heaved a thankful sigh as the heat of the day faded and a cool breeze sprang up. As twilight gathered, the bears found a place to sleep in the middle of a juniper thicket.

"This is good," Kallik said approvingly. "The smell of the bushes will hide our scent."

"But we have to hunt before we sleep," Toklo reminded her. "I'm starving!"

Kallik and Toklo set off, leaving Lusa and Yakone dragging ferns into their temporary den to make it more comfortable. Toklo headed into the trees, while Kallik prowled around closer to the bushes. While she hunted, she stayed alert for the sound of more flat-faces.

The undergrowth was full of the scent of prey, and before long Kallik picked up the traces of a partridge. Setting down her paws as lightly as she could, she crept up on the ground-nesting bird, her jaws watering with anticipation. But the partridge must have heard her approach, because when Kallik was still just out of reach, it let out an alarm call and exploded upward in a flurry of wings. Kallik leaped and batted the bird out of the air, holding it down with one paw while she ended its struggles with a bite to its neck.

When she returned to the den with the partridge dangling from her jaws, she met Toklo on his way back, carrying a squirrel.

"Good job," he mumbled around his catch. "We'll eat well tonight."

Inside the thick covering of the juniper bushes, the four bears shared their prey. Kallik felt almost too exhausted to eat, but she felt a warm satisfaction that they had crossed the river safely.

"Lusa, you won't forget your underwater swim in a hurry," Toklo teased. "Maybe you'll show me how to do it sometime."

"Oh, sure," Lusa retorted sleepily. "Right after you and Yakone show me how to hunt horses!"

A harsh squawk from somewhere overhead woke Kallik. Stretching her jaws in a yawn, she looked around to see pale light filtering through the branches of their den. Her companions were still sleeping. The harsh call came again, along with a flutter of wings as the unseen bird took off.

We've never been in such a noisy place! Kallik thought crossly, wishing she could go back to sleep. *My ears are ringing!*

The second call had roused her friends, and they all pushed their way into the open. The air was cool and clear, and above their heads the sky was pale blue without a trace of cloud. Kallik felt brighter as they set out, enjoying the fresh scents all around her and the shade of the trees.

More narrow, stony trails crossed their path, and Kallik's paws itched to follow one that seemed to be going in the right direction. "It would be great not to have to struggle through brambles the whole time," she sighed.

Toklo shook his head. "It's too dangerous, you know that. Besides, we can't be sure it would go the right way."

Reluctantly Kallik agreed. The scents of horses, mules, and flat-faces were too strong to risk it, and she followed Toklo without protest as he headed across the trail and back into the undergrowth.

Only a few bearlengths later Toklo halted, pointing with his snout to a set of clawmarks scored into the bark of a pine tree. A familiar scent drifted into Kallik's nostrils. "There's a brown bear living around here," Toklo said. "We'd better stay out of his territory."

"Did you meet him last time?" Kallik asked.

Toklo shook his head. "He must have moved in since then," he replied. "Or maybe we just missed the edge of his territory."

Following Toklo, they veered to the side, tracking the scent marks and scratches on the trees in an effort to skirt the brown bear's territory. Kallik's fur prickled with apprehension as she padded quietly along, hoping not to attract the bear's attention.

I hope he's over on the other side of his territory. We have enough problems without getting into a fight.

"If I were this bear," Toklo said as they came to a small stream bubbling along among rocks, "I would make this my boundary. A stream makes a good barrier."

"Let's check!" Lusa bounded on ahead for a few bearlengths and halted underneath a gnarled oak tree. "You're right!" she called back. "Here are some more markings!"

"Lusa," Toklo grunted as the others caught up to her. "Don't go dashing off like that again. We *know* there could be a hostile bear about."

"Okay," Lusa muttered. "Sorry."

Toklo fell silent as they walked along the edge of the brown bear's territory. Kallik wondered if he was thinking about the territory waiting for him—and maybe the she-bear Aiyanna who was guarding his brother's burial mound.

"One day you'll have your own territory," she said to Toklo. "And bears will have to avoid *your* scent."

Toklo nodded. "I won't fight any bear unless I have to, though," he said. "I'm not like Chogan."

A short way farther on, the stream vanished into a patch of swamp surrounded by brambles and spindly dogwood. The bears circled around it warily, looking for the next set of clawmarks.

"Let's check over there," Yakone suggested, pointing with

his snout at a lightning-blasted tree on the edge of the swamp. "It's the only spot where you could put a clawmark."

Heading for the tree, Kallik saw that Yakone was right. The bear had scored his claws deep into the trunk of the dead tree. She could see the next set of clawmarks, too, on a pine tree well away from the direction she and her friends were traveling.

"Thank the spirits!" she exclaimed. "The boundary curves away here."

"And we haven't met the bear," Toklo added with satisfaction.

As they left the unseen bear's territory, Kallik began to hear more sounds from up ahead: horses clattering along a stony trail with their hard paws, and the occasional bark from a flat-face. *Not again* . . . As they approached the sounds grew louder, and they were somehow different, harsher and more confused, from what they had heard before.

Peering out of the bushes, Kallik was astonished to see a plump flat-face on a horse followed by a long, long line of mules, far more than she could count, all linked together by vine tendrils. Each mule carried a bundle on its back, each bundle almost the size of a black bear. Farther down the line, more flat-faces on horses flanked the mules.

The bears crouched down to hide in the bushes to watch them all plod past.

"Seal rot!" Yakone muttered. "We'll have to wait until they've gone."

Kallik's fur prickled with anxiety. The line of mules seemed never ending. *How many more can there be?* she wondered.

Then one of the mules balked, sidestepping and tugging on its vines as if it wanted to flee.

"It knows we're here," Toklo growled. "Now the flat-faces are sure to spot us."

Kallik tried to press herself closer to the ground as the panic spread through the line of mules, more of them throwing up their heads and letting out high-pitched whinnies. The vines that held them snapped taut, holding them in place with skittering paws. Kallik heard annoyed barking from the flat-face at the front.

"I can hear more flat-faces. Coming up behind us!" Lusa whispered, her eyes wide with dismay.

Kallik swiveled around. She picked up the flat-face scent, then stiffened as several bright-pelted flat-faces emerged through the trees, chattering away and heading straight for her and her friends. They didn't seem to be aware of the bears or the mules. "Now what do we do?" she hissed.

On both sides the undergrowth pressed in on them, its thorny walls a barrier that was impossible to break through. There was nowhere to go but forward, but the long mule train was still blocking their route.

"Will it ever end?" Toklo muttered.

The flat-faces behind them drew closer and closer, until Kallik could hear them breathing. *Much closer and they'll step on us!*

"We can't stay here," Toklo growled. "We'll have to charge the line of mules."

"But we won't be able to get through!" Yakone objected.

"It's the only way. We'll have to charge at a gap between two of them." Toklo glanced from Kallik to Lusa. "Ready? We'll meet up on the other side of the trail."

Lusa nodded, her eyes wide with fear.

"Okay," Kallik said, trying to crush down the terror that was surging up inside her.

Yakone gave a nod as well.

"Now!" Toklo roared.

Together all four bears plunged out of their hiding pace and down onto the trail, crashing into the line of mules. The mules reared up and let out screeches of alarm, their fore-legs kicking at the air. Struggling to escape from the bears, they became entangled in the vines that bound them, quickly changing from an ordered line into a shifting, impenetrable mass.

Kallik, in the lead with Toklo, found herself caught up in the vines that attached the mules to one another; within a heartbeat they became wrapped around her legs so she could hardly move. Toklo was trapped, too, roaring as he tried to bite through the vines and escape from the terrified, thrash-ing mules.

BOOM!

The crack of a firestick sounded above the shrieking of the mules. Panic washed over Kallik, and she found herself crash-ing into the other bears as they all tried to flee. She caught a glimpse of the plump flat-face running down the trail toward them, aiming his firestick again.

"Get back to the bushes!" Toklo bellowed.

But it was impossible to retreat. Rocks and undergrowth hemmed them in, and they were trapped with the panicking, kicking mules all around them.

BOOM!

Kallik saw a paw-sized chunk of rock fly off a nearby boulder a heartbeat after the firestick explosion. It flew through the air toward her, and before she could duck, it struck her on the side of the head. Her vision blurred and she stumbled; then she felt Toklo and Yakone grabbing at her, pulling at her fur. Noise and an echoing darkness swirled all around her.

Oh, spirits, come and save us!

CHAPTER FOUR

Lusa

Panic flooded through Lusa when she saw the flat-face raising his firestick. She tried to run, but one of the mules' vines was wrapped around her front paw. Drawing on all her strength, she wrenched at it until the vine snapped, and with a desperate, scrambling wriggle she managed to reach the edge of the mule train. At the roar of the firestick she ran as fast as she could back up the slope to where they had started.

Behind her the air was full of the bellowing of bears and flat-faces and the trampling of many paws. A bird screeched in alarm. All Lusa wanted was to hide. But as she hurtled forward she saw the group of bright-pelted flat-faces that had been behind them scattering in front of her. One of them let out a yell and waved its forelegs above its head.

Lusa ducked behind a large tree, her heart thumping with fear. Then she scrabbled through a bush, swerving away from the flat-faces, ignoring thorns that tore at her pelt. For a moment she thought she had escaped; then the ground gave way under her paws, and she rolled down a steep bank and back onto the trail, where the bears and mules were still in a mix of chaos. She landed with a thud that drove the breath out of her body.

The paws of the rampaging mules stamped a snout's length from Lusa's head. Rolling away from them, she scrambled to her paws. A few bearlengths away she could see her friends, struggling in the midst of mules that flailed at them with their hard paws. Flat-faces were shouting and the mules were letting out high-pitched whinnies, while the bears bellowed as they fought to escape.

Lusa stared in horror as one of the mules near her started bucking madly, breaking free from the vines that tethered it. The mule reared up, shrieking. Its forelegs kicked out, and one of its sharp, rocklike paws hit Lusa on the head.

Pain sliced through Lusa. She staggered and fell onto her side, her vision blurring, and a sound like rushing water filling her ears. She struggled to stand up, but her legs felt too weak to support her. She stumbled back to the ground again and took a moment, breathing hard, before she managed to push herself to her paws.

Beneath the roaring in her ears, Lusa thought she could hear her friends running through the trees on her side of the path. They must have given up on getting across. Her eyes were streaming, but she managed to pick out vague, swirling shapes in the shadows. She hauled herself up the bank once again and began to run.

Behind her, the sounds of struggling pulsed loud and soft in her ears. The forest around her seemed to shift and blur, and though she blinked she couldn't clear her vision. Unable to find a safe path, she crashed from tree to tree, with brambles ripping at her fur.

Oh, Arcturus, help me!

Lusa stumbled on past many trees, thinking this must be the way she'd seen her friends go. Gradually the roaring in her ears died away, and she could see clearly again. Blinking, she halted and looked around.

"Toklo? Kallik?"

There was no reply. Bewildered, Lusa turned around to face the way she had come. *They must be behind me. They're on their way, right?*

But agonizing moments passed, and there was no sign of Toklo, Kallik, or Yakone. Lusa crouched, motionless, pain still throbbing through her head as she tried to control her breathing and the pounding of her heart so that she could listen. But the only sounds that came to her ears were the trampling and braying of the mules in the distance, along with the irritated grumbles of the flat-faces who were trying to get them under control.

Lusa sniffed the air, but all she could pick up was the fear-scent of the mules and the acrid tang of firesticks. There was no scent of any of her friends.

I've lost them! Lusa thought helplessly, staring into the dark trees.

"Toklo! Kallik! Yakone!" she called again, but her voice was lost in the echoes from the dense trees, and beneath the squawk of birds startled by her roar. Trees loomed over her head, and a whirling darkness threatened to engulf her.

The pain in Lusa's head where the mule had kicked her grew worse and worse. It felt like an aching heartbeat in her skull, or a stabbing claw hurting her again and again, clouding her mind so she couldn't think. She reached up with her forepaws to the place where the pain was, but it didn't help, only unbalanced her and sent her stumbling through the trees.

Lusa slumped down on her side and looked around. The sound of the mules had faded away, and now she wasn't even sure which direction she had come from. *Oh, spirits—how am I going to find the others?* She was afraid that they had run and run like she did, thinking that they were all still together. *They could be* anywhere *by now!*

Growing more desperate with each moment, Lusa heaved herself up again and went on searching and calling, crawling through bramble thickets and scrambling over rocks in her frantic search for some trace of her friends. *There must be something—a pawprint or a lingering scent.*

At last, exhausted, Lusa collapsed to the ground. Dazed and terrified, she tried to figure out where she was. She needed to find the other bears. Peering up through the branches, she tried to recognize the peaks that were just visible above the trees. Could she figure out which way they'd been heading before they met the mules?

"If I go in the same direction," she said aloud, trying to sound confident, "I'll meet up with them . . . won't I?"

Lusa rose to her paws and staggered through the trees on

unsteady legs, only to halt as another frightening thought came to her.

What if they've noticed I'm not with them, and they've turned back to look for me? What if the flat-faces find them? They could be risking their lives for me.

Trying hard to squash her fears down by doing something practical, Lusa checked the angle of the sun and studied the shape of the mountains and the way the trees grew. *There should be a peak shaped like a squirrel's tail,* she thought, trying to focus on her distant memories of her first journey to the lake. Lusa couldn't see that particular mountain from where she was, but she set off again on what she hoped was the right path. She blundered through the trees, trying to avoid the worst of the thornbushes and brambles, but as she waded through a stretch of long grass, she failed to notice the edge of a bank and half fell, half slid into a muddy stream, landing in the water with a splash.

Lusa dragged herself out, her pelt covered in mud, and scraped her paws on a patch of low-growing, thorny plants that covered the far bank. Her head still spun, and she realized she had lost all sense of direction again. She wished that it was night, so that she could follow the Pathway Star.

As Lusa tried to regain her bearings, a flicker of movement caught her eye. She turned her head to see a flat-face appear from behind a nearby tree. Startled, Lusa shrank back. *I should have picked up his scent long before he got this close.*

The newcomer was big for a flat-face, with gray head-fur and a bright-scarlet pelt. He stood still for a moment, shock and fear in his eyes. Then he raised his forepaws and let out a roar.

Lusa flinched away from him, pressing herself against the tree trunk behind her. *It's okay! I'm not going to hurt you. Just leave me alone!*

Then another flat-face appeared, smaller than the first one. When it opened its jaws and began yapping at the first flat-face, Lusa guessed that she was a female because of her higher voice. She had put one of her paws on the tall flat-face's arm and was looking at Lusa with kindness in her gaze.

I think she's asking that fierce flat-face not to hurt me.

Lusa took a lumbering step sideways, shifting away from the flat-faces and keeping her head low in an attempt to show them she wasn't a threat. She moved slowly and carefully, aware that it was important not to spook them.

But her head was hurting so badly now that she could hardly stand up. Her vision blurred again, shadows pressed around her as if they wanted to swallow her, and her hind legs felt too wobbly to hold her up. She staggered, took another wavering pawstep, and collapsed onto her flank.

Lusa was dimly aware of the flat-faces approaching her, slowly and cautiously. She knew she should run away, but she felt too exhausted, and was in too much pain, to move a single step. The flat-faces were talking to each other again; their voices were gentle and low-pitched, and she had a sudden memory of being in the Bear Bowl, where the flat-faces brought her food and spoke to her in the same gentle tones.

Ashia should be here, Lusa thought woozily. *And Yogi and King . . .*

Where are they all? And is that fruit I smell?

Her senses were drifting away when she felt flat-face paws pushing at her, and she realized that they were rolling her onto a flat, shiny pelt. A moment later she felt herself being dragged over the bumpy ground. As she lurched to one side, she let out a groan and felt a flat-face paw, warm and hairless, touching the side of her face. The female flat-face made a sound that Lusa guessed was meant to be soothing.

This is all wrong, Lusa thought. *I should be running away, finding the others. . . .*

But her head hurt so much, and she didn't even have the strength to raise a paw. Everything around her was blurred, and with a long sigh Lusa let herself slip into the waiting shadows. As she drifted into sleep, she heard a bear roar at the very edge of her hearing. She tried to stir, but the darkness tugged at her limbs and dragged her down. . . .

CHAPTER FIVE

Toklo

Rock-hard paws slammed into Toklo on all sides. Vines clung to his legs, and the air throbbed with the screeches of mules and the yells of the flat-face with the firestick. In the chaos he had lost sight of the other bears.

Enough!

Toklo braced himself, standing solidly on all four paws. Drawing air into his lungs, he let out a massive bellow.

The mules scattered, panic-stricken, scrabbling and screeching as they tried to get away from him. He spotted Yakone through the shifting mass of bodies; the white bear was untangling a vine that was wrapped around Kallik's legs. There was no sign of Lusa, but Toklo guessed that she must be hidden somewhere among the mules. "This way!" he roared.

Toklo saw Kallik break away, but Yakone was blocked by a huge black mule. Teeth snapping, eyes rolling, it lashed out at him with sharp paws. Yakone tried to dodge around it, but it charged at him and he tripped over a trailing vine. The mule's flailing hooves kicked him hard in the side.

Realizing that Yakone wasn't following her, Kallik veered back, while Toklo halted and roared again with all his strength. The black mule by Yakone panicked even more, sidestepping so that Yakone could scramble to his paws and flee.

With both white bears now hard on his paws, Toklo charged into the bushes at the far side of the trail. *Well, that was a disaster,* he thought sourly.

Hearing the others crashing through the undergrowth behind him, he plunged deeper into the bushes, the shouts of the flat-faces and whinnies of the mules fading behind him as he forced his way through. Toklo's ears were ringing, he felt battered, and every hair on his pelt was on end. He halted, panting, in a clearing surrounded by dense trees and waited for the others to catch up with him.

Within moments, Kallik and Yakone pushed their way into the open. Yakone was limping, but Toklo noticed with relief that his injured paw wasn't bleeding.

"Where's Lusa?" he asked when the black bear didn't follow the two white bears out of the undergrowth.

Kallik and Yakone gazed around in bewilderment. "I thought she was with you," Kallik said.

Toklo shook his head. "She must be around here somewhere," he said, trying to ignore the first faint stirrings of anxiety. "I didn't see her out there. Let's wait for her here and give her a chance to catch up."

Both white bears flopped down with huffs of relief and began checking each other over for injuries.

"Are you both okay?" Toklo asked them. "Are you hurt?"

Kallik raised a paw to rub the side of her head; Toklo saw that one of her eyes was almost closed. "I got knocked over when a mule ran into me, but the pain's not so bad now," she replied. "I think I'm okay. Yakone, I saw you take a bad kick."

"Stupid mule," Yakone growled. "But it's nothing. Don't worry." He began to lick Kallik's damaged eye, drawing his tongue across it with strong, gentle strokes.

Toklo sat beside them, noticing for the first time a gash in one of his forelegs. His pelt around it was matted with blood, but the bleeding had stopped. He felt as if every inch of him was covered with bumps and scrapes, but as he flexed his muscles he realized he wasn't badly hurt. "We need Lusa here to find the right kind of herbs for healing," he murmured.

Where is she? His anxiety returned, stronger now, like a claw striking deep into his belly. Raising his head, he listened for the sound of Lusa's paws breaking through the undergrowth, and sniffed to pick up a trace of her scent. But there was nothing.

"Lusa!" he called. "We're over here!"

There was no reply.

"Maybe she ended up farther down the trail," Kallik said. Her voice was confident, but Toklo could hear the concern underneath it. "She'll need time to get back."

Toklo tried to distract himself by cleaning his matted pelt, breaking off now and then to listen for Lusa. But the small black bear still didn't appear. *She should have found us by now,* he thought.

Kallik rose to her paws and called out Lusa's name again, but there was no response.

"She's not coming," Yakone said at last.

Now real fear bit into Toklo like a coyote's jaws. "Stay where you are," he ordered the others, and headed back the way they had come. "Lusa! Lusa!" he called again as loud as he dared, not wanting to attract the attention of the flat-face with the firestick.

Kallik and Yakone hadn't obeyed his order, catching up with him at the edge of the trail. By this time the mules and flat-faces had gone, leaving behind them trampled under-growth and scraps of broken vines.

"Let's spread out, and then meet back here, beside this juniper bush," Kallik said. "Surely Lusa crossed the trail . . . she can't be far away. Maybe she got stuck in some brambles."

"Okay, we'll meet when the sun gets to the top of those trees," Toklo agreed, pointing with his paw.

Kallik and Yakone took off along the trail in different directions, while Toklo headed farther into the trees. He expected to find Lusa battling her way through the undergrowth, look-ing for him and the others. But though he searched under bushes and in thickets of bramble, calling Lusa's name, he found no trace of her, not even her scent.

Deeper anxiety still welled up inside him when he reached the meeting point to discover that no one else had been able to track down the little black bear.

Kallik voiced Toklo's own fear. "What if she was badly

hurt? Too badly to travel on her own?" The white bear was ignoring her own eye injury.

"You might be right," Toklo admitted grimly. "We'll have to search harder, and look for places she might try to hide if she was injured."

"And we should look for scraps of fur or traces of blood," Kallik added, looking sick.

"Okay, but let's stay together this time," Yakone suggested. "We don't want to lose each other as well."

Together the bears headed away from the trail this time, deeper into the forest. Toklo began peering up trees, in case Lusa had tried to climb away from danger.

Their hopes rose when they came upon a steep ravine, its sides covered with rocks and thick bushes. But though they searched carefully on both sides, from the top to the bottom, peering under every bush and behind every boulder, there was no sign of Lusa.

"Maybe she *didn't* cross the trail," Kallik said as they headed wearily back to their starting point. "Maybe we should be looking on the other side."

"That doesn't make sense," Toklo objected. "Lusa knew what the plan was."

"Do you have any better ideas?" Kallik challenged him.

Toklo's shoulders sagged. "No," he admitted.

They went back to the path and Kallik and Yakone exchanged a glance, then headed along the trail in the direction the mules had been traveling. Toklo watched them for a moment as they sniffed carefully at the stones and the vegetation beside the path. Then he crossed the trail, making for the thorn thicket where they had hidden from the mules and the flat-faces.

Maybe I can follow Lusa's scent from there, he thought.

But before Toklo reached the thicket, he halted at the sound of Kallik calling his name.

"Hey, we've picked up Lusa's scent!" Yakone told him. "It leads up into the trees, here on the far side."

"She didn't cross with us," Kallik murmured as Toklo hurried to join her and Yakone.

"Look at this," Yakone said, pointing with his snout to a spot beside the trail. Trampled ferns and a scrap of broken vine showed that some kind of scuffle had happened there, and a few of the fern fronds were flecked with blood.

"She must have been injured!" Kallik exclaimed.

Toklo picked up the rising anxiety in Kallik's voice and fought to keep himself calm. "Come on," he said. "She couldn't have gone far. She'd know we'd look for her."

Yakone led the way along Lusa's scent trail, back toward the edge of the brown bear's territory that they had passed earlier in the day. The trail was strong and full of Lusa's fear-scent.

"I need to find some herbs to help her." Kallik was glancing from side to side as they followed Lusa's scent into the trees. "But Lusa knows so much more about them than I do!" There was a sharp edge of panic in her voice.

"There's still daylight left," Toklo said encouragingly. "We need to find Lusa as fast as we can. Then she'll be able to tell us what herbs she needs."

Pressing on into the undergrowth, they kept on following Lusa's scent trail. To Toklo's relief, it soon veered away in another direction. *Thank the spirits!* he thought. *I was afraid she might have wandered into that other bear's territory.*

Toklo spotted tufts of black fur clinging to a berry bush. "Look," he grunted, pointing to it with his snout. "We're on the right track."

As he spoke, Toklo heard the cough of a waking firebeast, then a gentle roar as it moved off. Though it was faint in the distance, his fur prickled. "Is there a BlackPath in this part of the forest?"

Yakone let out a low growl. "There are BlackPaths *everywhere.*"

Up ahead, the undergrowth thinned out, and light trickled through the gaps in the trees. Toklo caught glimpses of firebeasts running back and forth and realized that a huge BlackPath cut through the forest.

"What if Lusa was hurt by a firebeast?" Kallik's voice quivered. "If she was badly injured by a mule, she might have stumbled onto the BlackPath without knowing where she was."

Toklo ran forward toward the BlackPath; Kallik kept pace with him while Yakone, still limping, dropped a little way behind. On the BlackPath, firebeasts charged in both directions, the rumbling of their bellies loud and threatening. Their acrid scent filled the air, and their bright, unnatural colors dazzled Toklo's eyes.

"Now what?" he asked. "Do we follow this BlackPath?"

"What good would it do?" Kallik retorted. "How can we listen for Lusa, or pick up her scent, with all the racket and reek from the firebeasts?"

Toklo's shoulders sagged. "You're right."

All three bears backed up into the forest again, looking around vainly for Lusa. Then Toklo spotted a flattened patch of grass underneath a tree and bounded over to it. "Lusa's scent is here!" he reported with a flicker of excitement. "She must have lain down to rest."

Kallik and Yakone padded over to inspect the flattened grass for themselves.

"But she's not here now," Yakone said worriedly. "So where did she go?"

Closing her eyes, Kallik lifted her snout into the air and stood still, concentrating. Toklo waited impatiently; he knew Kallik could pick up the scent of a seal across empty ice. If any bear could track Lusa, she could.

Finally Kallik shook her head. "I can hardly pick up Lusa's scent at all," she admitted. "It's these spirit-cursed firebeasts. Their awful reek swamps everything else. I'm going to cross the BlackPath and see if I can find her trail on the other side."

Yakone opened his jaws to protest, then hesitated. "Be careful," was all he said.

Toklo followed Kallik to the edge of the BlackPath, where she crouched, waiting while the glittering firebeasts flashed to and fro. At last there was a lull.

"Now!" Toklo said.

Kallik plunged forward, her paws pushing her along in

massive leaps until she reached the far side of the BlackPath. Toklo watched her through the racing firebeasts as she nosed among the stones and vegetation at the edge of the hard black surface, his claws digging into the ground with anxiety. She wandered in both directions for many bearlengths, eventually returning to a spot just across from Toklo. She waited for a gap in firebeasts, then bounded back to him.

"Well?" Toklo asked urgently.

Kallik fixed Toklo with a sorrowful gaze. "Nothing," she reported. "Lusa didn't cross here."

"Then what happened to her?"

Before Kallik could reply, Toklo heard Yakone calling to them, a note of excitement in his voice. "Kallik! Toklo! Come here!"

"He's found her!" Kallik gasped.

She galloped back into the trees, with Toklo hard on her paws, but when they reached Yakone, standing beside the flattened grass they had found earlier, the white male was alone.

"I managed to pick up Lusa's scent from here," Yakone said, while Toklo struggled with crushing disappointment. "Though it's very faint, it goes this way . . . and look at how the grass stems are pressed down. Then here . . ."

Yakone led the way back toward the BlackPath and halted to sniff the ground, where Toklo saw the deep grooves of a firebeast's rolling paws and another tiny tuft of black fur on the spiky leaves of a thistle. "This is where the trail stops," Yakone finished.

Toklo stared at the fur, so close to the twin gouge marks in the soft earth. "Was Lusa taken away by a *firebeast*?" he asked hoarsely.

Kallik and Yakone stared at him in dismay. "It seems like the only way her trail could have gotten so cold, so quickly," Yakone responded at last. "Look at those tracks. The firebeast stopped, grabbed Lusa, and then went off that way, back to the BlackPath."

"But why would it do something like that?" Kallik whimpered. "Lusa knows not to attract the attention of a firebeast."

Toklo grunted. "I was taken by a firebeast once, remember? Flat-faces dragged me onto its back."

"That's right," said Kallik. "We followed its tracks and found you where it had crashed into the river."

Yakone blinked. "Wow. Well, if you were able to rescue Toklo then, we must be able to save Lusa now."

"It won't be so easy," Kallik warned, frowning at the Black-Path. "There are no tracks this time."

"That doesn't mean we can't try," Toklo insisted.

Kallik pressed against Yakone. "We shouldn't have let Lusa out of our sight on the mule track."

"Whatever's happened, whatever we should have done, we'll get her back," Toklo growled.

His words were nearly drowned by the roar of the biggest firebeast Toklo had ever seen. It was so long that he wondered if it might be half firesnake. It charged along the BlackPath, bellowing as it drooled out clouds of choking black smoke. Toklo coughed as the hideous fumes caught in his throat, and he recoiled into the trees with Kallik and Yakone at his side.

"That looked big enough to swallow Lusa whole!" Kallik exclaimed, staring after the huge beast in dismay.

"For a firebeast, it was slow," Yakone said thoughtfully. "But it still ran a lot faster than any bear ever could. If Lusa was taken away by one of those, and it left no tracks, do we have any chance of catching up with her?"

"Of course we do," Toklo grunted, refusing to admit, even to himself, that Yakone was voicing his own fears. "We haven't come this far only to lose each other now." *And I did not leave the place that will be my home only to lose one of my best friends.*

He sniffed at the air again, desperately trying to sift through the firebeast scents to find Lusa's. After a moment the two white bears padded up to him.

Kallik rested her chin on the top of his head. "It'll be okay," she whispered.

But it sounded more like a question than reassurance. Toklo felt his shoulders slump.

The silence dragged on until Yakone broke it abruptly. "Which way should we head now?"

Fury surged up inside Toklo and he rounded on the white male, almost knocking Kallik over. "What are you saying?" he demanded. "Are you suggesting we continue our journey without Lusa?"

"Of course not!" Yakone growled. "That's not what I meant at all! But you can't pretend that we don't have a difficult job ahead of us. No, not difficult; practically impossible. So we need to be realistic. Charging after Lusa without stopping to think about what we're doing could get us into even bigger trouble. You can see how dangerous these mountains are, with all the flat-faces and firebeasts."

Kallik shifted her paws nervously as Yakone spoke. She looked worried that claws would come out. *I'm not the one starting a fight,* Toklo thought irritably. *But maybe Yakone has a point. . . .*

"Come on," Toklo grunted. "Let's climb to higher ground. If she *wasn't* taken by a firebeast, we might be able to spot Lusa from up there." He tried to sound hopeful, but he knew his words were empty.

"Okay," Yakone agreed. "And let's hunt while we're doing that. We need to keep our strength up."

Toklo headed for a fern-covered slope that led back into the forest, and the white bears followed him. But the ascent was steep, the ferns hiding stones where the bears stubbed their paws. In spite of the shade of the trees, the air was hot and stifling. A narrow stream cut across the slope, with a much higher bank on the far side. Leaping across it drained what little strength they had left. Toklo couldn't remember feeling so exhausted, but they had to keep going.

As they plodded on, all three bears tried to stay alert for the signs of prey, but though Toklo picked up traces of birds or small animals, there was nothing that would fill the bellies of three hungry bears.

After a while they left the trees and undergrowth and reached an area of sheer rock, with stretches of scree that rolled away from under their paws as they tried to climb. Toklo's spirits rose a little as he picked up the scent of a mountain goat, though his heart sank when he realized the scent led

straight up almost sheer cliffs where it was difficult for the
bears to follow.

The white bears had picked up the scent, too. "Do we really
have to go all the way up there?" Kallik asked with a sigh.

"We'll get a good view of the area," Yakone reminded her.
"And a goat would keep us going for a long time."

Toklo took the lead again as they followed the scent, hauling themselves up steep rock faces and over boulders. But
after all their efforts, they lost the scent in a patch of sharp
stones and scree.

"Seal rot!" Yakone snapped.

"It's okay," Kallik responded, clearly trying to hide her disappointment. "We've climbed a long way, and if we go on to
the ridge, we might spot Lusa *and* the goat."

As they continued, Toklo realized that Yakone was struggling to make progress with his mangled paw, stumbling and
veering toward the edge of a precipice. As the white bear's
paws slipped under him he let out a yelp of alarm, scrabbling
to regain his balance.

Toklo lunged forward, crossing the scree slope in three
strides to block Yakone from the sheer drop. Bracing his paws
against the slippery stones, he used all his weight to shove
Yakone back to the safety of stable ground.

Yakone ducked his head in embarrassment. "Thanks,
Toklo."

The sun was going down as they reached the crest of the
climb and stood looking down at the BlackPath with wind
buffeting their fur. The dark swath of the forest stretched

below them, the branches swaying slightly in a chill breeze. Beyond the trees, firebeasts charged back and forth on the BlackPath, shafts of light from their eyes piercing the gathering twilight. There was no sign of Lusa, and seeing the land stretched out all around them was overwhelming. *She could be anywhere.*

"We should rest," Kallik said. Her flanks were heaving and her swollen eye had started to weep. "We can't go on all night."

Toklo quivered with frustration. "We have to keep looking," he insisted. "You didn't give up on me when I was taken by a firebeast, did you? We're not going to give up on Lusa."

He let his voice trail off as he struggled against black despair. If the firebeast was still moving, every passing moment was drawing Lusa farther away from them. But they were all tired and injured from the fight with the mules. And getting back down to the forest again would be even more treacherous in the dark. Toklo didn't let himself think about how impossible their situation was. He knew that if he did, he might feel so hopeless that he would give in and turn his back on his friend.

And I'll never do that.

"Okay," he sighed. "Let's stop for the night."

The bears found a sheltered spot in the lee of a rocky outcrop and huddled together in the dark.

"I know we'll do everything we can to find Lusa," Yakone said quietly, his hesitant voice telling Toklo how hard he found it to speak his thoughts. "But what if we don't find her? If she was taken by a firebeast, she could be anywhere."

"I'll never give up looking for her!" Toklo snarled.

"It's not what I want," Yakone responded, a slight edge creeping into his tone. "But Toklo, you seem to be forgetting—the Longest Day won't wait for us."

To Toklo's relief, Kallik spoke up in his defense. "We can't give up on Lusa, and we *won't*—even if it means missing the Longest Day Gathering. After all," she added, "the main reason we're going to Great Bear Lake is so Lusa can find some other black bears. We all have homes waiting for us. It's only Lusa who doesn't."

As she spoke, Toklo thought of Aiyanna and the territory waiting for him back in the mountains, and his heart ached even more for Lusa. She didn't know where her home was going to be, and now she had lost the three bears who were her family in the wild. Ujurak's words echoed in his mind as well, that there was a particular reason why Toklo needed to be at Great Bear Lake this fishleap. Toklo pushed his curiosity out of his mind. Nothing was more important than finding Lusa.

Finally the bears fell into an uneasy sleep, the cold wind probing deep into their fur.

Dawn light woke Toklo; he forced his eyes open to see Kallik and Yakone stirring beside him.

"We have to hunt." Yakone's words were interrupted by a giant yawn. "We can't travel on empty bellies."

Toklo's paws were itching to continue the search for Lusa, but he knew Yakone was right. "Okay," he agreed, his stomach rumbling at the thought of the mountain goat he had scented the day before.

The three of them headed off in different directions. Toklo couldn't imagine why any creature would want to live among the bare rocks, but satisfaction flooded through him when he rounded a boulder to see a mountain goat no more than a couple of bearlengths away.

You thought you could escape us, did you?

The goat bounded off, surefooted in the stony landscape, with Toklo in pursuit. *Seal rot! I'm losing it,* he thought frustratedly as his paws skidded on loose scree and he dropped farther back.

Just then Toklo heard a roar from somewhere ahead of him. Yakone surged out from a gap between two rocks and brought the goat down almost before it realized he was there.

"Great catch!" Toklo panted as he padded up to join Yakone.

"A lucky catch," Yakone corrected him with a nod of satisfaction.

They dragged the goat back to the rocky outcrop where they had spent the night, in time to meet Kallik, who was returning empty-pawed. Her eyes brightened when she spotted the prey.

"Hey, good job!" she exclaimed. "I'm so hungry I can feel my belly flapping."

The goat provided ample food for all of them, and Toklo was feeling comfortably full as they set off again, heading down toward the forest once more.

"We need to get back to the BlackPath," Toklo said. "We're pretty sure what direction the firebeast went. Sooner or later it'll have to stop to feed or sleep."

Kallik and Yakone exchanged a doubtful glance. "At least the BlackPath is going in the right direction for Great Bear Lake," Kallik commented.

"For now," Yakone added.

"We've got to find Lusa," Toklo insisted. "We'll follow the BlackPath wherever it leads."

They were close to the tree line when Toklo paused to sniff the air and froze, every hair on his pelt beginning to rise.

That's bear scent!

Glancing around, he spotted a familiar shape: a small black bear prowling alone across the flat, rocky ground. For a moment his heart swelled with joy. "It's Lusa!" he exclaimed. "We found her!"

He was about to leap forward to join his friend when Kallik blocked him with her shoulder. "No, Toklo." Her voice was full of disappointment. "It's not Lusa."

At the same moment Toklo realized that the scent wasn't Lusa's. This wasn't his friend, but another black she-bear.

"You're right," Toklo said. "But she might have seen something. We need to talk to her."

With Kallik and Yakone a pace behind him, Toklo began padding up to the strange bear. But when the black bear glanced up and saw them, she let out a screech of terror and scurried for the nearest tree, scrambling up to hide herself in the branches. Toklo blinked at the strength of her fear-scent.

Signaling to the white bears to keep back, Toklo approached the tree by himself. "My name's Toklo," he called, trying to make his voice sound quiet and friendly. "I'm looking for a black bear who's a stranger around here like me. Have you seen her?"

The bear peered down at him, her face poking out from a cluster of leaves. "I'm Enola," she replied. "Why are you with those white bears?" Her voice shook with fear. "I've heard about white bears, but I've never seen them. What are they doing here?"

"We're looking for our friend Lusa," Toklo told her. "We lost her yesterday when we ran into some mules. She might have been trapped in a firebeast."

Enola's eyes were huge among the shadowy branches. "Taken away by a firebeast?" Her voice rose to a shrill squeak. "You'll never find her!"

"We have to try," Toklo responded, keeping his voice calm and gentle.

Enola blinked, her panic seeming to recede a little. *Maybe she can see we're not going to hurt her,* Toklo hoped. She even lowered herself by a couple of branches, though she was careful to stay out of the reach of Toklo's paws.

"Are you sure she was taken by a firebeast?"

"No," Toklo admitted. "But Lusa vanished into thin air after she ran from the mules. Her trail ended by the Black-Path, where there were marks from a firebeast's paws."

"I'm really sorry you lost her," Enola continued. "I'll keep an eye out and let you know if I see her."

"Thanks, but we probably won't stay around for much longer," Toklo told her. "We're on our way to Great Bear Lake, for the Longest Day Gathering."

Enola's eyes were bright with interest. "I've heard about that," she said, "but I've never been. It's too far to go alone," she added regretfully. For a moment, she sounded very lonely and young, but cheered up almost immediately. "Is that where you met Lusa? At Great Bear Lake?" she asked.

Toklo shook his head. "No, Lusa met up with me and . . . another friend, long before that," he told Enola. "I met Kallik at Great Bear Lake—that's the white she-bear," he finished with a glance at Kallik and Yakone, who were still waiting a few bearlengths away.

Once more Enola let herself down to a lower branch, looking much more confident now. "You're lucky to have traveled so far," she said.

"Oh, our journey took us much farther than that," Toklo responded, beginning to feel friendly toward the eager young she-bear, who reminded him so strongly of Lusa. "We traveled right up to the Endless Ice and saw the spirits dancing in the sky."

Enola's eyes widened, and she let out a wistful sigh. "That must have been wonderful! I wish I could come along with you to Great Bear Lake," she added, giving Toklo a speculative look. "I know all the places where black bears might hide!"

For a moment Toklo was tempted to invite her to travel with them. But then he glanced back toward Kallik and Yakone, thinking how far they had come together, and how close they were to the end of their journey. *I can't take the risk of having a young, inexperienced bear joining us now.*

Toklo remembered Chenoa, too, the other black she-bear

who had shared their journey for a while.

Chenoa died when she was swept over the waterfall. If we hadn't taken her with us, she might still be alive.

A shiver ran through Toklo as he realized afresh that now he had lost Lusa, too. "Thanks for the offer," he said to Enola. "But we need to finish our journey alone."

"Okay." Enola was visibly struggling with disappointment. "Maybe I'll get to the lake one day."

"I hope so," Toklo said, feeling sorry for her, but knowing he had made the right decision. *This is Enola's home. Not all bears need to travel forever to find a place to live.*

"And I'll look out for your friend," Enola added. "If I see her, I'll tell her which way you went."

"Thank you," Toklo said. "Good-bye, and may the spirits be with you."

"Good-bye," Enola responded. "I hope you find Lusa."

Toklo rejoined Kallik and Yakone, who pressed up to him eagerly.

"What did she say?" Kallik asked. "Has she seen Lusa?"

"No," Toklo replied, feeling disappointed all over again as he saw the hope die from his friends' faces. "But she said she'd keep an eye out for her."

"That doesn't help us much," Yakone grunted. "What were you talking about for so long?"

"She wanted to come to Great Bear Lake with us. But I didn't think it would be a good idea."

"You were right," Kallik said. "We can't take care of her and look for Lusa."

As the three of them padded away together, Toklo was aware of Enola watching him from her tree, but when he glanced back over his shoulder, her small black shape was already out of sight among the branches. He felt a moment's regret, followed by a fiercer determination.

There's one black bear who does need to get to Great Bear Lake. We have to find Lusa!

Plunging farther down the hill, Toklo and the others came back within sight of the BlackPath and followed it in the direction they figured the firebeast must have gone, while remaining a couple of bearlengths away, under cover of the trees.

"We don't even know if we're going the right way," Kallik said after a while.

"But this is our best guess," Toklo reminded her. "There's nothing else we can do. Keep your eyes open for any firebeast tracks leaving the BlackPath."

But though the bears plodded along through the suffocating heat of the day until the sun slid down the sky and cast long shadows through the trees, they saw no firebeast tracks, and no places near the BlackPath where a firebeast might have taken Lusa.

I wonder if Ujurak knows where Lusa is, Toklo thought. *I wish he were here now. If he took the shape of a bird, he could help us look for her.* "Where are you, Ujurak?" he asked aloud, wishing he could understand why the star-bear had abandoned them when they needed his help so much.

"I wish he were here, too," Kallik said softly.

"Then why isn't he?" Toklo asked, slashing angrily at a clump of long grass as he trudged past it.

"I don't know," Kallik admitted. "Maybe he knows that we can find Lusa on our own."

Toklo grunted.

The long day was drawing to an end when the bears reached a place where the BlackPath swooped down the mountain until it reached the edge of a vast plain.

By the time they were halfway to the plain, night had fallen. The bears paused in a gap among the trees; Toklo gazed down at the constant stream of firebeasts. In the darkness their fierce, glowing eyes lit up the ground in front of them.

Is Lusa really in one of those? Toklo wondered. He tore his gaze away from the rushing firebeasts and gazed up at the night sky. Above his head Ujurak's shape blazed out, cold and expressionless. *Why don't you help us?* he asked despairingly.

Behind Toklo, Kallik began trampling down the undergrowth in the shelter of a thorn thicket, dragging in ferns to make a temporary den. Yakone vanished and reappeared a short time later with a grouse dangling from his jaws.

"Thanks, Yakone," Toklo said. It seemed like a long time since they had feasted on the goat.

"You're welcome," Yakone grunted.

Almost too tired to eat, the three of them gathered around to share the prey. Toklo could barely choke down the meat; he missed Lusa too much, happily crunching fern roots beside them. He hated that while they were resting they were doing nothing to find her.

But we can't keep going all day and all night.

While Kallik gathered more leaves—which she hoped would help treat Yakone's injured paw—Toklo settled down to sleep. His mind kept whirling with images of Lusa being attacked by a firebeast, or lying injured and frightened in the forest, but he was so exhausted that nothing could stop him from drifting off to sleep. He dreamed that he was standing on the edge of a great plain. A herd of caribou was moving across it, covering the ground as far as Toklo could see. The clicking sound of their feet echoed around him.

Then a small black bear emerged from the middle of the herd, while the caribou walked calmly around it without showing any fear.

"Lusa!" Toklo whispered.

But as the black bear drew closer, Toklo realized that it wasn't Lusa. This bear was gazing at him with the warm brown eyes of Ujurak.

Toklo bounded forward to meet his friend at the edge of the herd. "Ujurak! Can you tell me where Lusa is?" he called.

Ujurak shook his head. "I can sense her," he replied. "I know she's alive, but she has been taken far away."

"Can you speak to her for me?" Toklo begged.

But Ujurak was already beginning to fade away. "Look for the place where the caribou walk," he whispered, "beneath the stars that shine where the sun will rise."

"Is that where Lusa is?" Toklo asked. "With the caribou?"

Ujurak's voice seemed to come from a distance now, echoing through the night. His figure was no more than a faint outline on the edge of the caribou herd. "Find the caribou. . . ."

His voice became one with the wind that swept across the plain, over the crisscrossing BlackPaths lined with flat-face dens, and then the last traces of his form vanished. Toklo woke into a gray dawn, with Kallik and Yakone still sleeping beside him.

CHAPTER SIX

Lusa

"Lusa! Lusa!"

Her mother's voice was calling to her, and Lusa realized that she was back in the Bear Bowl, crouching at the foot of the tree. She tried to focus on Ashia's voice, but she could hardly hear it over the roaring of an angry bear.

Her heart thumping in panic, Lusa looked around and spotted the huge, ragged figure of Oka, throwing herself at the fence over and over again as she tried to break through it in a frenzy of grief and fury.

"It's okay!" Lusa barked to her. "I found Toklo! He's alive—he's fine."

But Oka didn't seem to hear her. She just went on bellowing and raging against the fence. Then all the black bears surrounded Lusa: King and Ashia, Stella and Yogi, all of them roaring, too, until Lusa thought that her ears would burst.

She started to panic. "Help me!" she squealed, flailing her paws because she felt something enfolding her tightly. "Let me go!"

Pain stabbed through her head, making her lie still again, and with a growing feeling of horror she realized that she wasn't in the Bear Bowl at all. Instead she was lying on the back of a firebeast, wrapped in some kind of thin, shiny pelt that trapped her paws and pressed against her flanks. The bellowing of bears in Lusa's dream was really the noise of the firebeast as it rumbled over the BlackPath.

Agony sliced through Lusa's head again as she tried to raise it, and the sky above her was so dazzlingly bright that it hurt her eyes.

Toklo, Kallik, Yakone—where are you? What is happening to me?

Moaning, Lusa let herself drift back into the darkness inside her head. When she woke again, the firebeast was still moving, but she felt strong enough to prop herself up as much as the shiny pelt allowed and look around her, craning her neck to peer over the side of the firebeast's hollow back. With a start, she saw that they had left the mountains behind and were rolling across a flat plain. Lusa sniffed the air, trying to detect trees or water or anything familiar, but all she could pick up was the eye-watering stench of the firebeast.

"Where is it taking me?" she whimpered. She remembered the two flat-faces in the forest—a large male and a smaller female—and wondered if they were in the firebeast as well. Had it attacked them all? Or did the firebeast belong to the flat-faces, the way firebeasts often seemed to be commanded by the hairless creatures?

Desperately thirsty, Lusa drifted in and out of consciousness. Suddenly the firebeast swerved, sending her sliding across its back, before it shuddered to a halt. The rumbling sound died away, and after a moment Lusa could hear flat-face voices. A little while later a flat-face came and looked down at her.

This was a flat-face Lusa hadn't seen before, with gray fur around a brown face. All her instincts told her to hide, or to snap at him if he tried to touch her, but his voice was low and kind. Something familiar about his scent reminded Lusa once again of the Bear Bowl, and his soft tones made her relax almost against her will.

But in spite of her urge to trust this flat-face, Lusa could feel her heart pounding as she looked for a way to escape. *I have to get out of here! Then I can find herbs for the pain in my head and start looking for the others.*

The gray-furred flat-face started to peel off the shiny pelt. As soon as Lusa's legs were freed she lashed out, and the flat-face retreated rapidly. A flat-face cub appeared, looking over the side of the firebeast and squeaking at Lusa, until yet another flat-face pulled the cub away. Then the gray-furred flat-face reappeared, bending over Lusa. She felt something sharp prick her neck, and almost at once shadows began to gather around her and the inside of her head felt like it was filling with fog. Lusa struggled to stay awake, but the shadows overwhelmed her and she slipped away.

Lusa blinked as she raised her head and tried to work out where she was. As her vision cleared, she made out bars all around her and a roof above her head, clustered with shadows.

I'm in a cage . . . like the time I was captured on the ice.

She remembered how back then Ujurak had appeared to her in the shape of a flat-face and rescued her from the flat-faces who had captured her.

Maybe he'll help me again, she thought, trying to feel more hopeful. *But what if he doesn't know I'm here?*

With an enormous effort, Lusa managed to sit up. Her muscles shrieked at her as she moved stiffly, and her head still felt full of cloudfluff. The floor of her cage was made of some hard, gray stuff, though the corner where she had been lying was covered by a thick bundle of straw. Beside her was a shiny silver bowl, brimming with water. Lusa managed to get up on shaky legs, plunged her muzzle into the bowl, and took a long, long drink.

When she looked up again, swiping her tongue around her jaws, she realized that the light around her was fading. But she could still see enough to tell her that she was inside a long, low den lined with cages on either side.

I need to find a way out. But I'm so tired, and I ache all over. . . .

Lusa sniffed the stale air, but the scents of so many animals were mingled that she couldn't tell them apart. She wondered how long she had been asleep since she had seen the flat-faces.

Her head still throbbed with pain from where the mule had kicked her. Her vision was blurry in the eye on that side, and she staggered a little when she tried to move.

But I'm not hurt too bad, she told herself firmly. *I can keep traveling, if only I can get out of this den.*

Then another scent drifted into her nose. *It's another black bear!*

"Who's there?" she called, wondering too late if it was safe to raise her voice.

"Never mind," came the gruff reply.

Squinting through the bars on one side of her cage, she could just make out the hunched shape of another black bear. "Do you know the way out of here?" Lusa whispered.

A long silence followed her words, and Lusa thought she might have somehow offended the other bear. When he finally spoke again, he seemed confused.

"Way out? Of course there's no way out! Anyway, why would you or any bear want to leave?"

Because bears don't belong in cages! Lusa thought. *Why isn't this bear doing everything he can to escape?*

There was a loud click, and light flooded into Lusa's cage from a bright white strip overhead. She had to shut her eyes and duck her head against the unexpected glare, while all around her noise broke out: the skittering of claws, flapping of wings, the screeching and roaring of many different creatures.

Lusa opened her eyes again, and as she got used to the light she caught her breath in astonishment. Though she had scented other animals, she hadn't realized how daunting it would be to see them. *Oh wow...*

In the cage on her other side was a coyote biting at the bars that separated them, its cold eyes fixed on her. Lusa shuddered, hoping the bars were too strong for its sharp yellow teeth. On the opposite side of the den, a flock of pigeons were fluttering around an enclosure, and beside them an eagle perched on a branch in a cage, harsh cries coming from its gaping beak. In the next cage along, a raccoon was scrabbling in the straw on the floor. Rhythmic thumping came from farther down the den, on the same side as Lusa so that she couldn't see what was making the noise, but she guessed that some large animal was throwing itself at the door of its cage, over and over.

Lusa opened her eyes wide in astonishment. *How long have these animals and birds been kept here?*

The black bear in the cage beside Lusa let out a grunt, drawing her attention back to him. Now that she could see him clearly, she made out gray speckles in his fur, and to her surprise his eyes were the same shade of gray, not black and shiny like hers. They stared blankly at Lusa as the bear lifted his head toward her, sniffing.

"You're a black bear, aren't you?" he muttered.

Why can't he see that? Lusa wondered. "Are you blind?" she asked tentatively.

"Oh, aren't you the clever one?" the other bear growled.

Lusa's fur bristled. "There's no need to be mean!" she snapped.

Before the other bear could respond, the door to the den opened. The noise from the other creatures grew even louder until Lusa wanted to cover her ears with her paws.

A pair of flat-faces stepped inside the den and walked right up to Lusa's cage. One of them was the gray-furred male she had seen before, outside by the firebeast. The other was a smaller female, with the same brown skin and gray head-fur.

Both of them stared at Lusa, making strange noises at each other and occasionally pointing at her with their paws. Lusa shrank to the back of the cage, until the cold stone wall pressed against her fur.

Moving slowly, the male flat-face opened a flap at the bottom of the door of Lusa's cage and pushed a bowl inside. Closing the flap again, he walked away down the row of cages with the female flat-face at his side. Lusa watched them peering inside the other cages as they murmured to each other.

She tottered across the cage to investigate the new bowl. Before she reached it, she could pick up the delicious scent of fruit, and her mouth watered.

"I bet you're not so eager to leave now, are you?" the old black bear grunted.

Lusa didn't reply. Her belly was howling with hunger, especially now that she wasn't thirsty anymore. But it had been so long since she'd eaten this kind of food, it seemed like it belonged to another life. Memory flashed into Lusa's mind of her mother Ashia saying, *"Eat, little one! Try the berries first; they're very juicy."*

"But I'm a wild bear now!" Lusa protested out loud.

"Eh? What?" barked the old bear, tilting his head toward her.

Lusa ignored him and, unable to resist the sweet fruit, pushed her snout into the bowl and took a big mouthful. The fruit's sweetness thrilled through her, a much stronger taste than she remembered. *Mmm . . . wonderful!* she thought, her head spinning.

Gulping down the mouthful, Lusa turned back to the bear in the next cage. "My name's Lusa," she told him. "What's yours?"

"Taktuq," he muttered.

"And what is this place?" Lusa asked him, feeling encouraged that he had answered her question.

Taktuq shrugged. "It's my home."

Lusa felt a chill run through her fur. "This isn't another Bear Bowl, is it?"

The old bear tipped his head on one side as if he didn't understand. "What's a Bear Bowl?"

"It's a place where lots of bears live," Lusa replied. "Flat-faces feed them, and other flat-faces come and look at them."

"Then this is no Bear Bowl," Taktuq grunted. "We don't get flat-faces looking at us, just the ones that feed us."

"Then why are all these animals here?" Lusa asked, gazing down the row of creatures again. The coyote had stopped biting the cage bars, though it was still glaring at her; the eagle was shifting on its perch, half raising its wings as if it wanted to fly, while the raccoon still scrabbled among its straw.

"Most of them have something wrong with them when they arrive," Taktuq told her. "Some of them leave when they get better, and a few stay—like me."

Lusa gulped down the rest of the fruit. "What will happen to me when I get better?" she asked when she had licked sticky juice from her muzzle. "Where will I go?"

Taktuq shrugged. "How should I know?"

"Where is this place?" Lusa persisted. "I left my friends in the mountains, and they have to find me. Or I have to find them!"

"You're a long way from the mountains now," Taktuq told her. "Unless your friends are caribou? They pass near here at this season." He paused, letting out a long sigh. "I remember hearing the caribou with my mother," he murmured. "So many hooves clicking past . . . Vast herds of animals, traveling, traveling. I wanted to go with them, but my mother wouldn't let me. I used to think it was because I couldn't see."

Lusa looked at the old bear, studying his unseeing eyes. As if he was conscious of her gaze, Taktuq let out a bitter chuff of amusement. "No, there's nothing they can do for me. Even flat-faces can't cure blindness. I figure that's why I'm still here. But it's okay," he added. "I have food and shelter here, and a place to go outside when it's daylight."

He nodded toward the back wall of the cage. Lusa looked at the same spot in her own cage and noticed the outline of a door in the wall. Her legs still feeling unsteady, she staggered over to it and shoved it with all her weight. It didn't open.

"No use trying that," Taktuq observed. "The doors only open for the flat-faces."

Ignoring him, Lusa sniffed carefully along the bottom of the door and as far up the sides as she could reach. There was a flap set into it, bigger than the one the flat-faces had used to deliver her food, but there didn't seem to be any way of unfastening it. She continued investigating all around the sides of the cage, careful not to get too close to the coyote, until she reached Taktuq once more.

The old bear had been sniffing the air, and Lusa realized that he must have tracked her progress all around the cage by her scent. "Found a way out yet?" he teased. "I told you, there isn't one. Not unless the flat-faces let you out."

Lusa bit back an angry response. "What's it like to be blind?" she asked curiously. "I can't imagine it."

Taktuq let out a huff. "What's it like to see?" he countered. "No, don't answer that," he went on before Lusa could form a reply. "I don't need to know. I can recognize other animals by their scent and the sound they make, and I can sense what's going on by the way the air moves around me."

"Really?" Lusa's fascination made her forget for a moment her need to escape. "I want to try."

"Good luck with that," the old bear grunted as Lusa closed her eyes.

In the darkness she strained to pick out the sounds and scents of the other animals, but they were all mixed up. Apart from Taktuq's scent, and the reek of the coyote on her other side, Lusa couldn't distinguish any of them. And though she could feel slight movement of the air against her fur, it meant nothing to her.

"This is too difficult," she sighed, opening her eyes again. Turning to Taktuq, she added admiringly, "You must be really smart."

Taktuq snorted, then curled up and drifted off to sleep without saying any more. Lusa gazed at him for a moment longer, trying to imagine herself in his world, then gave herself a brisk shake.

This isn't getting me out of here.

Convinced that there must be a way to escape from the cage if she could only find it, Lusa continued to examine every paw's width of the floor, the bars, and the flap where the flat-faces had given her the food. But before long she began to realize that the outlines of everything around her were growing blurred. She looked up and saw that the lights were still blazing above her, but it was becoming harder and harder to see.

Oh no . . . Lusa blinked, trying to clear her vision. *I must be going blind, too!* Panic lurched in her belly. She struggled to stay on her paws, but they crumpled beneath her and she sank to the floor of the cage. Sleep was tugging at her fur, and after a feeble effort to resist, she gave herself up to it.

Loud clicking sounded all around Lusa, and she opened her eyes to find herself walking in the midst of a vast herd of caribou. They pressed so close to her that she could hardly breathe, and she was afraid that their clicking feet would trample her.

"Help!" she wailed. "I have to find my friends!"

The caribou ignored her, as if she was invisible, as they went on and on, sweeping Lusa along in the center of the herd, covering plains, fording rivers, and forging onward over fields of ice.

Then Lusa spotted another black bear's face among the legs of the caribou. With a cry of relief she recognized the bear's warm brown eyes.

"Ujurak! Help me!"

Somehow Ujurak managed to find a path between the

moving legs and nudged Lusa sideways until both of them reached the edge of the herd. He stood beside Lusa, watching as the caribou moved away in a cloud of dust and the sound of their clicking feet faded into silence.

"Now what?" Lusa asked, turning to face Ujurak. "Tell me how to find the others!"

Ujurak didn't reply, but gently nudged Lusa again until she was facing the opposite way, gazing along the dark swath of the caribou trail. Lusa half hoped to see her friends padding toward her, but nothing moved in all the landscape.

"Ujurak, I don't understand," she began, and turned back toward the star-bear, only to see that he had vanished, though his scent still wreathed around her.

"Where are you?" Lusa gazed back and forth with the beginning of panic. "Don't leave me!" she begged.

"I won't," Ujurak's voice murmured in her ear, as close as if he was right beside her. "I am always with you."

CHAPTER SEVEN

Kallik

Kallik woke to see that the first faint traces of dawn had begun to creep into the sky, though above her head the stars still glittered. Groaning softly as she stretched her cramped limbs, she scrambled to her paws and shook off scraps of fern from their makeshift nest.

Toklo was sitting up next to her, his solid shape outlined against the growing light as he gazed out over the plain, but before she could speak to him, she was distracted by Yakone shifting and mumbling by her side. Bending her head, Kallik examined Yakone's injured paw, giving the wound a good sniff. To her relief, the scent of infection had faded.

Those leaves did a good job, Kallik thought.

Toklo padded forward and stood at the edge of the clearing, overlooking the misty gray plain. Kallik joined him. "Do you think Lusa is somewhere out there?" she murmured.

To her surprise, there was a new confidence in Toklo's eyes as he turned to her. "I know she is," he replied. "Ujurak told me."

Kallik felt a spark of hope flare inside her. "You spoke to Ujurak?"

Toklo nodded. "He came to me in a dream. He said there would be caribou where Lusa is. That we have to find the caribou."

All the cramps and stiffness in Kallik disappeared. "So do you know which way we should go?" she asked. "Did you meet caribou on your first journey to Great Bear Lake?"

"No, but Ujurak said we would find them beneath the stars that shine where the sun will rise." Toklo set his jaw. "We *will* find her, Kallik. We haven't come all this way only to lose her so close to the end of our journey."

The bears stared out across the plain. Kallik gazed at all the flat-face denning places, all the crisscrossing BlackPaths, all the vast stretches of empty land, and her optimism began to leak away.

There are so few places for us to hide. We'll be so vulnerable. . . .

"We'll stay in the mountains for as long as we can," Toklo said, as if he could read Kallik's thoughts. "There'll be more prey up here, and more places to shelter. And when we have to leave, we'll be guided by the stars where the sun will rise."

Kallik squeezed back into the bramble thicket and thrust her muzzle into Yakone's shoulder to wake him. "Guess what?" she announced. "Ujurak appeared to Toklo in a dream and told him that we have to find the caribou to find Lusa. We don't have to follow the BlackPath anymore."

"Great!" Yakone heaved himself to his paws. "What are we waiting for? Let's get going!"

"We'll hunt first," Toklo decided, appearing at the edge of the thicket. "We'll travel faster on full bellies."

"I hope Lusa has food and shelter," Kallik said.

Yakone nodded, his eyes solemn. "If she's somewhere out there alone . . . Anything could have happened to her."

Kallik knew what Yakone was suggesting but didn't dare let herself think that Lusa could be beyond rescuing. "Ujurak wouldn't send us to find her if she was dead," she told Yakone. "We have to trust him."

"I trust *you*," Yakone responded. "And that means I know this is the right thing to do."

Kallik leaned into him, grateful for his strength and understanding. "Come on, let's hunt," she said.

As the bears spread out quietly among the trees, Kallik was the first to spot prey. A ground squirrel was scrabbling in the roots of a mountain maple, and she killed it quickly with a single blow of her paw.

"Thank you, spirits, for this prey," she murmured, then called to her friends to come and share.

Though the squirrel barely took the edge off their hunger, none of the bears wanted to spend any more time hunting.

"We can catch something else on the way," Toklo said.

By now the stars had faded and a glow on the horizon showed where the sun would rise. Kallik and the others headed toward it.

Toklo took the lead, and almost at once began to take them upward again. "Lusa and I traveled along the peaks the last time we made the journey to Great Bear Lake," he told the others. "There are fewer trees up there so you can see more clearly, and there aren't as many flat-faces."

As they climbed higher in the cool dawn, Kallik felt new strength flowing into her legs. The clean-tasting air invigorated her, a welcome change after the suffocating heat from the last few days of walking. It didn't take long to leave the thick forest behind, entering a region of steep slopes and tilted slabs of rock, where the occasional stunted tree or sparse bushes were all that managed to root themselves in the thin soil.

Toklo seemed tireless as he hauled himself over boulders and plunged down into the steep ravines that crossed their path. He never faltered, as though he knew exactly where he was going.

The air was so still and silent around them, without even the sound of birdsong or falling water, that Kallik felt as though the three of them were all that moved in that bleak landscape beneath the blue sky and scudding white clouds.

She and Yakone walked side by side in Toklo's pawsteps. A particularly hard scramble led them up onto the ridge at the very top of the mountain, where Yakone paused briefly, puffing out his breath.

"Are you okay?" Kallik prompted. "Is your paw hurting?"

Yakone shook his head and started to follow Toklo again. "My paw's fine. But I'm frightened for Lusa. How will we ever find her among all this?" He swung his head around, taking in the huge stretches of the mountains. "Firebeasts can travel so much faster than us. She could be all the way to the Melting Sea by now!"

Kallik paused. "But you'll keep on looking for her, right?" she asked in a small voice.

Yakone padded on for a few more paces, then glanced sideways at Kallik. "I have faith in Ujurak to get us there," he grunted. "It's just that . . . the mountains are so big, and Lusa is so small."

"I know." Kallik touched Yakone's shoulder with her muzzle. "But we *will* find her. I'm sure we will. We have Ujurak's help now."

A little farther on, the craggy slopes leveled out into a rocky plateau, where small creeping plants struggled to grow in the cracks.

"I remember this place!" Toklo exclaimed, coming to a halt. "It's where Ujurak turned into a goat."

"I wish I could turn into one," Yakone said, with a rueful glance at his stunted paw. "I'd do a lot better among all these rocks."

Crossing the flat plateau was easy, but after that they reached a place where the ridge became too spiky for them to walk, and they had to scramble down until they reached a path a few bearlengths below.

"I remember this place, too," Toklo said, sniffing. "It's where we were chased by wolves. Ujurak turned into a mule deer and led them away."

"Do you think there are still wolves here?" Kallik asked nervously.

"If there are, we'll give them something to remember," Toklo responded grimly. "We're a lot bigger than Lusa and I were back then...."

His voice trailed off and he paused, his eyes clouding with sadness. Kallik knew he must be wrestling with the fact that neither Ujurak nor Lusa was with them now.

"It's not your fault that we've lost them," Kallik pointed out gently. "And we'll find Lusa again."

"We were so close to the end of our journeys!" Toklo snarled, stamping on a scrap of dead branch that splintered under his paw.

"Exactly," Kallik said. "And Ujurak won't let us finish without Lusa."

Toklo hesitated, his spurt of angry despair fading. Then he swung around and headed along the path once more.

The mention of wolves had made Kallik more alert, and before long she began to pick up traces of scent like that of abandoned prey, or blood on the pelt of a predator. "Toklo..." she began.

"I know," Toklo growled. "I can smell it, too. But it's stale scent... a day or two old. There aren't any wolves around now."

"I'd still be happier if we got away from here," Kallik said, remembering their fierce battles against the wolves in Toklo's forest.

"The wolves might have left some prey behind," Yakone suggested. "I'm getting hungry, and I haven't seen a single thing to eat up here."

Toklo thought for a moment. "No," he decided at last. "It's

not worth the risk to follow the scent. We'll look for a place to turn off this path, and then try to hunt."

But at first there seemed to be no way of getting off their narrow trail. Sheer rock stretched upward on one side, while on the other the ground fell away in a precipice to the pine forests below. Kallik's fur began to prickle with anxiety as the wolf scent grew stronger. Like it or not, the bears seemed to be heading right for them.

Sunhigh was almost upon them when they spotted a narrow gully leading upward. It wasn't a direction that would likely lead them to food, but at least they'd get a good look at their surroundings—and get off the wolf trail. Toklo immediately began scrambling up, scattering loose stones from his paws as he clambered higher. Kallik held back to let Yakone go next.

If he slips because of his injured paw, I'll be there to catch him.

But the white bear hauled himself up behind Toklo without any trouble. Kallik brought up the rear, trying not to think about the plunging drop behind her.

Up on the ridge, the bears stood still with the wind tugging at their fur while they looked out across the landscape ahead. On the opposite side of the ridge the slopes were gentler, and not far below was the dark line of the pine forest.

"Let's go that way," Toklo said, with a jerk of his head toward the trees. "There should be prey there."

As they descended among the trunks, Kallik heard a muffled roaring sound, which grew louder as they walked. They followed a stony path through the trees and emerged beside a

foaming stream that thundered down in a sheer, narrow cas-
cade into a pool below. The air was full of spray and the scent
of water.

Cautiously, because the rocks beside the waterfall were
slick with moisture, the bears scrambled down to the edge of
the pool. As Kallik bent her head to drink, relishing the cold
taste, she imagined how wonderful it would feel to plunge
right into it and feel the icy torrent soaking into her fur.

Without hesitating, she slid off the rocks and lowered herself into the pool. The churning water tossed her to and fro,
but she battled it with strong paws, exhilarated by the struggle. She could feel the force of the stream lifting away the grit
from her fur.

"Come on, Yakone!" she called.

Yakone plunged into the water and surfaced beside Kallik
with a whoosh, splashing water into her face.

"I'll get you for that!" she spluttered, diving at him.

Yakone ducked down and reappeared on Kallik's other
side. "You can try!"

But Kallik knew that they couldn't go on playing forever.
She turned to swim back to the rocks, and almost at once
caught sight of a silver flicker in the white foam of the pool.
Snapping her jaws instinctively, she closed her teeth on a fish.
Satisfied, Kallik hauled herself out of the pool with water
streaming from her pelt and dropped the fish at Toklo's paws.
Toklo's eyes gleamed as he looked at her prey.

"Nice catch," he said. "Now we don't need to waste time
hunting."

The bears shared the fish—a plump trout—and set out again, among the trees.

"We can't keep traveling this far down from the ridge," Toklo muttered after a short while. "The trees close us in, and we can't see where we have to go. Now that we've eaten, we need to find a way back up."

Beams of sunlight slanted at an angle through the pine trees, and Kallik realized that the day was drawing to an end. *We'll have to make a den for the night soon.* Before long a path opened up, winding its way through the trees and eventually bringing the bears out onto the edge of a long plateau that stretched in front of them as far as they could see. Trees encircled it, but the ground ahead was clear except for small rocks scattered across it with larger outcrops of boulders here and there.

Toklo was peering into the distance. "What's that?" he asked, pointing with his snout.

Looking in that direction, Kallik saw a cloud of dust billowing into the air. At the same moment, she felt the ground vibrating through her pads. Yakone let out a grunt of surprise; clearly he could feel it, too.

"There are a lot of animals in that cloud," he said.

"I'm going to get a better look." Toklo headed for the nearest pine tree and began to haul himself up the trunk. "We need Lusa," he huffed. "She's the best at climbing."

Kallik felt a renewed pang of loss as she watched Toklo heaving himself slowly from branch to branch and remembered how nimbly Lusa could bound up a tree trunk.

A moment later Toklo's voice came down in a joyful bellow.

"Caribou! We've found the caribou! Ujurak said we had to track them down in order to find Lusa!"

For a moment Kallik could hardly believe it. *Can it really be that easy?*

Toklo half fell, half scrambled down from the tree, and the bears set off again, heading in the direction of the caribou herd. The floor of the plateau was littered with stones and bigger boulders, and here and there were pools of ice. Kallik sniffed the air; it was much colder here, and a thin wind ruffled their fur, tasting of ice and stone.

"This is better," she said, beginning to feel more hopeful at the familiar tang.

"Yeah." Yakone's voice was full of satisfaction. "It almost feels like home."

The bears picked up their pace until the caribou came into sight. The herd was heading away from them, with stragglers pausing to graze. The sound of their clicking feet carried faintly on the wind.

"So where's Lusa?" Toklo asked, halting and gazing around.

Yakone raised his head and let out a mighty bellow. "Lusa! Lusa!"

His roar echoed around the plateau, but no small black bear emerged from among the rocks.

Toklo clawed at the ground in frustration. "She should be here! Something isn't right."

Kallik fought back despair and tried to focus on what was important: finding Lusa. "Toklo, what did Ujurak say exactly?" she asked.

Toklo hesitated, clearly deep in thought. "He told me to look for the place where the caribou walk," he replied at last. "And he said we should find the caribou. But we've done that, and Lusa isn't here!"

"Then Ujurak didn't actually *say* that Lusa would be with the caribou?" Kallik persisted. When Toklo shook his head, understanding began to grow inside her. "Don't you see, Toklo? This is a sign, like the ones Ujurak followed before." Turning to Yakone, she explained quickly, "Ujurak was always good at spotting signs, like the shape of trees or the position of rocks, that told us which way to go."

Toklo huffed out a breath. "So the caribou are another sign, showing us which way to go. If we want to find Lusa, we have to *follow* the caribou!"

"Well, that shouldn't be too hard," said Yakone. "We can hardly lose a herd that size!"

"Let's go!" Kallik urged.

She took the lead as they set out, picking up the pace again so that they drew closer to the herd. But as they emerged from the gap between two huge boulders, Toklo stopped, his gaze fixed on an outlier of the herd that was tearing at the leaves of a spiky bush. He swiped his tongue around his jaws.

"Don't even think about it," Kallik warned him. "If we try to hunt, we could spook the whole herd. They might stampede in the wrong direction."

Toklo heaved a long sigh. "I suppose you're right. But I really want to sink my teeth into a nice fat caribou."

"You'll just have to keep wanting," Kallik retorted sharply.

"For now, these caribou aren't prey. They're our guides."

"So where are they leading us?" Yakone asked.

Kallik shook her head in confusion. "I have no idea. But it must be where Lusa is, and that's good enough for me. I trust Ujurak."

The bears padded along in the wake of the caribou, keeping their distance so as not to spook the herd.

"It's a good thing we're downwind of them," Toklo commented.

The landscape gradually changed, the flat plateau surrounded now by mountains, the topmost ridges still streaked with snow. Between two of the peaks Kallik spotted a wide river of ice leading away into the distance. Ridges of ice like frozen waves reflected the dying sun, and the dark cracks of crevasses zigzagged across it.

"It's a glacier!" she exclaimed.

"Wow!" Yakone said. "There's a glacier on Star Island, but it's much smaller than that one."

It's like a sign, Kallik thought. *A wonderful sign to tell us that we're on the right track.*

Toklo tipped his head to one side. "We didn't come this way last time." He glanced around and finally pointed his snout toward another ridge, not far off, running in the same direction as the glacier. "I think we traveled along there."

"Then we're going the same way, more or less," Kallik said. "I think the glacier is another sign," she added, voicing her earlier thought. "Showing us the way, just like all the other signs we've seen on our journey."

The caribou continued their trek toward the glacier, and the bears followed. As they walked on, the landscape continued to change. A glittering turquoise lake appeared below them, and big white birds swooped overhead. Kallik took long breaths of the cold air.

It's almost like being back on the ice!

Suddenly a new sound jerked her back to the present, sharp and jarring in the peaceful dusk.

Flat-faces!

Their raucous chatter was the first warning the bears had that flat-faces were nearby. A moment later a small herd of them wearing brightly colored pelts appeared along a path that zigzagged down from the nearest ridge.

"Hide!" Toklo ordered.

Kallik glanced around wildly. They had come too far away from the trees to reach them without being spotted, and the flat plain didn't offer much cover big enough to hide three bears.

"There!" Yakone hissed, jerking his muzzle toward a cluster of rocks a few bearlengths away.

He took the lead as the bears galloped toward the rocks and forced themselves into a tiny space beneath an overhang. Crushed together, they peered out at the flat-faces.

Kallik couldn't believe that they were really hidden in their narrow refuge. She felt like the flat-faces would spot them at any moment, and waited tensely for their bellowing to break out.

I can't see any firesticks, but that doesn't mean these flat-faces don't have any.

But the flat-faces passed by, chattering happily, not paying any attention to the bears.

"Honestly," Toklo muttered, scrambling out from the overhang when the sounds of the flat-faces' pawsteps had died away, "are they blind and deaf? Couldn't they even scent us?"

"I don't think they can scent anything with those tiny snouts, thank the stars," Kallik said, shaking her pelt.

Yakone was gazing around. "We have to rethink our route to stay away from the flat-faces," he decided. "The caribou aren't moving as fast as us, so that means we can take a longer route with more shelter."

Toklo nodded. "Back among the rocks," he agreed. "Then we can hide more easily if we need to."

Together the bears left the open plateau and climbed part of the way up to the ridge. They had to scramble among rocks and around trees, and sometimes plunge through patches of snow to get to more comfortable ground. Kallik's pelt prickled with the effort of staying alert for the signs of more flat-faces. *The awful creatures are everywhere!*

As they rounded a bramble thicket, a sudden squawk startled them as a grouse exploded from the ground and battered its wings around Toklo's head. Toklo lashed out a paw, but the bird swerved away and vanished into the trees. Kallik's heart pounded as they gazed after it.

"Too bad I wasn't faster," Toklo grunted. "That would have helped to fill our bellies."

"Never mind the grouse," Yakone said, padding onward. "What about the caribou? We can't see them from here. I'm afraid we've gone too high."

Toklo led the way through a patch of scrubby bushes to a jutting rock where they could look down onto the plateau. There was the caribou herd. Toklo gave a grunt of satisfaction at the sight of them, very small from this distance, surrounded by their dust cloud.

"We haven't lost them," he said.

Watching the progress of the caribou, Kallik felt a new surge of determination.

Hold on, Lusa! We're coming!

CHAPTER EIGHT

Lusa

A *shaft of burning light pierced* Lusa's skull. Slowly she struggled back to consciousness and saw that a beam of sunlight was shining through a gap in the wall, high over her head. The noise of animals and birds filled the air.

Taktuq's gruff voice came from close beside her. "Oh, you're awake."

Lusa's heart thumped with shock as she remembered where she was. She scrabbled to her paws and turned to the old black bear, who was crouched beside the bars of his own cage.

"I have to get out of here!" she gasped. "I have to find my friends!"

But her head still hurt so much she could barely stand, and her fur had a strange smell that reminded her of the flat-face healing den at the Bear Bowl.

"Did something happen to me?" she asked, sniffing her chest.

"The flat-faces took you out of your cage at sunrise," Taktuq replied. "You're injured, right?"

"A mule kicked me," Lusa said.

Taktuq gave a grunt of surprise. "What were you doing that close to a mule?"

"I was traveling with three other bears . . ." Lusa began, and launched into the story of meeting the long line of mules and trying to batter their way through to escape from the herd of flat-faces. "I ran away and lost my friends in the chaos," she finished. "Flat-faces found me and brought me here."

"And it's these friends that you want to find, right?" Taktuq checked.

Lusa decided not to tell him that one of the other bears was brown and two were white. "Yes. They're like my family," she explained. "We were on our way to Great Bear Lake. That's why I have to escape, or I'll never get there."

"The flat-faces will have treated your injury," Taktuq told her. "That's what they do."

A spark of hope woke inside Lusa. "And if I'm okay, they'll take me back to the mountains?"

Taktuq twitched his ears. "I don't know."

The noise from the other creatures was making Lusa's headache worse. She flopped down beside the cage bars, too miserable to look for a way to break out.

"Why don't you go outside?" Taktuq suggested, sounding more sympathetic. "The fresh air might make you feel better."

Lusa raised her head. "Outside? We can get out?"

"Sure. I told you before, remember? Look, it's this way."

Taktuq stood up and lumbered to the back wall, where he

pushed against the flap in the cage door. It swung open, and he scrambled through.

Lusa padded to the back of her own cage and pressed her forepaws against the flap that had been solid and unmoving the night before. This time it swung away from her easily, allowing her to wriggle through the flap and into the open. Sitting on the warm, damp grass, Lusa took in long gulps of air. It wasn't really fresh: She could pick up the scents of flat-faces and firebeasts, but it was certainly better than the stale air inside the den. There wasn't as much noise out here, either.

Ahead of Lusa stretched a long, thin pen enclosed on three sides by tall walls of silver mesh. Behind her was the wall of the den. Taktuq was in a similar enclosure on one side of her, and the coyote was on the other side. A line of other enclosures stretched in both directions.

Lusa glared as the scrawny, reddish-gray coyote padded up to the mesh and gave her a sniff, then turned away as if it was bored. Lusa noticed that it was walking unevenly and turned to Taktuq.

"The coyote's limping. What happened to it?"

"I have no idea," Taktuq replied. He didn't sound as if he cared, either.

Being surrounded by all these different creatures was making Lusa deeply uneasy. She tried to tell herself that it was just the same as the Bear Bowl, but she wasn't able to convince herself. In the Bear Bowl, there were no savage creatures like the coyote to bother her.

Besides, I've seen so much since then. I could never be content in the Bear Bowl now.

Meanwhile, Taktuq had stretched out in a patch of sunlight, turning so that his gray-furred belly was warmed by the rays. "Tell me about this Bear Bowl you come from," he said. "Why did the flat-faces put you there?"

"I was born there," Lusa corrected him. "My whole family was there." She didn't want to go too deeply into her memories of the Bear Bowl, because she knew she'd never make Taktuq understand. Even though she was glad of his company, the effort of talking to him was making her headache worse again. "I'm a wild bear now," she murmured. *And I have to escape, or I'll never see my friends again. And I'll never get to Great Bear Lake to meet Miki and his family.*

Lusa began to investigate the enclosure, sniffing around the mesh and looking for places where she could break through or dig her way out. But the mesh went right down into the earth, and she couldn't find any weak points. At the far end of the enclosure was a door, but it was shut tight, and far too small to escape through anyway.

As she snuffled her way around the enclosure, she caught a sudden strong whiff of coyote scent and jumped back as the creature beside her snapped its jaws at her, a paw's width away from the mesh. "Get away from me!" Lusa barked, scuttling out of range.

She heard Taktuq chuffing with amusement.

"It's not funny!" Lusa yelped. "I was hunted by a pack of coyotes once."

"Really?" Taktuq sounded impressed. "How did you escape?"

"We jumped onto a firesnake," Lusa announced proudly, then added, "Do you know about firesnakes?"

The old bear nodded. "My mother told me about them. And I remember hearing them screech sometimes, before I lived here. I can't believe it agreed to carry you."

"It didn't *agree*. I'm not sure it even knew we were riding on its back. It was scary! But we couldn't run any farther, because my friend Yakone hurt his paw in a flat-face thing with teeth."

Taktuq looked puzzled, then obviously decided to let it go. For a few moments he was silent. "You're lucky to be alive, if all that's true. Sounds like you'd be better off staying here," he said at last.

In one corner of Lusa's enclosure there was a small wooden shelter, and beside it a log lying on the ground. Nearby was a bucket of water. She went to get a drink, then began padding the length of the silver mesh restlessly, hating the feeling of being shut in when she had traveled freely all the way to the Endless Ice and back. *How did I ever survive in the Bear Bowl?*

"For the spirits' sake, settle down," Taktuq muttered irritably. "Listening to you walk in circles is making me tired."

Lusa ignored him. The coyote was bothering her, too; it had taken to padding alongside her, keeping pace with her on its own side of the mesh. It kept casting quick glances at her, its jaws wide and its pink tongue lolling. *It can't reach me through the mesh,* she thought. *At least, I don't think it can,* she added with a shiver.

Trying to take her mind off the disgusting creature, Lusa

remembered her vivid dream of Ujurak among the caribou. "Can you tell me more about the caribou?" she asked, swerving back to Taktuq's side of the enclosure.

"I think there was one here," the old bear replied. "But that was a few seasons ago. It didn't stay long."

"No, I'm looking for a whole herd of them," Lusa responded. "You said they come here at this season."

Taktuq let out a snort. "What do you want with caribou? Black bears don't eat them, and they're big enough to trample you."

"I know," Lusa said. "But I think I'll find my friends if I can find the caribou."

There was a stir from the other enclosures, and the two gray-furred flat-faces appeared, carrying bowls of food. They began pushing the bowls through the small door at the end of the pens.

Investigating her bowl, Lusa found it filled with grapes and chunks of apple, which she chewed up happily. In his enclosure, Taktuq was gulping his food down with cheerful snorting noises.

A rank scent drifted into Lusa's nostrils, and she looked sideways to see that the coyote was crouching over a bowl of raw, strong-smelling meat. *That's right . . . eat it up,* she thought. *You can't have black bear today!*

A third flat-face had come out with the older, gray-furred ones and stood watching Lusa while she ate. This flat-face was the cub Lusa had seen when she first arrived. It had long, dark head-fur, and spoke in a soft, high-pitched voice, which made Lusa think this was another female. After a few moments she came right up to Lusa's enclosure. The older flat-faces looked on warily at first, but when the young flat-face reached her hairless paw through the mesh, the older female darted forward and drew her gently away. She seemed to be explaining something in a quiet voice, touching the young flat-face's paw several times.

Lusa watched curiously, half-frightened and half-fascinated to be so close to these flat-faces. As she finished her bowl of fruit, the older female gave the young one an apple and pointed at Lusa with encouraging sounds. The young flat-face crouched down and rolled the apple through the mesh.

Lusa hesitated, wondering if it was a trap. *But I'm still hungry, and the fruit is so delicious. . . .* She crept closer to the mesh, reached out a paw to snatch the apple, then darted away again. The young flat-face let out a happy yelping sound.

"Becoming a pet now, are you?" Taktuq grunted. His head was tilted intently to pick up all the details of what was happening.

Lusa didn't know what he was talking about. *It was just some fruit, right?*

The young flat-face leaned on the mesh, watching Lusa eat the apple, and with the pressure of her body, Lusa noticed that the mesh was coming away from where it was attached in the top corner. Dropping the remains of the apple, she launched herself upward, scrabbling for the weak point.

Instantly the two older flat-faces dashed forward and pulled the younger one away, making shocked noises. The male grabbed a pronged stick and came toward Lusa with it. Lusa ignored him, clinging to the mesh while she tried to loosen it with her teeth and claws. But the next moment the male flat-face had pushed her gently to the ground with the end of the stick.

Lusa scrambled back onto her paws and roared at the flat-face. "You have to let me out of here!" she growled, biting at the end of the stick in a fit of anger.

The young flat-face wailed something to the older female.

"Stop it," Taktuq said. "Calm down. You're scaring them."

"They can't keep me here!" Lusa protested.

"They can," Taktuq contradicted her flatly.

The three flat-faces left in a hurry, the two older ones pushing the young one ahead of them.

"Come back!" Lusa barked after them. "Let me out! I have to find my friends!"

Fury erupted in Lusa's brain with the force of an exploding star. She stormed around her enclosure, ramming into the wooden shelter and knocking it over. She lashed out at the water bucket, spilling the water, and raked her claws down the log that lay on the ground.

I have to get out! I have to get out!

But all Lusa's fit of rage did was exhaust her. She collapsed on the ground, her head throbbing and her heart racing.

Taktuq pressed himself against the mesh until some of his fur poked through and brushed her side. "Steady, little one," he grunted, his voice unexpectedly gentle. "You're obviously not badly hurt. Perhaps they'll let you go."

Lusa raised her head. "I can't wait for the flat-faces to decide," she said. "I have to escape *now!*"

"You won't do that by scaring them," Taktuq told her. He was silent for a few moments, then added, "Sit up, Lusa. I want to show you something."

Weary and discouraged, Lusa pushed herself up from the ground. "What?"

"Watch the fox down there," Taktuq said, pointing with his snout down the line of enclosures. "I've heard the flat-faces talking to it. They treat it like a friend, from what I can tell."

Lusa spotted a small brown fox several cages away. *Taktuq knows it's there? He can hear and scent so much!*

The young female flat-face had reappeared and was heading toward the fox. Lusa watched, her interest piqued, as the young female opened a full-size door in the mesh and walked up to the animal. The fox leaped to its paws and ran over to her with an eager *yip.*

Taktuq's right! Lusa thought, astonished.

The young flat-face stooped down and stroked the fox's head, then fastened some kind of vine around its neck and guided it out of the enclosure with gentle tugs.

"She's letting it out!" Lusa exclaimed. A memory flashed into her head of seeing flat-faces walking like this with dogs, more than once on her journey. "It's like . . . like a dog!"

Beyond the mesh was a wide stretch of grass, where the fox and the flat-face played happily together, running alongside each other and jumping over logs laid on the ground.

"Why doesn't the fox bite through the vine and escape?" Lusa wondered aloud. "It could, easily. They're just running up and down."

"Maybe it likes being here," Taktuq responded.

How can it, if it is wild? Lusa thought.

Tired and discouraged, Lusa let her snout rest on her paws. Throbbing pain struck through her head where the mule had kicked her, and her legs felt too heavy for her to move. For a long time she dozed there on the grass, half listening to the sounds of birds and animals around her.

When Lusa woke, the daylight was beginning to fade, and a few stars had appeared. She lay on her back and stared up at them, but because darkness hadn't fallen, it was hard to make out any shapes. Then, as Lusa watched, some of the stars seemed to blaze extra bright, as if they were trying to catch her attention. Huge, glittering outlines began to appear against the darkening sky. *Oh . . . that's Ujurak! And his mother!* Clear above her head, they shone more brightly than any of the other stars.

That must be a sign from Ujurak, Lusa thought, quivering with excitement. *He knows where I am! He's watching over me!* She waited to see if Ujurak would speak to her, but no words came into her mind. Still, she felt a surge of hope. *I just need the flat-faces to let me out of the cage; then it would be much easier to escape.*

Lusa let out a long sigh. "I won't be here much longer!"

"I know what you're thinking," Taktuq grunted. "Do you really think you can persuade the flat-faces to trust you?

You're a bear, not a little fox! And you scared them today."

Lusa knew he was right; she was furious with herself for being so fluff-brained. *But I'm not giving up. I know what to do now, and I'm going to try. . . .*

CHAPTER NINE

Toklo

Night fell, and with clouds covering the moon, it became too difficult for the bears to continue traveling. Peering ahead through the darkness, Toklo realized that the caribou must have stopped, too. The clicking noise of their paws had fallen silent, and instead he could hear crunching as the animals grazed, along with the occasional bellow. His jaws watered as strong caribou scent was carried to him on the breeze.

"We could sneak down there," Toklo muttered, half to himself, "and pick one off, right on the edge of the herd. The rest of them wouldn't know a thing about it."

"I told you before," Kallik spoke sternly as she padded up beside Toklo. "We *need* the caribou. We'll have to hunt for something else instead."

"Okay, okay," Toklo grumbled.

"I'll go," Yakone offered, his white pelt fading swiftly into the darkness.

Meanwhile, Toklo and Kallik began to prepare a den in a thicket of berry bushes at the edge of the trees. As Toklo trampled down the undergrowth to make a flat place to sleep, he spotted some berries growing on one of the nearby bushes. His belly ached with hunger, so he pulled off a cluster and chomped it down, curling his lip at the bitter taste.

"Lusa would enjoy them," he murmured. "I hope she has enough to eat, wherever she is."

By the time the den was ready, Yakone had returned with a couple of ground squirrels. *They're not as satisfying as a caribou would be,* Toklo thought as he tore off his share of the meat, though he didn't say so out loud to Yakone.

When the food was finished, the two white bears curled up and went to sleep, but Toklo stayed awake for a while, watching the clouds drift across the night sky. In the gaps between them he caught glimpses of Ujurak and Ursa, and though he couldn't sense Ujurak anywhere close to him, he was sure that those stars were shining the brightest, reassuring them that they were on the right track.

"We are coming, Lusa," he whispered.

Toklo slept at last, but it seemed he had barely closed his eyes before he was roused by Yakone stirring beside him.

"The nights are so short a bear can hardly get a wink of sleep," the white male grumbled as he raised his head and peered around blearily.

"That's why we have to hurry up and find Lusa," Toklo responded. "The Longest Day can't be far off."

With a nod to each other, the two bears heaved themselves to their paws and slipped into the trees, muzzles raised and jaws open for any sign of prey.

Yakone tilted his snout toward a clump of long grass, and Toklo spotted the outline of a grouse in the gray dawn light. Setting his paws down as lightly as he could, he crept around in a wide circle until he was in position on the other side of the bird.

Growling fiercely, Yakone leaped forward. The grouse shot upward with a loud alarm call, heading straight for Toklo, who swatted it out of the air with one paw. Feeling thoroughly satisfied, he picked up his catch and carried it back to Kallik with Yakone padding by his side.

"We're a good team," Yakone commented.

Once they had eaten, the bears had to wait for the caribou to set out again. Toklo found a spot on an overhanging bluff where he had a good view of the herd. One or two of them were already on the move. Toklo spotted a young calf dart away from its mother and come skittering on unsteady legs almost as far as the bottom of the bluff where he was crouching. His paws itched to leap down on top of it, but he stayed where he was.

Kallik would claw my pelt off if I touched it!

A moment later the mother caribou let out a bellow and galloped up to her calf, chasing it back into the herd again. At the same time Toklo noticed that an old bull had wandered away from the group to pull at the leaves of a sage bush. Two younger males followed it and guided it back, just as the mother had done with her calf.

They look after each other, Toklo thought, surprised. He had always thought of caribou as stupid and couldn't imagine how they recognized one another when their herds were so big. *Weird . . . But I don't care what they do, just as long as they guide us to Lusa.*

The caribou started moving at last, and the bears followed. The sun rose higher in the sky, but it wasn't hot like it had been earlier in their journey. Toklo was relieved to see that the white bears were moving confidently over the icy patches that became more frequent as they headed closer to the glacier. A cold wind swept over them from the ice field; Kallik and Yakone raised their muzzles and sniffed at it happily.

It was almost sunhigh when they reached the glacier. Toklo eyed it warily, trying to hide how daunted he felt by the wall of ice that loomed above him. It was like a river that had been frozen and cut off midflow. But it was stained and dirty, dotted with stones and boulders. Instead of the sound of water, the vast body of ice creaked and strained, sounding like tree branches rubbing together, or rocks grinding over sand. Toklo hoped they wouldn't have to go any closer to the ice. He didn't trust it; it was too much like a living creature, waiting and watching the puny bears pass by.

He was relieved when the caribou skirted the edge of the glacier, and the bears trekked after them. But before they had gone far, Toklo spotted a long line of flat-faces heading alongside the glacier, their bright pelts standing out against the gray-white of the ice. They were fastened together with long vines, just like the mules had been on the day the bears lost Lusa.

"What are they doing now?" Toklo muttered.

"I don't know," Kallik responded, "but we'd better avoid them."

Toklo let out a low growl from deep in his throat. He knew Kallik was right, but that meant heading away from the caribou's direct route to find somewhere they could hide. The flat land beside the glacier offered no cover at all.

The caribou flowed on like a river, unstoppable and single-minded, apparently unaware of the flat-faces, who were much closer to the edge of the glacier. The flat-faces paused to watch the caribou for several moments, then moved on, getting closer and closer to the bears.

Yakone let out a growl, bunching his muscles as if he was ready to attack.

"No!" Kallik said sharply. "They might have firesticks!"

"Do you have a better idea?" Yakone asked.

Toklo cast a final desperate glance around and came to a decision. "We'll have to climb onto the glacier."

Kallik narrowed her eyes at the massive boulders that edged the creaking river of ice, then turned to look at Yakone. Toklo knew that she was wondering whether he would be able to handle the hard scramble.

"Fine," Yakone said firmly, as if he, too, understood what Kallik was thinking. "Let's go, before the flat-faces get any closer."

Giant boulders loomed up in front of the bears as they approached the glacier. For a moment Toklo worried about being able to hoist themselves over the smooth contours, slick with melting ice. Then he spotted a gap between two of the biggest rocks.

"This way!" he called.

The gap was narrow, and Toklo felt his fur brushing the rock walls on either side. Ahead of him the ice spilled down in frozen waves with smaller chunks of rock trapped inside it, which provided pawholds for them to climb.

Toklo clambered up as quickly as he could and turned to fasten his teeth in Yakone's scruff to help him up the last bear-length. Kallik followed, panting, and all three bears crowded together behind another boulder, listening to the chatter of the flat-faces as they passed by below.

"That was close," Yakone breathed out.

"Now that we're up here, maybe we should stay," Kallik suggested as the noise of the flat-faces began to die away. "Yakone and I can travel more easily on the ice, and we'll be safe from flat-faces."

"But what about the caribou?" Toklo asked. "They won't come up here, and we can't risk losing them."

"We won't," Kallik replied confidently. "We'll be traveling alongside them and can easily keep up."

Toklo glanced around. Harsh, dirty ice stretched away beneath their paws, while boulders blocked their path and their sight of the caribou. The surface of the glacier was riven with bottomless cracks, like empty streams with sheer sides. The landscape was tough and unwelcoming, but Kallik was right that they would be safer here on the glacier.

"Okay," he said. "Let's give it a try."

They had not been traveling long before Toklo wondered if they had made the right decision. Scrambling over the icy rocks slowed them down, and he began to worry that the caribou would leave them behind. But when he clambered up to the top of a boulder more than three bearlengths high, he saw that the herd was still in sight and the track left by their clicking feet was clear on the ground. The flat-faces were disappearing into the distance.

Toklo turned to speak to Yakone, who was hauling himself up onto the boulder beside him. "We might be okay to—" he began, but broke off as Yakone's paws skidded out from under him. Yakone scrabbled frantically at the ice-covered surface, but he couldn't get a grip.

"Kallik!" Toklo roared.

At the same moment he flung himself at Yakone and sank his claws hard into the white bear's shoulder. But Yakone was still slipping, his eyes wide with fear as he struggled to hold on to the rock.

A glance down revealed a narrow gap below them between two spiky pinnacles of rock. If he fell, Yakone might be crushed in the gap, or pierced by one of the sharp points.

Then Kallik was by Toklo's side, grabbing Yakone by his other shoulder. Together she and Toklo managed to haul Yakone up, paw's width by paw's width, until he could collapse safely on the top of the boulder.

"Thanks!" he gasped.

"Are you okay?" Toklo asked.

Yakone flexed his limbs, letting his weight rest on each in turn. His wounded paw was seeping blood again, staining the surface of the rock, but apart from that he seemed okay.

"I'm fine," he said firmly. "Just scared out of my fur!"

As the bears continued, Toklo kept a careful eye on Yakone, who was in the lead, and saw that he was limping again. Worse, he seemed to be finding it hard to keep his balance.

Did he wrench his shoulder?

Dropping back to pad along beside Kallik, Toklo leaned close to her and whispered, "I think one of us needs to lead the way, to look for the easiest route for Yakone. But we can't let him know that's what we're doing, because he won't want us to think that he's slowing us down."

Kallik flashed him a grateful look. "Thanks for understanding," she murmured.

Toklo let himself fall a little farther behind, while Kallik trotted ahead to catch up with Yakone and boost him over the next rock that was blocking their path.

Now Toklo could just barely make out the caribou herd in the distance, beyond the end of the glacier, and though he kept scanning the terrain, he couldn't see any easy way back to the flatter ground where they were. Boulders blocked his view in every direction, along with dark, jagged cracks in the ice that warned him of rifts where a bear might easily be swallowed up.

We'll have to move fast to catch up, he thought. *But how can we, when the going is this rough? Maybe we made a mistake, coming up here. . . .*

Toklo made an effort to pick up the pace, but his paws

slipped painfully on the ice. This was nothing like walking on the Frozen Sea. The surface was rutted and scored and full of sharp little stones that made Toklo wince as he set his pads down. Gritting his teeth, he struggled to catch up to the others again. "We're going to lose the caribou at this rate," he panted. "Do you know anything about dealing with this kind of ice?"

"I've never come across a place like this," Kallik admitted, shaking her head.

Both she and Yakone were looking confused, as if they couldn't imagine how their beloved ice was turning out to be so hostile.

Yakone murmured agreement. "I wonder if there are any other white bears here who can help?"

"Even if there are, we don't have time to stop and look for them," Kallik replied. "We've got to keep chasing the caribou. Come on!"

She lengthened her stride, loping along determinedly. Toklo and Yakone kept pace with her, Yakone trotting along unsteadily but managing to keep up. But the ice grew even more deeply rutted, so they kept stumbling into gullies or hurting their paws on the sharp upper edges.

Climbing down the side of a ridge, Toklo spotted a deep crevasse at the bottom of it, and at the same moment felt his paws slipping. He let out a roar of alarm and dug his claws hard into the ice, though he still kept sliding. "Stay back!" he bellowed to Kallik and Yakone.

The yawning gap was less than a bearlength away when

Toklo managed to stop himself, his claws gouging furrows into the ice. Peering down, he couldn't see the bottom of the crevasse, and his pelt grew hot at the thought of plummeting into the dark depths. The rift stretched away in both directions as far as he could see, but it was narrow, less than a bearlength to the other side.

Toklo let out a growl of frustration, anger pushing away his fear. *Why did we take this spirit-cursed path?* he asked himself.

Kallik and Yakone clambered down more cautiously and reached his side.

"We'll have to jump," Toklo said, conscious that all the time the caribou were getting farther away from them. "Yakone, can you make it?"

"I'll be fine," the white male responded grimly.

"I'll go first." Kallik took a run up to the crevasse and launched herself into the air. A moment later she landed safely on the other side.

"Now you," Toklo said to Yakone.

The white bear approached the cleft at a shambling run, while Kallik waited on the other side, ready to grab him if he fell short. Yakone pushed off and staggered as his forepaws struck the ice on the far side. Kallik steadied him, shoving him farther from the crevasse.

Toklo let out a breath of relief, then lumbered up to the rift and bunched his muscles for the leap. He caught a glimpse of the dizzying depths below him, then landed with a thump on the far side. "Made it!" he exclaimed with satisfaction.

Kallik headed off as soon as she saw that Toklo was safe.

"Come on!" she called over her shoulder. "We have to keep the caribou in sight!"

Her last words were followed by a roar of alarm. One moment she was bounding over the ice. The next, the glacier had opened beneath her paws and Kallik lurched over the edge of the yawning gap.

CHAPTER TEN

Kallik

Kallik let out a yelp of alarm as the ground vanished from beneath her front paws. Panic surged through her at the sight of sheer ice walls stretching down below her into darkness.

Another crevasse!

With a frantic effort she scrabbled at the solid ice behind her with her back paws. Reaching out with her forelegs, she managed to grab the opposite edge of the rift. Desperately she stabbed her claws into the ice and managed to halt her downward slide, but she lost her grip with her hind claws, and her haunches slipped down into the gap. Now her back legs were dangling down into the chasm. Her claws strained from supporting her weight.

"Help!" she called. "I can't hold on!"

"I'm coming!" Yakone's voice sounded from above Kallik's head, and she saw him leaping to the other side of the crevasse. A moment later he appeared and leaned over the edge, reaching his paws down toward her. "Hang on!"

Yakone fastened his claws into Kallik's forelegs, but his

mangled paw couldn't keep a strong grasp. Kallik saw him gritting his teeth against the pain as he struggled to pull her up.

A roar from Toklo came dimly to Kallik's ears. "I'm almost there! Hold on!"

But Kallik felt Yakone's claws begin sliding along her flesh and fur. "I'm losing my grip!" he gasped.

His voice changed to a roar of terror as a clump of fur tore away from Kallik's leg, and she fell.

The darkness from below filled Kallik's vision, and she lost sight of Yakone. Her body thumped against the opposite side of the crevasse, and she slid down it until finally her hindpaws collided with solid rock. Kallik tried to brace herself, but the speed of her fall was too great. She was thrown forward by the impact, and her head struck the wall of ice. A starburst of light exploded behind her eyes, followed by thick, suffocating darkness.

Kallik blinked and rubbed her eyes. *What happened . . . ? Where . . . ?* Then memory began to seep back, and she realized that she had fallen into the crevasse.

Cold terror poured into Kallik as she looked up and saw the narrow stretch of blue sky far above her head. She knew she had to get up and find a way out, but the pain in her head left her dazed and trembling. When she tried to scramble to her paws, she felt so groggy and her legs felt so weak that she sank down again and rested her head on her paws.

I'll try to get out in a little while, she told herself. *But I need to sleep first. . . .*

"Kallik! Kallik!"

Frantic cries echoing down into the crevasse tugged her back to consciousness. She recognized Yakone's and Toklo's voices, full of fear and anxiety.

"Kallik, can you hear us?"

Kallik angled her head upward. "I'm down here!" she called, her voice weak and shaky. "I'm alive. I'll find a way out, I promise."

"Thank the spirits!" Yakone's voice was full of relief. "We've been calling and calling."

"I can see the end of the crevasse, over in this direction," Toklo barked. "We can wait for you there."

"Wait! I can't see you! Can you see me?" Kallik asked as loudly as she could, not sure which direction Toklo meant.

There was no reply, just a tumble of dirty ice fragments down the wall beside her, which made her lurch back to avoid getting struck. Toklo and Yakone must have backed away from the edge. Kallik knew she had to force herself into action. As her eyes became used to the half-light, she saw the crevasse was very narrow, barely wide enough to hold her. Like the surface above, the walls were made of jagged ice with boulders wedged into it, and beneath her paws were small, loose stones, and grit covering solid rock.

I'm under the glacier, she thought wonderingly.

Kallik realized she was facing farther into the ice, but the rift was too narrow for her to turn. For several moments she kept trying anyway, forcing down panic, but all she was able to do was scrape her sides on the rough edges of the rock. At last she gave up, panting.

Toklo called down to her again. "Kallik, we'll walk along the crevasse and meet you at the end." His echoing voice was dying away behind Kallik.

"No—I can't go that way!" she cried out.

But Toklo and Yakone were already moving off. She could feel the vibrations of their pawsteps thudding away.

Desperately, Kallik did the only thing she could: push herself forward, up toward the source of the glacier. But the dim light made it almost impossible to see where she was going. More than once she tripped and stumbled over loose rocks, or the walls curved unexpectedly and she crashed into them with her muzzle or her shoulder.

Determined to keep going, Kallik pressed her flank against one of the ice walls. The rough edges of rocks and sharp blades of ice scraped at her fur and bruised her ribs, but she pushed on, refusing to step away and lose track of where she was.

Without warning, one wall curved sharply toward the other, and the path became only just wide enough for Kallik's body.

It's getting narrower! she realized, horror of being wedged down there flooding through her. Now her fur brushed the walls on both sides, and her face was scratched by jutting shards of ice and stone that scraped perilously close to her injured eye.

Kallik's breath came fast and shallow. She made another effort to turn around, but the walls were so much closer here that there was no chance of turning, and she soon gave up. She couldn't even slide back the way she came, because now that she'd squeezed through, she was unable to force her hips backward through the tiny gap.

Knowing it was her only choice, Kallik took a deep breath and surged forward, feeling the walls pressing against her from both sides. They had curved together above her head now, blocking out the sky. With every pawstep the crevasse grew narrower, and soon she had to force her way through, with the jagged rocks tearing at her. At last, she found herself completely stuck, unable to move forward or backward.

No! she thought. *This can't be happening!*

In a panic she began scrabbling at the walls in a desperate attempt to climb out, but all she did was exhaust herself.

Finally, half collapsing, her chest heaving as she fought for breath, Kallik peered into the dim depths of the passage ahead. *I have to get through!*

With a great deal of effort she pushed forward, feeling her pelt ripping on the rocks and her ribs getting crushed by the walls of ice. Breathing in, she took another step and another, forcing her way through inch by inch until the walls suddenly widened again and she stumbled clear.

Kallik halted, gulping in long breaths. Creaking noises drifted through the air, and a strange, eerie light filtered down through the ice, showing her the passage in front of her. At last there was space enough for her to turn around.

But I'm not going through there again! she thought, glancing back the way she had come.

Her sides bruised and scraped, her paws splitting on the sharp stones, Kallik stumbled on. The path led upward, though at the same time she was aware that the walls were getting higher. A wave of despair and fear began to swell inside her.

I'm buried under the ice!

Kallik closed her eyes and steadied her breathing, focusing on images of stars and calm ice to see if she could communicate with the spirits, but there were no bubbles or patterns in the ice of the crevasse that might whisper to her of white bears from the past. All she could hear was the ominous creaking, the gigantic moans of a vast creature moving around her.

This isn't the sort of ice that I know. . . .

The sounds made Kallik feel very small and vulnerable. All her life the ice had been her home, her friend, the place where she knew she belonged. But this ice was indifferent and hostile, trapping her as if she was a seal without a hole to escape. She realized with a new feeling of dread that there were no spirits here, nothing to protect her from the malignant presence all around her. The ice moaned again.

It's like it's alive!

As she went on, she found herself setting her paws down as lightly as she could, hardly even daring to breathe, as if she might manage to avoid the attention of the huge being that surrounded her on all sides.

Panic surged up again inside Kallik. She wanted to run, to

SEEKERS: RETURN TO THE WILD: THE BURNING HORIZON 133

batter a way out through the walls of ice. But before she lost all control, she felt a warm body pressing against hers, urging her to go on padding steadily upward.

"Ujurak?" she said, her voice quavering.

"Yes, I'm here."

To her surprise, Kallik picked up fear in Ujurak's voice, as well as a slight tremble in the body that she felt but couldn't see. It was like he was a young, overwhelmed little bear again, perhaps because being underneath a glacier was so different from anything he had experienced before.

Strangely, the realization that her guide was frightened, too, helped to calm Kallik. She was reminded of how she had cared for the cub Kissimi on Star Island.

We can help each other.

"Does this path lead to the surface?" she asked Ujurak. "Is it much farther?"

"I don't know," the smaller bear replied. "But it's the best hope we have, so we'd better keep going."

"It's good to have you here," Kallik said.

For a moment she felt Ujurak's body press more closely to her side. "I'm glad to be with you again."

As the two bears stumbled on, Kallik noticed that the ice above her head was beginning to darken. Fresh terror crept over her as she realized that night was falling. "I'm so afraid," she whispered. "I can't handle being trapped here in the dark, alone."

Ujurak's voice was warm. "You're never alone."

Together Kallik and Ujurak climbed and climbed up the

slope as the light grew dimmer. Kallik struggled to keep putting one aching paw in front of the other, covering bearlength after bearlength without any sign that they were coming closer to the surface.

Stumbling over a loose rock, Kallik lost her balance and fell. For a moment she lay still, unable to gather the strength to rise to her paws and carry on. "I just want to lie here and sleep for a while," she murmured.

"No!" Ujurak gave her a hard shove. "You can't sleep here. If you do, you'll never wake."

He gave Kallik another shove, urging her to her paws again. Kallik got up and staggered on, but her head was spinning and she struggled to cling to consciousness.

A few paces ahead, she realized that her sides were brushing the walls of the crevasse. "It's getting narrower again," she choked out. "I'll get stuck!"

"No, you won't." Ujurak's voice was reassuring. "Just keep going."

Kallik pushed herself forward, wondering how Ujurak managed to stay by her side when there was hardly enough room for her to force herself through the narrow path.

Step by step they carried on. There was one horrible moment when Kallik became wedged in an angle of the passage. Sharp pain bit into her shoulder as she finally wrenched herself free. "Why is it so . . . hard?" she panted.

But the next section of the path was wider again, and the going became easier. Then Kallik realized that something felt different on her fur. Pausing to sniff the air, she realized a breeze was flowing over her, cool and fresh, smelling of ice and mountains.

"We must be close to a way out!" she exclaimed.

Kallik mustered her last reserves of strength and hauled herself upward in the twilight. She could see the sky above her now. It was pale, and she could make out a few glimmering stars. "We're going to get out!" she told Ujurak, then realized that he wasn't with her anymore. Brief sadness passed over her like a gust of wind, followed by a boundless gratitude that he had stayed with her through the worst of her ordeal.

"Thank you, Ujurak," she whispered.

The ice walls were lower now, though still higher than Kallik could reach if she balanced on her hindpaws. But with the surface so near, she pressed forward with new energy, certain she would be able to climb out soon.

At last Kallik heaved herself out of the crevasse, now no more than a shallow gully across the face of the glacier. She lay on the surface of the glacier, gasping for breath, with the mountain peaks looking down at her. Her head reeled, and the stars spun above her, but she could still make out the Pathway Star, and the blazing shapes of Ujurak and his mother.

"Thank you, Ujurak!" she breathed out once again.

CHAPTER ELEVEN

Lusa

Lusa lay on her side with the sun beating down on her until her fur was uncomfortably hot and her mouth was dry with thirst. She had spent the whole day waiting by the mesh for the flat-faces to return.

I have to show them that I'm friendly! I wasn't trying to attack them!

But the flat-faces never came.

"Don't get your hopes up," Taktuq advised her, a hint of amusement in his voice. "The flat-faces will let you out when they're ready. Besides, you're safe and well fed here. What's your problem?"

Lusa sprang to her paws and faced the old bear. "It's all wrong!" she snarled. "Bears should be wild."

"In the wild, I would be dead by now," Taktuq pointed out quietly.

Lusa glared at him for a moment longer, then relaxed, letting out a sigh. "I know, I'm sorry," she said. "But this life isn't for me."

Taktuq shook his head, baffled. "I'll never understand what's so wonderful about living in the wild."

Lusa drew in her breath for a hot protest.

"Okay, okay," Taktuq added quickly. "I know I'm never going to change your mind."

As the sun went down, Lusa heard movement from inside the den and picked up the scent of fruit drifting toward her. She realized that the flat-faces must have brought food to lure her back inside. The other animals had already retreated, even the coyote. Though every hair on her pelt wanted to stay in the open, she knew she needed to do whatever the flat-faces asked her to right now. She forced herself to go back in through the flap, looking as small and meek and unthreatening as she could.

But the flat-face—the gray-furred male—didn't speak to her or try to touch her. Frustrated, Lusa gazed at the fruit. She had no appetite for the sweet taste now, and although she told herself she had to eat to keep her strength up, the thought of it nauseated her. She slumped down in front of the bowl.

Taktuq lifted his head from his own bowl and turned his cloud-colored eyes toward her. "It will take time to win their trust," he said sympathetically.

"I don't have time!" Lusa retorted.

The old bear didn't respond at first, only finished his food in a few swift gulps, then shuffled over to the bars that separated him from Lusa and flopped down.

"Come here," he said. When Lusa didn't move, he added,

"Come on. I want you to talk to me."

Lusa felt so weary and miserable, it was easier to give in to him than to start arguing. She stumbled across her cage and sank down next to Taktuq. The old bear pressed up against the bars so that their pelts brushed.

At the touch some of Lusa's misery began to dissolve. She felt safe and protected, as if she was a cub again.

"Tell me about these other bears," Taktuq said gruffly.

Lusa sighed, deciding that she would tell Taktuq the truth after all. "At first I was with a brown bear and a . . . another brown bear," she began. "And at Great Bear Lake we met a white bear."

"What?" Outrage and surprise mingled in Taktuq's voice. "You mean you weren't traveling with *black* bears? Why in the name of Arcturus would you do that?"

"It just happened that way," Lusa said. "They're really good friends, believe me."

Taktuq gave a disbelieving snort.

"We've traveled so far together," Lusa told him. "All the way to the Endless Ice, and then back again."

"The Endless Ice really exists?" Taktuq asked, sounding astonished. "My mother used to tell me about it, but I thought it was just a story."

"Oh yes—it goes on forever. I never knew there was so much space in the world . . . so much sky. I nearly froze and starved to death, and I wanted so much to fall into the long-sleep, but I knew if I did, I would never wake up."

Taktuq poked his snout through the bars to nuzzle her

shoulder. "You must have been terrified."

"I was," Lusa responded. "But it was wonderful, too. We saw the spirits dancing in the sky, all the colors you could imagine, and the stars were so bright!" Suddenly she remembered Taktuq's blindness. "I'm sorry," she added. "I forgot you'll never be able to see that."

"That's not important," Taktuq grunted. He paused for a moment, then added, "How did you get here?"

"One of the brown bears died there, on an island in the Endless Ice." Fresh sadness swept over Lusa as she remembered Ujurak's small body, broken by the avalanche. "And another white bear joined us for this part of the journey. We were traveling to Great Bear Lake when I was injured by the mule, like I told you."

Taktuq sniffed, but he made no other comments about her traveling companions. "So . . . why Great Bear Lake?"

"We were looking for our homes," Lusa told him. "The others have all found theirs, but I haven't. Not yet."

There was admiration in Taktuq's voice, though his tone was still gruff, as if he was reluctant to admit his awe for what Lusa and her friends had experienced. "You really have done some extraordinary things."

"Yes," Lusa responded. She realized for the first time that Taktuq was much like Toklo in his gruffness and the friendliness hidden beneath it. "But it will all have been for nothing if I can't find a place where I truly belong."

Taktuq let out a sigh. "You can belong anywhere if you try hard enough," he said quietly.

* * *

When the next morning came, Lusa continued her plan, eager to show the flat-faces how friendly she was. She pressed up against the bars of her cage, waiting for the first appearance of her captors.

As soon as they opened the door of the den, the other creatures set up their usual racket, flapping about or scrabbling at their bars. Lusa refused to let it bother her and just sat quietly, trying to make a show of looking gentle and safe. But the flat-faces paid her no attention, just checking the rows of cages.

Disappointed, Lusa told herself she would have a better chance of impressing them once she was allowed outside. Scuffling her paws impatiently, she heard a clinking sound from the outer flap and realized that must mean the flap had been opened.

She skipped outside and waited for the flat-faces to appear with the morning food.

What did I do when I was in the Bear Bowl? she asked herself, trying to remember. *What made the flat-faces laugh?* Glancing around, she spotted the log she had clawed in her fit of rage the day before. *Maybe I could think of a game with that. . . .*

Lusa felt stiff and awkward as she padded up to the log and gave it a prod. The days when she had been a carefree cub playing in the Bear Bowl seemed like they had happened to a different bear. But the flat-faces had appeared now, delivering food bowls to each enclosure, and she knew she had to think of something quickly.

I know! I'll pretend that it's a salmon, and I'm going to catch it!

Lusa skipped from side to side, making little pounces at the log. Then she pretended that the river had knocked her off her paws, and rolled over on her back, waving her paws in the air. Though she was careful not to look at the flat-faces, she was aware that they had stopped to watch and heard them let out cheerful barking sounds.

A quick glance showed Lusa that the young female flat-face was hanging back behind the older ones, clearly still wary of her. Staying back from the mesh, Lusa carried on playing, then bounced over to her fruit bowl and began to eat, holding the fruit in her front paws like she was a ground squirrel.

The flat-faces at the Bear Bowl liked to see that—only the spirits know why!

But when she looked up with a chunk of apple in her paws, Lusa was disappointed to see that the older flat-faces had gone on to deliver the rest of the food bowls, and the young one had vanished altogether.

What's the point of being cute if no one is watching?

Leaving the rest of the fruit, Lusa slumped down beside the mesh near Taktuq. "I tried to make friends with that young one, but it didn't work," she complained.

"It didn't work *yet*," Taktuq corrected her.

Lusa shrugged. She watched as the young flat-face reappeared from one of the small flat-face dens that were clustered outside. She went into the fox's enclosure to take him out on the vine. Lusa's paws itched to join them as they ran up and down and played on the grass beyond the mesh. The fox rolled over, waving his paws happily as the young flat-face rubbed his belly.

A growl from the enclosure next to her distracted Lusa, and she spotted the coyote glaring at her again, its teeth bared. Lusa curled her lip at it, frustration at her captivity spilling over into anger.

I've fought fiercer coyotes than you, you mangy carrion-eater! she snarled inwardly. *But now I've got to be little and sweet and gentle, so consider yourself lucky!*

The day seemed to drag by. After the young flat-face returned the fox to his enclosure, she disappeared again. Bored and frustrated, Lusa flopped down and tried to sleep, slipping into an uneasy doze.

Sunhigh came and went before the young flat-face came out again. This time she was with the older male. They were playing with a small, round, scarlet-colored object, throwing it to each other on the grass outside the pens.

Lusa watched curiously as the gray-furred male threw the object too high. It soared over the young female's head and landed with a thump in Lusa's enclosure, making her jump. The young flat-face let out a cry of surprise.

Lusa trotted forward and patted the object. It was like a smooth, round, lightweight stone. It weighed less than an apple, and yielded slightly when Lusa pressed it with her paw. Fascinated, she rolled it about, aware of the flat-faces watching her. *Time to try again.* Using a bit more force, she made the thing roll away from her, then chased it.

I feel like such an idiot! Lusa thought. *What would Toklo say if he could see me now?*

But it was working. The young flat-face let out happy barks, and clapped her front paws together. In the next enclosure Taktuq tilted his head, listening. "Now what are you up to?" he asked.

Lusa paused, her breath coming in quick puffs. "I'm playing with this round thing the flat-faces threw," she explained. "They're watching me—they think it's fun."

"Then you're doing well," Taktuq grunted from behind his mesh. "Who would have thought a wild bear could think up tricks like that?"

Lusa couldn't tell if he was being sarcastic or sympathetic, so she ignored him, just as she ignored the coyote, still snarling and snapping on her other side.

She kept playing with the round thing, being as cute as possible, but then the young flat-face turned around and trotted away. Lusa shoved the round thing aside and clawed at the log in frustration, forgetting that the older male was still watching her.

"Careful," Taktuq warned her. "Don't spoil it now."

Moments later the young flat-face returned, followed by the older female. The young one had a piece of fruit in her hand, and she pushed it through the mesh to Lusa while both the older flat-faces stood watchfully nearby.

Lusa padded up to the mesh and very carefully took the

fruit from the young female's paw. While she was eating, the gray-furred male said something to the younger one, and they both walked away with the older female. The young flat-face looked back over her shoulder and waved one hairless paw at Lusa.

Lusa swallowed the last of the fruit and stretched out, feeling exhausted from so much thinking and pretending. *Is my plan working?* she fretted. *Will I escape?* She wondered where Toklo and Yakone and Kallik were, and what they were doing. *They must be looking for me, probably going out of their minds with worry. Will Ujurak tell them that I'm underneath his stars?*

Even if he did, Lusa knew that she couldn't expect her friends to come into this den and let her out. If they got caught, none of them would make it to Great Bear Lake. She would have to escape and find them. At least the stars were a sign to her that she shouldn't give up, because she knew that Ujurak and Ursa hadn't abandoned her.

Drifting into sleep, Lusa dreamed that she had turned into a bird. Instead of her familiar black fur and four sturdy legs, she had glossy feathers and strong wings, which she beat, reveling in the sensation of the air currents holding her up as she soared to the top of a tall tree.

She flew higher and higher, above denning places and the BlackPaths, up into the sky, the firebeasts below growing smaller and smaller until she couldn't see them anymore. She soared over mountains, rivers, plains, and ice, searching and searching for her friends. Her eyes were so powerful that she could pick out the tiniest leaf or pebble, the least flicker of movement as a vole slipped out from the shelter of a bush. But there were no bears in all the wide landscape below her.

"Where are you?" she called in her harsh bird voice. "Where are you?"

CHAPTER TWELVE

Toklo

"Kallik, we'll walk along the crevasse and meet you at the end!" Toklo bellowed down into the ice. He thought he could hear a faint response but couldn't make out the words. "I'm not sure if she can hear me," he added to Yakone, who looked stunned, his eyes full of horror at the way Kallik had simply disappeared.

"We have to do something to help her," he said.

"There's nothing we can do," Toklo responded grimly. "If we tried to get to her, we would all be trapped. All we can do is follow the crevasse and hope we can help her out at the end."

Yakone nodded reluctantly. Side by side the two bears padded along the edge of the crevasse toward the end that was closest. Though he was trying to stay calm for Yakone's sake, Toklo's head was reeling. *First Lusa, now Kallik! Am I going to lose every one of my friends?*

"It's all my fault," he muttered. "I shouldn't have made us come onto the glacier to begin with. If we'd headed down into the trees, we could have avoided the flat-faces more safely and kept the caribou in sight. Now we've lost Kallik, and the caribou herd that was leading us to Lusa will soon be long gone."

"It's *not* your fault," Yakone insisted, overhearing him. "We were all rushing, and if my dumb paw hadn't held us up . . ."

"You can't help being injured—" Toklo began, then broke off as he spotted another wide crack zigzagging across the ice, branching from Kallik's crevasse. He ran over to it and peered down into the dark depths. "Kallik!" he roared. "Kallik!"

Yakone joined him, and both bears bellowed their friend's name until they were hoarse. But there was no reply, only the echoes of their own voices.

"We have no way of knowing if she's making any progress. Maybe she's trapped down there . . . or worse," Yakone said, his eyes full of fear.

"Don't think that!" Toklo snapped. "Maybe she just hasn't reached this part yet." *I have to believe that,* he told himself determinedly. "We're here, Kallik! Keep going!" he called out again, just in case their friend could hear him.

This crack that crossed Kallik's crevasse was wider than the one they had jumped before. They decided Toklo would make the leap first, so he would be there to help Yakone on the other side. Toklo took a long run up to it and drew on all his strength as he pushed off into a leap. He landed safely, wincing as his paws thumped onto the rough surface. Then he turned to help Yakone.

The white male was already launching himself into the air. He came down on the very edge of the crack, letting out a yelp of pain as his wounded paw hit the ice. His hindpaws were perilously close to thin air, and Toklo grabbed his shoulder fur to haul him clear.

"Thanks!" Yakone panted.

"Do you need to rest?" Toklo asked, glancing at Yakone's injured paw, which was oozing blood again.

"I'm not going to rest for a single moment until we find Kallik!" Yakone growled.

Toklo nodded. "You're right. Let's keep going."

His belly was bawling with hunger, and he knew that Yakone must be just as famished. His mouth was dry, too, and both bears paused briefly to lick moisture from the ice. It hardly helped.

We can't waste time hunting, Toklo thought. *Besides, there's no prey out here, only a bird swooping overhead now and then.*

More and more rifts in the ice crossed their path, and Toklo was afraid that they would lose Kallik's crevasse in the confusing crisscrossing gaps, or when they had to leave the edge of it to skirt around boulders or tall ice ridges. His fear and sense of urgency was growing with every pawstep. *We have to believe she'll make it to the end,* he thought, struggling with a horrible picture in his mind of Kallik stuck and helpless. *If we're not there when she gets out, she might think we've left her behind.*

"Look!" Yakone pointed ahead with his muzzle.

Toklo's brief hope that the white bear had spotted Kallik died as he saw a herd of flat-faces clambering up the glacier, tied together with vines like the first group they had seen, and prodding at the ice with sharp sticks. Their bright-red pelts were like spots of blood on the surface of the glacier.

"They're up here, too? That's all we need!" he groaned.

"We have to hide," hissed Yakone.

But when Toklo looked around, he couldn't see a single place where they could take cover from the flat-faces. Between them and the looming mountain ridge, the glacier was strewn with boulders too small to duck behind, and the folds of ice weren't high enough to hide them, either.

The two bears stopped in panic as the flat-faces drew closer, calling to one another in their high, bird-like voices. Toklo could feel the ice trembling under his paws from their thumping pawsteps and the blows from their pointed sticks. All of Toklo's instincts were telling him to run before the flat-faces spotted them, but he knew that if they did, they would never find Kallik's crevasse again. Indecision and near panic froze his paws to the ground.

Then Yakone pointed downward with his snout toward a small crack in the ice. "We'll have to hide down there."

Toklo stared in disbelief. "We'll fall . . . we'll be trapped like Kallik."

"We won't fall." Yakone was trying to sound confident. "It's big enough to hide us, but too narrow for us to fall down. Now go!" He gave Toklo a shove.

Every hair on Toklo's pelt was bristling with terror as he lowered himself haunches first into the crack. It felt like a mouth gaping to swallow him up. The crack was just wide enough for him to fit through, and though Yakone was right that it narrowed just below his body, he still felt as if the glacier was pulling him down into its creaking, whispering belly.

He picked up a stale, stony smell from the cold, empty air beneath him.

Yakone almost squashed Toklo as he eased down into the crack beside him. Both bears dug their claws into the ice, clinging to the lip of the crevasse as the flat-faces trekked past, chattering and puffing. Toklo held his breath and listened to the sounds of the flat-faces as they faded into the distance. Then to his horror he felt his back claws sliding and chips of ice crumbling away under his weight.

"I'm slipping!" he gasped. "I've got to get out!"

Instantly Yakone clawed his way out of the crack and grabbed Toklo's scruff in his jaws, hauling him upward. Toklo scrabbled frantically with his hindpaws and collapsed, panting, on the surface of the glacier. Exhaustion and fear made his head whirl, and he was shaking beneath his fur. Yakone looked just as bad, his fur filthy, his wounded paw bleeding again, and his eyes filled with fear.

"Great spirits, Ujurak, where are you? Can't you see what's happening?" Toklo muttered, feeling anger building inside him. "Or have you given up any hope of saving us?"

Yakone rested a paw on his shoulder. "We can't give up," he said. "Not on Kallik, not on Lusa. And not on Ujurak."

Toklo let out a long sigh. "You're right," he grunted, hauling himself to his paws.

Dusk was falling as the bears set out again. The terrain grew rockier and rougher, and their pace dropped as they drew close to the edge of the glacier. Their paws slipped on the sloping surface, and boulders or folds in the ice made it hard to follow the edge of Kallik's crevasse. They kept on calling out to her in case she was close enough to hear them, but there was never a reply.

"I really don't want to stay on the glacier overnight," Toklo said, gazing around uneasily at the frozen river. In the still air the creaking and groaning sounds seemed louder, and the ice glowed eerily in the dim light. *I just know I can feel it shifting under my paws.*

"I don't like it, either," Yakone responded. "But we can't leave Kallik."

Suddenly Yakone stopped walking. "Toklo. Look!"

Just up ahead, the crevasse they had been following dwindled to the tiniest crack.

Toklo gazed at it in despair. *Even if Kallik made it this far, there's no way she could get out.*

"Are you sure this is Kallik's crevasse?" he asked Yakone, hoping for even the slightest possibility that somewhere they had taken a wrong turn.

"I'm sure," Yakone replied heavily, panic in his voice. "But maybe we should search the others."

Together the two bears skirted along the top of the glacier's edge, looking for other cracks that could possibly be Kallik's. Plenty of dark rifts zigzagged across the surface, but none of them went in the direction where Kallik had fallen.

For a moment Toklo felt too frightened to take a step. He loathed this waste of creaking ice and its treacherous crevasses, and he was rapidly losing all hope of finding Kallik.

But we have to find her! We can't lose Kallik, too!

Toklo forced himself to walk back to the skinny end of the crevasse, peering down it and trying to figure out what to do while Yakone continued to pad restlessly along the edge of the glacier, looking for other places where Kallik might emerge from the ice. Toklo waited for him, scanning the frozen waste for the shape of a white bear who never appeared.

At last Yakone limped back to Toklo's side. His eyes were full of despair, and he was clearly struggling to keep his voice even. "We should find somewhere to rest for the night," he said. "We'll keep looking for her when it's light."

"No, we should go farther back and look for other cracks where she might have broken off in another direction," Toklo argued. "You said you wouldn't rest for a moment until we found her."

"I was wrong." Yakone's voice was stern. "What good will we be to Kallik or Lusa if we starve or refuse to sleep? Kallik is smart enough to stop and rest when night falls. We won't lose her if we take time to do the same."

Toklo could see the sense in what Yakone said and allowed the white male to nudge him toward the edge of the glacier. Together they scrambled and slithered down the ice floe until their paws hit rock and soil. Toklo felt a massive relief to have earth under his pads. As he paused for a moment to catch his breath, he noticed a dark-brown mass moving just above the tree line in the distance.

"Yakone, look!" he shouted with a surge of relief. "It's the caribou! We haven't lost them after all!" Then he looked back to see the glacier looming vast and impenetrable above him, and his brief excitement leaked away.

But Kallik is still somewhere under there. . . .

Yakone led the way to a scatter of boulders a short distance from the foot of the glacier where a few scrawny bushes grew. Turning around and around in the middle of the bushes, Yakone trampled down a sleeping-place. Then he clambered out from the branches and disappeared into the gathering darkness without saying a word.

Toklo just stood gazing up at the glacier, peering through the gloom in the hope of seeing a white shape emerging from the gray ice, until Yakone returned with a ptarmigan in his jaws.

"It's not much, but it'll have to do," he said, dropping the tawny bird at Toklo's paws.

When they had shared the bird, the bears settled down in their makeshift den. Yakone curled himself around Toklo, and though Toklo thought worry would keep him awake, he slid swiftly into sleep.

He dreamed that he was standing on the Endless Ice, its gleaming surface stretching around him as far as he could see. He was all alone; above him, the night sky glittered with stars. He could hear a faint whispering, like wind sweeping across the frozen surface, but no breeze stirred his fur. Toklo pricked his ears and turned his head. The whispering grew louder, more desperate, until he was surrounded by shrieks of despair and fear.

To his horror, they were coming from the ice beneath his paws.

"Help me! I'm trapped!"

"Help me!"

"Don't leave me here!"

Looking down, Toklo bit back a cry of dismay. Kallik, Lusa, and Yakone were staring up at him with huge, terrified eyes beneath the barrier of ice.

"I'm here! I'll get you out!" Toklo bellowed. He reared up on his hind legs and plunged down on the ice, battering it with his front paws. Three pairs of eyes watched unblinking, in mute alarm. But though Toklo scrabbled at the ice until his claws broke and his paws began to bleed, he couldn't break through to free his friends.

There must be a way! he thought.

He ran back and forth, searching for a crack in the ice, a seal hole, anything to help him shatter the glimmering surface.

"Ujurak, where are you?" he roared.

Then cold horror bit even deeper as he saw the tiny starlit bear trapped and desperate beneath the ice beside his friends. He stared helplessly up at Toklo, looking even smaller than when he was alive. On his shoulders his brown fur had vanished and was replaced by glimmering fish scales, as if he had been frozen in a last desperate attempt to change shape.

"Ujurak," Toklo whispered. "You can't be stuck, too!"

Toklo forced himself to tip back his head and look up at the sky. There was nothing but darkness where Ujurak's star-shape should have been. Toklo was left cold and alone, while all his friends began to sink down into the shadowy ocean.

"No!" Toklo roared. He hurled himself down at the ice again, battering and clawing at the surface. "Wait! Don't go! I'll come with you!"

He thought he could read an accusation in their staring eyes.

You didn't help us....

Toklo woke with a jolt, clawing at the stones beneath the branches of their makeshift den. Yakone was sitting beside him, looking troubled.

"Are you okay?" he barked.

Toklo sat up, breathing deeply as shudders of horror rippled through his body. A surge of relief struck him as he realized that he still had Yakone. "Just a bad dream," he replied.

Yakone pushed his way out from the middle of the bushes, and Toklo followed him into the chilly gray dawn. Mist covered the ground, and in the distance they could just make out the dark herd of the caribou, already heading away. The sound of their clicking feet came faintly through the air.

Toklo and Yakone gazed at each other. When Toklo had seen the caribou after reaching the end of the glacier, it had felt like a miracle that he'd found them again. Was this their last chance to follow them? Toklo could tell Yakone was wondering the same thing.

"What do we do?" Yakone asked. "Follow the caribou to find Lusa, or stay here and keep looking for Kallik?"

I know what Yakone wants to do, Toklo thought, seeing the longing in the white bear's eyes as he turned to scan the ice. *But what about Lusa?*

"We can't leave Kallik under the glacier," he whispered.

Yakone met his gaze, his eyes full of despair. "But if we lose the caribou, we lose Lusa, too."

For a moment Toklo felt as if a massive claw was tearing him apart. *I want to save them both, but how can I?*

Then, looking up, Toklo spotted stars just showing in the pale sky and caught his breath in wonder as he recognized the outline. This was Ursa, the gigantic star-bear he had seen in the cave on Star Island. Her markings had swelled out of the cave wall and soared into the sky, with Ujurak in his starry form beside her. Now the star-bear seemed to beckon Toklo onward, reassuring him that she would guide him to Lusa.

Ujurak's message echoed in Toklo's ears once more: *Look for the place where the caribou walk, beneath the stars that shine where the sun will rise.* Toklo gazed at the stars glittering above the horizon that lightened first at dawn.

"It's Ursa!" he choked out. "Ujurak's mother. He told us what to look for right from the start. We don't need the caribou. We can follow the stars to Lusa instead!"

CHAPTER THIRTEEN

Lusa

Pale dawn light trickled down from the gap high in the wall of the den, but Lusa was already pacing up and down her cage impatiently. Her movement roused the coyote, which drew its lips back in a snarl as it rose and shook its pelt. Lusa bared her teeth at it.

Stay out of my fur, mangepelt!

The short night had reminded Lusa how close the Longest Day must be, and she knew she was still far away from Great Bear Lake. *Surely Toklo and Kallik and Yakone won't give up on me. This has to be the day I escape!*

"What's wrong with you?" Taktuq grumbled from where he was lying in an untidy huddle beside the bars that separated their cages. "How can a bear get any sleep with you prowling up and down like you have ants in your pelt?"

"Sorry," Lusa said. She halted for a moment before starting her pacing again.

"If you get better, the flat-faces might release you anyway," Taktuq pointed out. "Isn't that good enough?"

Lusa thought about that for a moment. Her head was hardly hurting at all this morning, and her legs thrummed with energy. *But how long will it be before the flat-faces think I'm well enough?* "No, I can't wait any longer," Lusa replied. "I have to escape. I just need to get them to let me out of the pen, like they do the fox."

Taktuq let out a grunt. "Well, don't lose your temper again," he said. "Head for their voices if you hear them, but don't get too close. And remember you'll have to win over the young flat-face," he added. "I've listened to all three of them for a long time, and I know the big ones are very protective of it."

Lusa thought that over. "Do the flat-faces ever let you out of your cage?" she asked.

Taktuq turned his face away. "Not anymore," he murmured.

Lusa sensed that she shouldn't ask any more questions. *Maybe something happened. . . . Maybe Taktuq lashed out like I did at first.*

The older flat-faces came in to check out the animals, and a few moments later Lusa heard the flap to the outside clicking open. She pushed her way through and scampered across the enclosure to where the flat-faces had left her bowl of fruit. The coyote emerged at the same time as Lusa. It hurled itself at the mesh between them, snapping and snarling, and Lusa glanced back to hiss at it before bounding on.

While she was eating her fruit, she kept an eye out for the young flat-face. When the little one finally appeared, she headed straight for the fox, playing with it through the mesh but not taking it out of the pen. The fox yipped, a flash of russet fur spinning in circles.

Lusa dug her claws into the ground in impatience as she peered down the cages and watched. *Leave that stupid fox alone and pay attention to me!*

But the young flat-face stayed beside the fox until a large white firebeast growled across the grass and up to the enclosures. The two gray-furred flat-faces got out of it and opened up an enclosure containing an eagle perched on a tree stump. The bird let out a harsh cry and flapped its wings as the flat-faces approached it, then settled again without trying to fly away.

Lusa watched, fascinated, as the older flat-faces wrapped the eagle in a furless pelt. *I wouldn't want to get that close to it,* she thought, remembering the huge birds she had seen in the mountains. *Eagles are scary!*

The flat-faces put the eagle into a small cage made of silver mesh like the walls of the enclosures, then loaded it into the white firebeast. As they started to climb into the firebeast's belly, the young flat-face came running up, barking something at them. The gray-furred male said something and gestured to her, then climbed into the firebeast, which woke up and slowly rolled away.

The young flat-face walked off, her head drooping dejectedly. Lusa yelped to attract her attention, but she disappeared into one of the small flat-face dens. Lusa let out a tiny growl of frustration.

For a while she played in the enclosure, knowing that she had to be ready at all times to show off for the flat-faces. She ran along the log and leaped off it, imagining that she was crossing a deep-set stream. Scrambling up again, she turned in a circle, balancing on her hind legs and stamping her paws to keep her muscles from stiffening up.

Taktuq let out huffs of amusement as she scurried around, as if he realized how hard she was playing, while the coyote snarled and threw itself at the mesh. Lusa ignored it. *Smelly thing! I wish they'd put you in the firebeast and take you away!*

At sunhigh, Lusa was ready to retreat into the den for some shade. But as she crossed the grass toward the flap, the young flat-face reappeared. Lusa halted and watched her.

At first she headed for the fox and dawdled by its pen for a while. After reaching through the mesh to ruffle the fox's thick fur, she wandered up the line of enclosures, paused to bark something at Taktuq, then approached Lusa. Glancing around for a plaything, Lusa realized that the round red thing from the day before had disappeared, so she picked an apple out of her fruit bowl instead. Careful not to get too close to the mesh, she rolled it on the ground toward the young flat-face, who bared her teeth at Lusa and yapped.

That's a happy sound, right? Lusa thought, stopping herself from flinching.

"Be careful," Taktuq warned her quietly. "I can tell she wants to trust you, or else she'd sound scared."

Lusa kept playing and realized that the young flat-face made the happiest sounds when Lusa missed the apple when she swiped at it and fell over her own paws, so she began to do it deliberately to please her.

At last the young female reached through the mesh with one

brown paw. Lusa approached carefully and let her fur brush against it. The flat-face let out a high-pitched squeal, making Lusa jump. She backed off and then slowly approached again when she saw that the young flat-face's paw was still reaching into her enclosure.

After a few more tries, Lusa managed to keep still while the flat-face rubbed her head and ears, and she even dared to lick her hairless paw. *This feels so strange,* Lusa thought. All her instincts were telling her to lurch away, but she forced herself to stand still and let the young flat-face stroke her.

The scent of the strange creature almost overwhelmed her. It reminded Lusa of flowers, though it wasn't quite the same. She had never been so close to a young flat-face before, and she was fascinated by her hairless face and huge brown eyes.

Lusa heard a whisper from Taktuq. "What's happening?"

But Lusa couldn't answer him. She knew she had to keep quiet and still, so as not to scare the flat-face.

But just when Lusa thought everything was going so well, the flat-face turned abruptly and ran off.

"Come back!" Lusa let out an urgent bark, then flattened her ears in disappointment. "Did I do something wrong?" she asked Taktuq. "She touched me and let me lick her paw, and then she just ran away."

"Don't give up," Taktuq encouraged her. "You're doing well if she let you get that close."

Moments later, Lusa heard a noise behind her in the big den, and recognized the sound of the cage door opening. Lusa ran in through the flap and saw the young female standing there, anxious and wide-eyed. Her mouth was set with tension, and Lusa could pick up her fear-scent.

Lusa padded forward and pushed her snout gently against the young flat-face's side. The flat-face took out a narrow length of vine, clipped one end around Lusa's neck, and held the other end.

She's trapped me like a dog! Lusa thought, her pelt crawling at the sensation, even though this was what she had been working toward. *This is* not *what a wild bear should do!*

When the flat-face tugged on the vine, Lusa balked, turning her head toward Taktuq, who had followed her inside on his side of the bars. "This feels all wrong," she whimpered.

"This is what you wanted, isn't it?" Taktuq prompted her gently. "Go on. This could be your chance to escape!"

Lusa let the flat-face lead her out of the cage and through the big den. So many animals and birds were watching her! The pigeons fluttered wildly, and a rabbit in the cage nearest the door hopped back out of the way.

Lusa hated the thing around her neck. *I'm sure those other animals are laughing at me!* Though the vine wasn't tight, she felt as though it would choke her.

But I'm a wild bear, she reminded herself. *I'm a wild bear, and my clever plan is working. Look, this is me escaping!*

Outside, Lusa scanned her surroundings. Apart from the huge den that held the cages, she could see several small dens that she guessed were used to store flat-face stuff, and a low, white den with windows where the flat-faces lived. Beyond the dens were fields where horses, cows, and sheep were grazing, and around the white den was a stretch of dusty, flat ground with a BlackPath leading away out of sight.

Looking up at the sun, Lusa worked out where the mountains must be.

I have to go back to the mountains where I left my friends in case they're waiting for me there. I'll travel back for a while to see if I can find them. If I can't, I'll head for the lake and hope that we'll all meet up. It sounded logical, but for a moment she gazed at the far-off horizon and felt daunted by the scale of her task. *But I'm not even sure I can remember the way, and I don't know how long I have before the Longest Day.* Then she reminded herself that she had already found Toklo and Ujurak once. *I will find all my friends again. And I know that somehow the caribou will help me to do this.*

The young flat-face tugged Lusa around the big den and onto the stretch of grass that lay behind the enclosures. She patted Lusa on the head with her soft brown paw and pulled out a piece of apple from somewhere within her pelt. Lusa took it delicately, making sure her teeth didn't touch the flat-face's paw.

Now that I'm out of the enclosure, what do I do? Lusa wondered, as the young female started to walk again, leading Lusa with the vine. *I don't want to hurt the little flat-face. Could I just pull myself free? How fast will I be able to get down the BlackPath?*

By this time the coyote had spotted her and was pacing to and fro in its pen, snarling and pawing at the mesh. The young flat-face barked at it as if she was scolding it, but the coyote just hissed through its teeth and kept pacing.

In his enclosure, Taktuq was standing close to the mesh,

his ears pricked to work out what was happening. "Lusa, are you okay?" he called.

"I'm fine," Lusa replied softly.

The young flat-face gave a gentle tug on the vine and bent closer to Lusa, part of one paw raised to her mouth. She made a hissing noise through her teeth as she led Lusa up to a tiny den with mesh sides. *Is she going to put me in there?* Lusa thought, horrified. *I'll never fit!*

As Lusa drew closer to the tiny den, two gray rabbits hopped into view inside it. The flat-face pointed to them and yapped out a few words. Lusa gazed at her, baffled.

Am I supposed to do something with the rabbits? I know how to hunt them . . . is that it? Does she want me to catch the rabbits so she can eat them?

The young flat-face let go of the end of the vine so that she could open the little den and take out a rabbit. She snuggled it close to her, just like a mother bear with a cub.

Lusa's paws tingled with excitement. *She's not holding me anymore! This is my chance to escape!*

She began edging away. With one more glance at the flat-face, who was nuzzling into the rabbit's fur, she took a deep breath and made a run for it.

At the same moment a terrifying howl split the air, followed by a roar from Taktuq. "Lusa! Look out!"

Lusa glanced back to see the coyote launching itself against the mesh of its pen over and over, ripping the mesh away from the wooden frame. The creature wriggled through the gap it had made, leaving behind tufts of sandy fur, and pelted toward the flat-face.

Lusa skidded to a halt. The young flat-face had dropped the rabbit and was staring at the coyote, frozen with horror. The animals in the other pens were barking and howling, and a flock of small black birds circled their enclosure in a frenzy, beating the mesh with their wings.

Lusa didn't hesitate. She launched herself at the coyote, catching it in midstride and knocking it off its paws. As the flat-face shrieked behind her, Lusa threw herself on top of the coyote, clawing at its throat. The coyote wriggled out from underneath her and scrambled back onto its paws, but Lusa darted in and gave it a sharp nip on its shoulder.

They always hunt in packs, she thought, remembering how she and her friends had fought the coyotes beside the firesnake. *It isn't as good on its own. I can deal with one, no problem.*

The coyote sprang at Lusa. Its claws raked her side, but Lusa spun around and lashed at it with her hindpaws, then spun back to butt it with her head and unbalance it again. It was snarling in a fury, its jaws slavering as it snapped at Lusa, gripping one of her forelegs in its fangs. Pain sliced through her, and she brought her claws down on the coyote's ear. The coyote let out a howl and loosened its grip, enough for Lusa to jump back.

"Mangepelt!" she growled.

Lusa charged forward again, ducking her head low to dodge the coyote's jaws. Knocking the creature off its paws again, she planted her hindpaws on its belly and raked its shoulders with her front claws. The coyote struggled briefly, but Lusa had it pinned and it soon gave up, snarling as it gazed up at her with hatred in its eyes. Behind her, she could hear the young flat-face whimpering. Lusa braced herself to tear out the coyote's throat if she needed to.

Suddenly Lusa heard the rumbling sound of a firebeast halting behind her. She'd been so focused on the fight that she hadn't heard its approach. Heavy flat-face footsteps raced toward her. A muffled crack rang out, and a long, pointed stick struck the coyote in the shoulder. One end pierced its fur, leaving the shaft quivering in the air. The coyote went on snarling for a few moments more; then its eyes rolled up and it went limp.

Great spirits, have they killed it? Lusa thought. Then she noticed that the creature was still breathing. Carefully, not wanting to wake it, she took a step backward.

The older flat-faces had run to the young one; the gray-furred female wrapped her forelimbs around her. They were all chattering urgently to one another.

"Run, Lusa!" Taktuq's harsh cry broke through to Lusa, who was still dazed from the fight. "Go now!"

Lusa realized that with the coyote unconscious and the flat-faces focused on one another, no one was paying any attention to her. *How did Taktuq know? He's amazing!*

She took off, running with all the speed she could muster across the open ground and down the BlackPath. Her foreleg was bleeding where the coyote had bitten her, she was panting, and her heart was pounding hard enough to burst out of her chest. But she was free.

"Good luck!" Taktuq's voice drifted after her. "I hope you find your friends!"

As Lusa left the flat-face dens behind, a firebeast suddenly appeared in front of her. She veered off the BlackPath onto rough, tussocky ground and buried herself under the branches of a thornbush, trembling as she waited for the firebeast to stop.

But it must not have seen her, because it kept going. Its roar soon died away in the distance, leaving Lusa limp and exhausted under the bush. Silence surrounded her except for the distant cry of a bird, and a warm breeze washed over her, filled with the scents of trees and dust.

An image of three beloved faces, one brown and two white, filled her mind. *I'm coming to find you,* she thought. *Wait for me.*

CHAPTER FOURTEEN

Kallik

Kallik opened her eyes, dazzled by the early rays of the sun. She was lying on the glacier, the ice cool against her fur. The sky above was so blue it was like looking into the sea. As her vision cleared, she could see black dots circling above her head and she gazed at them, puzzled, for a few moments. Then she tensed with horror as the dots dropped closer and she realized what they were.

Vultures!

Two of the birds let out a squawk and swooped so low over Kallik that she could smell their meaty stench and felt their talons scrape her fur. For a moment she couldn't remember where she was or why the vultures would be targeting her.

Then in a rush Kallik remembered her struggles under the glacier, how she had been trapped there and had finally managed to climb to the top. She had hauled herself out and collapsed in the dark, too exhausted to walk another step. At the same moment she became aware of how the scent of blood from her battered and bleeding body must be attracting the carrion birds.

Summoning all her strength and ignoring her aching muscles and the pain in her paws, Kallik forced herself to her paws. "I am not dead!" she roared.

Another vulture swooped down low, and Kallik raised a foreleg to swipe at it. She missed, but the vulture veered away with an angry shriek, gaining height again.

For a moment Kallik gathered herself, watching the vultures that still circled threateningly around her. *Where am I?* she asked herself. *Where are the others?*

Then, as she gazed around at the massive river of ice, she realized that she was at the top of the glacier, while Toklo and Yakone were going to be looking for her at the bottom. *But that was an entire day ago,* Kallik thought with a tremor of fear. *Will they still be there waiting?*

Gathering her last scraps of energy, Kallik bounded away down the glacier. Her legs shook with weakness from hunger and the effort of climbing out of the crevasse, but she knew she couldn't waste any time.

I have to find the others! She tried hard to convince herself that they would have waited for her at the bottom of the glacier. *I'm sure they would never leave me here.*

As the landscape opened out in front of her, Kallik spotted a dark haze in the distance, on the slopes that led down to the forest, and she recognized the dust cloud they had first seen back in the mountains.

The caribou!

Kallik quickened her pace, straining to see the shapes of two bears following the herd, but it was too far away. The ice between her paws was rough and jagged, dotted with sharp rocks and holes, but she was so desperate to find her friends that she forced herself to run.

She was so eager to keep the caribou in sight that she didn't see another crevasse opening up in front of her. She let out a yelp of terror as she felt herself plummeting into the depths; then all the breath was driven out of her as she thumped down on a boulder that was wedged in the gap.

For a few moments Kallik lay still, getting her breath back and recovering from the shock of falling again. The surface of the glacier was less than a bearlength above her head, and below her was a dark nothingness smelling of ice and rock. Panic throbbed through her. *I'm not going through that again. I can't.*

Making sure not to slip, Kallik slowly reared up onto her hindpaws and clawed herself up and out of the crevasse, gripping the rough edges on the inside of the rift. At last she stood safe on the surface again.

Cloud-brain! she scolded herself. *You have to be more careful.*

The blood thrummed in Kallik's ears and her belly was painful from hunger, but she kept going, more slowly and cautiously now. The end of the glacier came into view, a rock-strewn slope emerging from the ice.

Kallik halted, her sides heaving. "Yakone! Toklo!"

Nothing responded to her loud cry. Around her nothing stirred; all she could see were boulders, stones, bushes. . . .

"Yakone! Toklo!" she called again. Her head drooped as her voice echoed around the slope. It felt as if the glacier itself was mocking her, laughing at her isolation. *Don't give up!* Kallik told herself fiercely. *You escaped from the glacier. You can't stop now!*

Bracing her shoulders, she padded along the foot of the ice wall, stopping every few paces to bellow the names of her friends. Still there was no reply apart from the echoes. *Keep going.*

Walk, call, echo. Walk, call, echo. As the sun crept across the sky, Kallik felt her hopes melt away. *Did they think I was dead? Is that why they didn't wait for me?*

"Oh, Yakone, Toklo! Where are you?"

"Kallik?"

The call came from behind her. Spinning around, Kallik saw Toklo racing out from behind a tumble of rocks. Yakone followed him, lurching every time he put his injured paw to the ground.

You waited! You didn't abandon me! Kallik ran forward to meet them, and all three bears pressed themselves together, letting out joyful yelps and nuzzling one another.

"I thought I'd never find you!" Kallik exclaimed. Her throat felt thick and sore with emotion, and she couldn't stop breathing in the precious fur-scent of her friends.

"We were afraid you were lost down there," Toklo said, and Yakone added, "We walked to the end of your crevasse, but it disappeared to nothing and you weren't there. How did you get out?"

"I had to go up to the top of the glacier and climb out

there," Kallik explained. "It wasn't at all like the ice in the ocean. It was empty, like a . . . a dead thing." She paused, shivering at the memory, then went on, "I almost got stuck down there. I think I might have given up if Ujurak hadn't come to help me."

"He found you!" Toklo exclaimed.

Kallik nodded. "I think he was afraid, too, but he never left me until I was safe."

"I'm so sorry that we couldn't help you," Yakone said. "We didn't know what to do."

"Well, it's okay now." Kallik stood back a little and looked at her friends, relishing the feeling of relief that flooded through her. *We found each other,* she thought. *Against all odds, we did it! So maybe that means we can find Lusa, too.* "We should follow the caribou," Kallik went on. "I saw where they're heading from high up on the glacier."

She padded forward, ready to go right away, but Toklo stepped forward to block her. "You're not going anywhere until you've had a rest and something to eat," he told her sternly.

"But—"

Yakone didn't give her a chance to protest. "Toklo's right. You look exhausted, your paws are bleeding, and you haven't eaten for a day."

"Besides," Toklo added, "last night we saw Ursa's star-shape in the sky. Even if we lose the caribou, she'll guide us to Lusa."

Kallik drew in a long breath. "That's wonderful!"

Though she was still impatient to keep looking for Lusa,

Kallik knew that Toklo and Yakone were right. Toklo plunged into the bushes, saying he was going to hunt, while Yakone led Kallik to a trampled sleeping-place among some thorns and made her lie down. While she rested he cleaned her sore paws, rasping gently against them with his tongue. Kallik dozed, giving way to the shadows that clustered at the edge of her thoughts.

Before long Toklo returned with a ground squirrel, and the bears settled down to eat.

"This is good, Toklo," Kallik said, relishing every bite, "but we really should get going." *We need to make up for the day we lost because of me,* she added miserably to herself.

"It'll be okay," Toklo mumbled around a mouthful of squirrel. "We just have to put our trust in the stars." He gazed up and over the trees, as if he was trying to see the plains beyond and find Lusa playing in a beam of sunlight. "We'll find her."

Her belly full, Kallik rose to her paws, ready to set out, but Yakone pushed her firmly down again.

"Rest," he ordered her. "We aren't going anywhere until you've had some sleep."

Giving in with a sigh, Kallik dozed in the den and woke to see that sunhigh was past. She jumped to her paws. "I didn't mean to sleep so long! Now we really have to leave," she said. "Lusa's counting on us."

"Okay," Yakone responded, nosing carefully down one side of Kallik and then the other and giving her paws a careful check. "You seem fine," he added, "but you have to promise to let us know if you need to stop."

"You too," she retorted, gesturing toward Yakone's injured paw.

Together they set off downhill, leaving the glacier behind and pushing their way through bushes and rough grass until they came to the caribou trail. Toklo led the way, ears pricked and stubby tail twitching as he forced aside the scrub until they were standing at the edge of the hoofprints.

"We may have lost the caribou," Kallik murmured, "but their trail is easy enough to follow."

The strong scent of the caribou wreathed around the bears, and a wide swath of hoofprints led on into the distance, scattered with caribou droppings. Ahead was the shadowy line of the forest, clinging to the lower slopes of the ridge.

All three of them fell silent as they headed for the trees. *We could have a long, long way to go before we find Lusa.* Anxiety crept up on Kallik again, her relief and joy at finding Toklo and Yakone fading as she realized the massive task that still lay before them.

Yakone let out a snarl of annoyance as he banged his wounded paw on a stone lodged in the dirt, and when Toklo tangled himself up in some brambles, he threw them off with a roar of fury instead of carefully picking his way out. He was still growling under his breath as he stalked on. Kallik could tell the others shared her anxiety.

Kallik padded beside Toklo, touching her muzzle to his shoulder in a soothing gesture. "We're all worried about Lusa," she told him. "But we have to stay calm, for our sake as well as hers."

Toklo cast her a sidelong glance. "I know," he said. "Sorry."

For once, Toklo seemed small and young, not like the confident, almost full-grown bear who had guided them this far. Kallik let her shoulder fur brush against his for a few strides. *He looks after all of us, but he needs to be looked after, too.*

The ground began to slope upward, and the trek became exhausting in the hot sun. The trees never seemed to get any closer, and their steps lagged as they stirred up dust.

Finally the bears paused to rest at the crest of a hill, staring out over the tops of the trees. Ahead of them the forest stretched as far as they could see. The caribou were so far ahead now that even at this height they couldn't see any sign of them.

"This is it," Toklo said, pointing with a paw. "Ursa's star-shape would be in that direction, so this is where we leave the caribou trail and head into the trees. We have to trust Ujurak."

"At least there'll be plenty of prey in there," Yakone commented.

"But will we be able to see the stars?" Kallik wondered, feeling uneasy at the thought of leaving the strongly marked trail.

Yakone nudged her. "We know Ujurak is with us," he said quietly. "He'll show us the way."

Relief from the scorching sunlight washed over the bears as soon as they stepped into the dense shade cast by the pines. At first a deep hush seemed to envelop them, but after a while Kallik began to hear the rustling of tiny creatures and the whisper of pine needles as something small and light moved over the ground.

Although she belonged out on the ice, Kallik felt at home in the forest. *It's safer here than being exposed on open ground.*

Her two companions seemed to feel the same. Their mood lifted and they pressed on more quickly, padding purposefully through the trees.

"I'm so glad we found you," Yakone said to Kallik as he fell in beside her. "I would never have stopped looking, even if it meant I never returned to Star Island."

Kallik shuddered. "I don't ever want to be in such an awful place again," she responded. "I have no idea what I would have done if Ujurak hadn't been with me—and even he was scared."

Yakone padded closer so that their pelts were brushing. "If Ujurak really means to see us to the end of our journey, then he has his work cut out for him!" he observed, a note of humor in his voice.

Kallik hesitated, then asked, "You believe that Ujurak was with me under the glacier?"

Yakone paused and turned to her, fixing her with a solemn gaze. He nodded. "Yes. He saved your life. I believe that."

Toklo halted and gestured ahead with his muzzle. Kallik spotted a small deer picking its way through the trees. *Oh yes . . .* she thought, feeling her jaws start to water.

Without needing to say a word, the bears spread out, padding silently over the thick covering of pine needles until they surrounded the deer, which still seemed unaware of them. As they began to close in, the deer gave a start of surprise and plunged away, heading for the space between Toklo and Kal-lik. Both bears leaped at it and brought it down, and Toklo gave the killing blow to its neck.

"Thank you, spirits, for this prey," Kallik said.

The bears ate hungrily, though as the scent of blood rose into the air, Yakone began looking over his shoulder with a wary expression in his eyes.

"There aren't any coyotes around here," Toklo reassured him. "We would have smelled them by now."

When their bellies were stuffed, they kept walking until the sun began to set, sending shafts of scarlet light angling through the trees. The shadows thickened as the light faded, but before it was completely dark, the bears came to a small clearing where they could look up through the circle of trees and see the stars. They lay down together in the open and gazed up at Ursa and Ujurak shining down at them. Far from their homes, hardly knowing where their journey would take them next, the bears felt a sense of peacefulness and hope. No harm would come to them tonight, not under the gaze of their star companions.

"I hope Lusa is safe, too," Kallik whispered.

CHAPTER FIFTEEN

Lusa

As soon as Lusa got her breath back, she crawled out from underneath the thornbush. Sunhigh was long past, and all around her the land was flat and scorched to dusty brown by the heat. Gazing at the expanse made Lusa's head reel, and she could almost feel herself shrinking to nothing more than a tiny dot in this endless landscape.

The flat-face vine was still around Lusa's neck. Determinedly she clawed at it until it snapped, and she kicked the scraps away from her. Then she gave herself a shake and forced herself to think about what to do next.

I need to retrace the route to the mountains, where I last saw the others, she thought. *They don't know I was taken away by a firebeast. They might still be looking for me there.* A small worm of doubt crawled into her mind. *I hope they're still looking for me. . . .* She knew that the journey could take days, because she had no idea how far from the mountains she had come. *It might be quicker to try to find my way to Great Bear Lake from here. The Longest Day could be very soon. But I don't want to finish my journey without the others. I have to try to find them first.*

Lusa set out across the scrubby grass, staying alongside the BlackPath. Her pelt prickled with apprehension, and she kept her ears alert for approaching firebeasts. After a while, realizing how hungry she was, she stopped to nibble berries from a scrawny bush and dug down to find some juicy white roots. Beside the BlackPath she found a puddle and took a drink, curling her lip at the tang of firebeasts in the water.

Yuck!

While Lusa was drinking, she heard a firebeast growl toward her and stop nearby. Looking up, she recognized all three flat-faces peering out from its belly. "No!" Lusa yelped, fear and shock freezing her to the spot. "They've found me!"

The young flat-face scrambled out of the firebeast and pointed at Lusa. Before she could get any closer, Lusa took off, racing across the scrubland toward a huge expanse of glossy green plants that towered above her head. Plunging into the stalks, Lusa spotted yellow kernels underpaw. *Corn! I remember that from the Bear Bowl.*

Lusa pushed her way through the thick stems, deeper and deeper. Sharp-edged leaves scratched her face and caught in her fur, but Lusa didn't slow down. She could hear the flat-faces barking at the edge of the corn, their voices high-pitched against the soft rustle of stalks. They didn't seem to be following her in, but Lusa didn't want to risk it so she kept going, trying not to brush against the stems and give herself away by their movement.

On and on Lusa went until she stumbled to a halt, her

cheeks stinging from the leaves, and strained to listen over the rustling sound of the cornstalks. There was no sign of pursuit from the flat-faces.

"Okay!" Lusa blew out a breath of relief. "Now all I need to do is find a way out."

But as she looked around, Lusa realized that she had no idea which way to go. *I'm lost!*

Fighting down panic, she nibbled some of the corn and licked the leaves for moisture to quench her thirst. Then she chose a direction and set out, only to stop again, afraid that she was just heading deeper and deeper into the corn. She turned around, but everywhere she looked, stalks stretched away from her into the distance. Now the noise of the wind in the leaves seemed sinister and hostile, as if the corn was watching Lusa and surrounding her endlessly. . . . *It can't go on forever, can it?*

"Ujurak?" she called in a small voice. "Can you see me?"

There was no reply. Feeling desolate and foolish, Lusa curled herself into a tiny ball.

Though she hadn't intended to sleep, she must have dozed, because when she uncurled herself, it was dark. She shivered, spooked by the corn as it whispered all around her. It was nothing like the comforting murmurs of black bear spirits that she could hear in trees.

The cornstalks seemed to be pressing in on Lusa, making it hard to breathe. Desperate for some fresh air, she looked up. At once new courage flowed through her as she spotted Ujurak shining ahead of her, strong and bright, and Arcturus gleaming down, just as they had on every step of her journey. She gazed at the glittering points of light, overwhelmed by the memory of the time in the cave when Ursa had appeared in all her blazing splendor and guided her son back to his home in the stars.

"Ursa and Ujurak will show me the way!" Lusa exclaimed.

Setting out again, Lusa used the familiar star-shapes to guide her through the corn. The trek seemed to take forever. Lusa's snout grew sore from brushing against the leaves, and her neck got stiff from looking up, but she kept going.

I just have to get out before daylight comes and the stars vanish, she told herself.

Gradually Lusa began to hear other sounds besides the rustle of the cornstalks. Somewhere in the distance a dog barked. A firebeast coughed and roared away. *I must be close to the edge!*

Lusa began to run, forcing her way through the corn. Finally she blundered out and came to a dead stop, her sides heaving as she looked out across a stretch of smooth grassland. The breeze stroked her ruffled fur, and her eyes watered in the cool night air.

"Thank you, Ujurak," she whispered.

Lusa trekked across the grass in starlight, her body casting a huge shadow beside her. She felt exposed once she left the cover of the corn, but she knew she wasn't alone, because Ursa and Ujurak were watching over her. When she reached a BlackPath, she ducked down into the ditch that ran alongside it and waited until it was clear of firebeasts. Then she ran swiftly across the hard gray stone and headed onward across another murmuring expanse of grass, following the stars all the while.

As dawn appeared on the horizon, Lusa began to look for somewhere to shelter. She veered away from a flat-face den, then realized that it had been abandoned, with large holes in the walls and the roof beginning to fall in. She was wary of entering the den itself, but she found a dense patch of under-growth just behind it and crawled into cover beneath the overhanging stems.

At first Lusa found it hard to sleep. Her mind was filled with Taktuq, the young flat-face, and the coyote. *I wish I could have said good-bye to Taktuq. And I hope I didn't scare the flat-face by fighting the coyote. I did it to save her!* But most of all she wondered whether she would be able to find her friends. A dark space seemed to open up inside her when she thought about how far away they might be by now, though she had to believe Ujurak was leading her somewhere important.

Eventually Lusa sank into sleep. Her dreams were full of the clicking feet of caribou, and she hoped that she had understood the sign of the caribou herd Ujurak had sent her.

When Lusa woke, she scavenged some leaves and ber-ries from the patch of undergrowth where she had slept and waited impatiently until the stars appeared so she could set out once again.

The night before, the sky had been clear and the stars easy to follow. But now the tiny silver dots appeared fitfully through clouds, confusing her when she tried to figure out her bearings. Lusa headed in what she thought was the right direction, only to realize when the sky cleared briefly that she was completely wrong. She let out an annoyed growl as she turned back to face the outlines of Ujurak and Ursa again.

Gradually the grassland gave way to a barren, rocky area, though it was still mostly flat. Lusa plodded up to the top of a low hill and became aware of thickening shadows shifting in front of her. She paused for breath, and at that moment the clouds shifted. Moonlight lit up the land with a cold, silver radiance. Huge shadows were moving toward Lusa. She flinched back, terror coursing through her.

Great spirits!

The shadows drew closer, and an ominous rumbling, clicking sound came to Lusa's ears. For a moment she was even more frightened until she realized what it was.

Caribou! I found them!

Even though night had fallen, the animals were still moving, quiet and patient in the shadows. The herd was passing below Lusa, around the bottom of the rise. Lusa ran down toward them, getting as close as she dared and taking cover behind a scatter of rocks. The caribou took no notice of her, as if they didn't even sense she was there. On and on they passed; there were more of them than Lusa could possibly count. She peered into the throng of animals, wondering whether her friends could be hidden inside the herd, like Ujurak had been in her dream. *No, that's impossible,* she told herself. *Caribou would never travel with bears so close.*

Finally the last of the caribou passed by, leaving a trail behind them that stretched back into the darkness. Lusa waited, hoping breathlessly for her friends to appear, following the trail. As the moments dragged by, she called out, "Toklo! Kallik! Yakone!" but there was no reply.

I found the caribou, but now which way do I go?

With such a momentous decision in front of her, Lusa settled down in the grass beside the trail and let her thoughts turn over. She knew that if she made the wrong decision, she might lose her friends forever.

Should I follow the caribou and hope they'll take me to the others? Or follow the trail back and look for them that way?

As Lusa crouched there in an agony of indecision, she remembered how in her dream Ujurak had made her turn around and look back along the caribou trail. She sat up, suddenly alert, her heart beating faster. "Ujurak wanted me to follow the caribou trail in the opposite direction!" she exclaimed aloud, so excited to have pieced the signs together.

Taking a deep breath, Lusa rose to her paws, squared her shoulders, and turned to follow the hoofprints back the way they had come.

I found the caribou, Ujurak! she thought. *Now you have to help me find my friends!*

CHAPTER SIXTEEN

Kallik

"Caribou! Look!" Kallik halted *in front* of the others and looked down at the ground. Lots and lots of hoofprints were pressed into the soft mulch of the forest floor, and there was a strong scent of caribou.

The bears had been traveling through the forest for a day. They had followed the direction of the stars down a steep, rocky incline, narrowly managing to keep their footing on the loose scree. Kallik felt a huge sense of relief at finding the caribou trail again. It looked like they were traveling through the forest in the same direction but must have taken a detour because of the steep slope. Kallik was beginning to feel even more certain that the stars and the caribou would bring them to Lusa.

Toklo padded up beside her and gave the tracks a sniff. "Yes, we're certainly going the right way," he said with satisfaction. "It's great that our two signs have come together again. We *must* be close to finding Lusa."

They pressed on over the soft mossy ground. Even Kallik

and Yakone, who were used to the ice, found the going easier than the rough surface of the glacier.

And there are no crevasses to fall down! Kallik thought.

She soon realized that the light up ahead was growing brighter. "We're coming to the edge of the forest!" she barked.

All three bears paused at the tree line and gazed out across the vast open landscape, a gently rolling expanse of rippling green and gold. The horizon shimmered like smoke in the heat of the day.

Kallik felt dread churn in her belly. The hot sun weakened her and Yakone so much. She longed to stay in the shade of the trees. But they had no choice. That was where the trail led, so they had to strike out into the vulnerable emptiness and find Lusa.

"We'll have to leave the caribou trail," Yakone decided. "We know we're going in the right direction, and we have the stars to guide us. Right now it's more important for us to choose a route that gives us some cover."

"Let's head for those trees," Toklo suggested. "I don't like being out here like a bug on a leaf."

He led the way across the open ground until they reached a copse, but the trees were so spindly they hardly cast any shade. Kallik couldn't see any more cover in the direction they had to go if they were going to follow the caribou trail, but her belly still churned as they turned away from the hoof marks pressed into the brittle grass.

The bears didn't feel much better protected when they were among the tree trunks.

"Even if we don't follow the caribou trail, it still feels very exposed," Toklo grumbled, trying to hide under a scrubby bush.

"Maybe we should travel at night," Yakone murmured thoughtfully. "We'd be able to see Ujurak's mother, and the darkness would keep us hidden."

"I think that's a great idea!" Kallik said. "It'll be cooler, too."

"But think of the time we've already wasted!" Toklo exclaimed with a flash of fury. "We won't have any hope of finding Lusa if we keep stopping."

"We also won't find Lusa if we get caught by flat-faces," Yakone said gently.

"Yakone's right," Kallik agreed. "We want to find Lusa just as much as you do, Toklo."

Toklo gave a reluctant grunt of agreement, then began pacing up and down among the thin trees, as if he still wanted to be on the move.

"Settle down and rest," Kallik urged him. "We'll make much better time at night if we get some sleep now."

Toklo looked as if he wanted to argue, but he said nothing and curled up at the foot of a tree. He fell asleep quickly, and Kallik wondered whether he had slept at all the night before.

Kallik exchanged a glance with Yakone. "This heat is awful," she said, feeling like she was burning up as the hot sun struck her fur though the measly tree cover. "I don't think I'll be able to sleep."

"Let's see if there's more shade that way." Yakone nodded

down a slope where the trees seemed to grow more thickly.

"Okay."

Kallik rose to her paws and padded after Yakone, though she doubted they would find anywhere to escape the merciless sun. Then, at the bottom of the slope, she spotted a tiny pond with trees and long grasses growing around it.

Together she and Yakone slid into the pool. Kallik felt blissful relief from the heat as the water soaked into her fur, even though there wasn't quite enough to cover her.

"This is better!" she breathed. Then she lifted a paw, wrinkling her nose at the green scum that covered it from the stagnant pond water. "We'll turn into green bears if we're not careful," she said.

Yakone nuzzled her shoulder. "I don't mind being a green bear if you're one, too."

Kallik and Yakone dozed in the water and woke to hear Toklo's voice calling to them through the trees. Darkness was falling, and when they emerged from the copse they could see the outlines of Ujurak and Ursa shining in the sky.

As they struck out across the open grassland, Toklo broke into a run. Kallik and Yakone picked up their pace to match his.

But they had not gone very far when Kallik noticed that Yakone was limping again. He was beginning to drop back, panting with the effort of running on his mangled paw.

"Toklo!" Kallik shouted. "Slow down! We can't go that fast."

To her relief, Toklo wheeled around and trotted back to

them. "I'm sorry," he said. "I just want to find Lusa as soon as we can."

"Ujurak hasn't told us to stop looking for Lusa," Kallik pointed out. "We have to trust that she's okay and that we're going to find her."

Toklo heaved a deep, frustrated sigh. "You're right," he admitted. "Okay, you set the pace."

The going was easy over the soft, flat ground, with a cool breeze whispering around them, but soon the bears began to feel hungry. "There doesn't seem to be any prey out here," Yakone complained. "I'd give anything for a good fat seal."

So would I, Kallik thought, and began to sniff carefully as they padded on. There was no hope of a seal, but there might be some other prey hidden in the long grass. After a while she picked up a faint scent and signaled to the others to stop. "Ground birds!" she whispered, pointing with her muzzle in the direction the scent came from.

Kallik stalked forward as slowly as if she was creeping up on a basking seal. Eventually she could make out the shape of the bird sitting among the grass, and slid forward in a single fluid movement to plant her paw on top of it.

Got it!

Toklo and Yakone padded up to examine her catch, a plump grouse. As Kallik picked it up, she noticed that it had been sitting on eggs.

"Good catch!" Toklo grunted, crunching up one of the eggs. "Spirits, that tastes good!"

All three bears felt on edge in the open grassland, casting

quick glances around them. *It's like being on the ice,* Kallik thought, sinking her teeth into the grouse. *Only out on the ice, there aren't any flat-faces to spot us.*

Kallik remembered the very beginning of her journey, after the silver bird crashed and killed Nanuk, when she walked for days across dusty, empty ground.

At least I have Yakone and Toklo now, she thought. *But I should have Lusa, too. . . .*

Not long after the bears set out again, they came to the top of a long, shallow slope and saw a large flat-face denning area spread out in front of them. The caribou trail veered sharply away from it in a completely new direction.

"Have you seen this place before?" Kallik asked Toklo.

The brown bear shook his head. "We must be away from the path I followed last time."

Lights glittered in the darkness, shining on crisscrossing BlackPaths and more dens than they could count. At the far side was a tall, slender tower with an ominous red light smoldering at the top of it.

"Looks like we should go straight through there," Yakone pointed out, gazing up at the stars.

"No way!" Toklo retorted. "We'll have to go around like the caribou."

"But we'll lose time if we do," Kallik told him.

"We'll lose even more if we get caught by flat-faces," Toklo flashed back at her.

Reluctantly Yakone nodded. "He's right."

Kallik had to give in, sighing as their paws turned into the new route. *Why can't anything be easy?*

By the time the sky began to pale toward dawn they were still skirting the denning place. It seemed to go on forever, with the smells of flat-faces and firebeasts, the danger of crossing BlackPaths, and the never-ending worry that they would be spotted. The ground was dusty where firebeasts had trampled the grass into dirt, and the dust stung Kallik's injured eye. There were no signs of prey.

"We have to find somewhere to hide," Toklo said. "We're bound to meet flat-faces around here in daylight."

Kallik glanced around and saw a small stretch of woods not far from the outermost flat-face dens. "In there would be a good place," she suggested.

She led the way into the trees, but before they had gone many bearlengths, she picked up the scent of flat-faces again and noticed the gray walls of a tumbledown den not far ahead.

"Seal rot!" she muttered. "Flat-faces are everywhere."

"Maybe the den is abandoned," Yakone murmured hopefully.

Before Kallik could point out that the scents were fresh, loud barking split the air, and a dog shot out from behind the den and raced straight for the bears.

"Get away!" Yakone snarled at the dog, raising one paw. "Or I'll flatten you!"

"No!" Kallik gave Yakone a hard shove. "Don't touch it. That'll only make its flat-face master chase us."

Yakone nodded, and together the bears plunged into the bushes, heading away from the flat-face den as fast as they could. The dog followed them for a little while, barking loudly enough to wake every flat-face in the denning area, then gave up and turned back to its den.

"Thank the spirits!" Kallik exclaimed.

Their flight had brought the bears back to the edge of the woodland. The ground ahead of them was flat and open, with nothing at all that could give them cover. A small BlackPath crossed the middle of it, where firebeasts were already running to and fro as the sun rose.

"We're too exposed here," Toklo said, flexing his claws angrily.

Gazing desperately around, Kallik saw some large dens on the edge of the denning area, on the other side of the Black-Path. They didn't look to her like the sort of places where flat-faces lived. They were too big, and there were no small, square holes in the sides. *We've hidden in places like that before.*

"We'll have to go in there," she told her friends, pointing with one paw.

"Are you completely cloud-brained?" Toklo growled, his eyes wide with amazement. "Those are flat-face places."

Yakone nodded uneasily, agreeing with Toklo. "I don't like the look of them."

"Like it or not, they're our only choice," Kallik retorted, biting back her irritation. "It's too hot to be outside all day, and the flat-faces are bound to see us if we hang around here much longer."

Reluctantly, Yakone and Toklo gave in. Kallik took the lead as they crept out into the open, trying to crouch close to the ground so they wouldn't be seen. As they approached the BlackPath, they found a narrow gully where they could squeeze down and wait for a lull in the stream of firebeasts. The sun had barely cleared the horizon, but already there seemed to be no end to the growling, stinking monsters.

Kallik froze as a flat-face in the belly of a firebeast let out a yell and pointed at them. *He spotted us!* But the firebeast swept by without even slowing down. Kallik relaxed, puffing out a breath of relief. *Maybe that firebeast isn't interested in bears.*

When they finally managed to cross the BlackPath, they had to skirt around a group of flat-faces who were standing beside a huge firebeast, peering at something underneath its belly. Then finally they had a clear path to the big dens.

Shoulder to shoulder, the bears galloped across the open ground and pushed hard at the door of the first den. But it wouldn't open.

"What's the matter with it?" Kallik asked, rearing up in frustration and battering at the door with her forepaws.

"Come on, let's try the next one," Toklo said tensely.

But as they headed toward the second den, they heard a whistling sound and the thump of heavy pawsteps. Just in time they ducked behind a sleeping firebeast as a flat-face came around the corner of the den.

"Why is he making that funny noise?" Kallik wondered aloud, thinking how weird the flat-face looked with his mouth puckered up. "Is he trying to be a bird?"

"Nothing would surprise me about flat-faces," Toklo responded.

The flat-face climbed into the belly of the firebeast they were hiding behind. As it woke up with a cough, the bears scrambled away and raced around the corner of the next den. Kallik peered out to watch the firebeast roll away, retching at the vile-smelling fumes that came out of its rear.

Meanwhile Toklo was trying to open the door of the second den, but it stuck fast. "Seal rot!" he exclaimed, giving it a bang with one paw. "Now what do we do?"

"Let me look at it." Yakone stepped forward and pushed his nose into a narrow gap between the door and the wall. "If I can just shift this . . ."

Kallik watched, holding her breath. Suddenly there was a loud click, and the door swung open. "Good job, Yakone!" she exclaimed.

With Yakone in the lead, the bears sneaked into the shadows of the big den. Kallik pushed the door shut behind her. Rows and rows of flat-face objects stretched out in front of them. There were piles of wooden things like flat cages, and stacks of shiny metal cans that reminded Kallik of how Lusa used to scavenge for food among flat-face rubbish.

I wonder if there's food in these.

But all she could smell was the tang of firebeasts and an oily scent that made her feel nauseous.

"I don't want to stay here all day," she said. "We'll need to find a better place."

"I don't like it here either," Yakone said, and Toklo nodded in agreement.

But when they opened the door again and peered out,

SEEKERS: RETURN TO THE WILD: THE BURNING HORIZON 195

several more firebeasts had appeared, with flat-faces climbing out of their bellies. Two or three of them were unloading huge stuffed pouches from the back of one of the firebeasts.

"We can't go out there now," Toklo muttered, withdrawing into the shadows again.

"Okay," Kallik sighed.

The bears retreated as far into the den as they could and squeezed into a gap between some of the shiny cans. One of them tipped over and rolled onto the floor with a clang. All the bears froze; Kallik fixed her gaze on the door, certain that a flat-face would come in to see what the noise was about.

None appeared, but Kallik still couldn't relax. She crouched beside Yakone and Toklo, all of them too scared to go to sleep.

"I'm sorry," Kallik whispered. "This was a bad idea."

"We'd have been spotted right away if we put a paw outside," Toklo pointed out grimly. "And there's nowhere else to hide. All we can do is wait here until it's dark."

CHAPTER SEVENTEEN

Toklo

A sickening stench wreathed around Toklo; he could feel it clinging to his pelt. He was walking in the middle of a herd of caribou, surrounded by gray-brown bodies and the sound of their clicking hooves. With the caribou pressing around him, he had lost sight of Lusa and the white bears, and when he tried to call out to them, there was no reply.

Toklo stumbled onward, swept along by the plodding caribou. He ducked down and tried to peer through the spindly brown legs to find his friends, when suddenly the ground gave way under his feet. He fell with a splash into terrible stinking black liquid, waves of it slapping against his fur. It was thicker than water, greasy and warm, sliding into his nose and ears and dragging him beneath the surface. Though he flailed his paws frantically, he could feel himself sinking until the fetid liquid closed over his head.

"Help me!"

With a yelp, Toklo woke to find himself in the cramped,

dark hiding place in the flat-face den. Yakone had risen to his paws and was peering into the den from behind the barrier of cans.

"I think it must be night outside," he reported, glancing back over his shoulder. "There aren't any gaps in the walls that light could come through, but it's all quiet. I think we should get out of here."

Toklo staggered to his paws, trying to push the horror of his dream from his mind, and followed Yakone and Kallik through the den on legs that ached with stiffness.

Yakone tried to nose the door open, but it didn't move. "I don't understand," he said, looking puzzled. "When we came in, I lifted that little silver stick there, but now it won't budge."

Toklo shouldered past him. "Let me try."

Fear and anger began to build up inside Toklo as he pushed and pulled at the door fastening with his snout and paws. But Yakone was right. No matter what Toklo did, it wouldn't move. "We're trapped," he growled. "There's no way out!"

Letting his fury spill over, Toklo turned on Kallik. "We should never have come in here!" he snarled at her.

"Leave her alone!" Yakone pushed himself between Toklo and Kallik. "We all agreed—"

"I can answer for myself," Kallik interrupted with an annoyed look at Yakone. "Toklo, this place was crawling with flat-faces this morning, and there was nowhere else to hide. We didn't have a choice, remember?"

"And now we're stuck!" Toklo knew he was being unfair,

but his fear of being trapped in this flat-face place and his need to get out and continue the search for Lusa were making him desperate.

"Maybe there's another way out," Yakone suggested. "Or maybe the door will open if we just push it harder."

He threw himself at the door; it shook but still held fast. After a moment Toklo joined him, and the two bears battered at the door over and over until they were both bruised.

"This is no use," Toklo panted, exhausted.

Kallik and Yakone both looked utterly defeated, and as despairing as Toklo felt.

"Okay, let's look for another way out," Toklo mumbled.

He headed down one side of the den, between piles of the flat wooden cages. A faint hint of light was seeping in from tiny translucent globes attached to the ceiling, but it was barely enough to see anything. Toklo had to rely on vague memories of the space from the day before, and he longed for the open air and starlight.

He kept bumping into the flat-face stuff and brought another of the shiny cans clattering down, striking him on the shoulder. His eyes watered from the weird flat-face smells.

There has to be another way out.

Toklo blundered on, searching along the walls, sniffing for a current of fresh air that would lead him to a gap. He could hear Kallik and Yakone padding around on the other side of the den as they, too, searched for a way out.

As Toklo fumbled his way along the last side of the den, dispirited and dizzy from the stench, two pale shapes loomed in front of him. Yakone and Kallik had returned to the door and were talking to each other in low, worried tones.

"This is the only way out," Toklo declared roughly. "So we'd better get it open before we're stuck in here forever." He braced his shoulders and launched himself at the door again.

But as he hurled himself forward, Toklo tripped on something, and he ended up crashing sideways into the wall. His body hit something small that clicked under his weight. There was a flicker like lightning, a loud buzzing noise, and then the whole den was flooded with a harsh, white light.

Toklo let out a yelp of alarm, wincing at the sudden brightness. For a moment he stayed where he was, sprawled on the ground, frozen with shock. Kallik and Yakone looked just as astonished.

"What happened?" Kallik whispered after a moment. She had screwed up her eyes against the dazzling light. "Did the roof blow off? Is it the sun?"

"No, it's coming from inside the den," said Yakone, squinting upward. "I don't know what it is, but we need to hide. The flat-faces must have realized we're here."

The bears ran back toward their hiding place, their paw-steps echoing in the large space. They wedged back into the narrow gap where they'd spent the day. After a few moments Toklo tilted his head to one side.

"Listen!" he urged.

Kallik pricked her ears. "I don't hear anything."

"Exactly," said Toklo. "I don't think there are any flat-faces here, and I haven't heard any firebeasts outside." He looked around the brightly lit den. "I don't know what made this place light up," he began, "but at least we can see now." He slid out into the open again. "Let's search for another way out."

"But the flat-faces—" Yakone protested.

"Toklo's right," Kallik interrupted. "If they were coming, they'd be here by now. Let's search!"

The bears split up to investigate the inside of the den further, padding along the narrow passages between the piles of flat-face stuff. Now that they could see where they were going, it was much easier to be quiet and not knock over the piles.

Not finding a way out, Toklo's optimism was just beginning to die away when he heard Yakone's voice from the other side of the den.

"I found something!"

Toklo trotted over and found Yakone standing in front of a door that had a bar across it made of some black flat-face stuff. Kallik joined them a moment later. Her white fur was smeared with dark, sticky grease, and her injured eye looked red and sore. Toklo wondered what state they'd be in by the time they found Lusa. *Because we will find her. Ujurak won't let us down.*

"Does it open?" Kallik demanded. She gave the door a push with her head, but it didn't move.

Yakone nosed around the edges of the door. "It doesn't have a fastening like the other one," he reported after a while.

"What's this for?" Kallik wondered, touching the black bar with one paw.

Toklo swallowed an angry growl. Every hair on his pelt

bristled as he thought of the night passing and being trapped inside for another day. Suddenly his frustration spilled over, and he hurled himself at the door with a mighty bellow. To his astonishment, as he put his weight on the bar it lurched downward with a loud click, and the door flew open. Toklo tumbled out of the den and rolled into the cold night air.

At the same moment a horrific, earsplitting shriek exploded around them, making all three bears stagger back in shock. Glaring red eyes flashed along the outside of the den, rolling madly as if they were trying to find who had made the noise.

"What's happening?" Kallik cried.

"I don't know," Toklo snapped. "But we have to get out of here. Come on!"

Kallik and Yakone stumbled into the open and began to run. Toklo galloped alongside them, rejoicing in the breeze against his fur and the sense of freedom. The terrible shrieking and the swirling red eyes faded into the distance. Shadows enveloped them as they fled from the lights of the big den, leaving the denning place far behind. As Toklo felt the dusty ground give way to cool grass beneath his paws, he pulled up, his chest heaving. Kallik and Yakone panted to a halt beside him.

"Thank the spirits that's over!" Toklo said. "Now we can keep looking for Lusa."

But when he looked up to find the stars, he was dismayed to see nothing but a glow from the moon as clouds scudded across it. There were only a few glimmers from the stars, and he couldn't make out Ujurak's or Ursa's star-shapes.

"Now what do we do?" he wailed.

"Well, we know we have to go around the denning place," Kallik reminded him.

Toklo sighed. "Yes, but how *far* around? Without Ursa, how will we know when we need to head toward the horizon again?"

Kallik turned back to study the lights of the denning place. "I think we're quite a ways around already," she said. "I bet we could start heading away from it now."

"Don't be cloud-brained!" Toklo's irritation spilled over. "Leaving the denning place now is nowhere near the same direction we were headed before."

"I'm pretty sure it is," Kallik insisted.

"Arguing isn't going to help," Yakone growled. "Look, there's that tower with the red light on top of it. We saw that when we arrived, remember? If we skirt the dens until we're close to that, and then head away, I think we'll be on the right track."

Toklo pictured his first sight of the denning place. Back then the tower had been on the far side, looking almost like a glowing paw pointing the way.

Is it one of Ujurak's signs?

"You're right," he said to Yakone. "Let's go."

Toklo's frustration faded once they were on the move again, but his empty belly was aching with hunger. He still felt nauseous and light-headed from the fumes inside the den, and he could guess that his friends weren't any better off. *We really need to hunt,* he thought, but there was no sign of prey.

Before long, as they trekked across a stretch of scrubland, Toklo spotted a cluster of flat-face dens that was several bear-lengths away from the main denning area. His ears pricked as he picked up the sounds of squawking.

"Chickens!" he hissed, halting.

Kallik turned to him, looking surprised. "But they're so close to flat-faces! We can't risk it," she protested.

"I'm so hungry I'll eat you if we don't find some prey soon," Toklo replied.

"We could take a look," Yakone suggested.

Kallik didn't object again, so Toklo led the way closer to the dens. Lights were showing through the square gaps in the walls, and he realized the flat-faces inside must be awake.

"Don't make a sound," he whispered.

The bears crept around the side of one of the dens until they came to a mesh enclosure. Light from the den showed the chickens flapping around a small wooden shelter. As the bears approached, the birds squawked madly and tried to cram themselves into a small, square hole in the wall of the shelter.

"What's the plan?" Yakone hissed.

Toklo's paws tingled as he wondered if the noise from the chickens would alert the flat-faces, but there were no signs of movement from the flat-face den. "We have to get into the pen," he decided.

Kallik padded up to the door of the enclosure and nosed around the edge of it. She found that the door was closed with a loop of metal links. When Kallik tugged at it, it didn't give way.

"We can't get in through there," she said.

"And the fence is too high to jump," Yakone added.

The scent of chicken was making Toklo's jaws water, and every hair on his pelt stood on end with the thrill of the hunt. *I wish Lusa was here,* he thought. *She was always the best at planning raids near flat-face dens.* A pang of grief for the missing black bear shot through him, but for now he had to ignore it.

"If all of us charge the mesh together, we should be able to knock it down," he said to the others. "Then each of us can grab a chicken and run."

"What if we get separated?" Kallik asked.

"Then we'll meet near the tower with the red light," Toklo replied. "Are you ready?"

Kallik and Yakone got in position alongside Toklo.

"Go!"

Together the bears hurled themselves at the mesh, rearing up and pushing it with their forepaws. After a brief moment of strain, the mesh buckled beneath their weight and crumpled to the ground. With his friends beside him, Toklo bounded through, the sharp edges of the mesh scraping his belly, and raced for the shelter where the terrified chickens were still trying to hide.

The simple wooden shelter splintered apart with a few swipes from the bears' paws, and the chickens practically exploded upward, their wings flapping as they let out panic-stricken screeches. Feathers whirled around Toklo's head. Then a chicken flew straight at him; Toklo grabbed it out of the air and crushed its neck with a snap of his teeth.

As he looked around for the others, Toklo heard shouting from the flat-face den. Somewhere a door banged.

The flat-faces are coming!

"Run!" he choked out around his prey.

Toklo scrambled back over the mesh, half-blinded by the flapping birds, and raced into the darkness. Kallik and Yakone flanked him on either side, each of them also carrying a chicken. He expected to hear the explosions of firesticks, but nothing happened. The shouting and squawking died away behind them.

Toklo felt a surge of elation as he and his friends bounded away. *We did it!* At last they reached a dip in the ground and halted, their sides heaving as they caught their breath. Around them everything was dark and silent.

"Good call, Toklo," Yakone said, tearing into his chicken.

Feathers tickling his throat while he ate his prey, Toklo felt massively relieved that his plan had worked. "It was a big risk," he mumbled.

"But it paid off," said Kallik. "We can't travel without food."

After a time, still coughing on feathers, the bears set out again. To Toklo's relief, a wind sprang up, blowing the clouds away, so that Ursa could shine down on them again. Toklo felt a spring in his step as they walked onward, and he could see that Kallik and Yakone were feeling more positive, too.

The scrubland gave way to a huge expanse of wheat, the prickly yellow stalks stretching halfway up the bears' flanks as they pushed through. Toklo glanced back at the three distinct trails of crushed wheat they left behind them; they were lucky nothing was trying to track them, because they couldn't be easier to follow.

On the other side of the wheat there was a narrow river, and beyond it the ground sloped steeply upward, with rocks poking through the thin soil. All three bears plunged through the water; it was so shallow they didn't need to swim, but they took the chance to duck beneath the surface and wash the dust and flat-face odor from their fur. They drank deeply at the water's edge before pushing on up the slope.

As they climbed, Toklo realized that the short night was coming to an end; the horizon was already edged with milky-pale light. "We need to find another place to hide soon," he warned.

There were no trees in sight, but halfway up the slope they came to a large, crumbling hole tucked below one of the rocks. Sniffing, Toklo picked up traces of flat-face scents, but they were faint and stale.

"This reminds me too much of the Island of Shadows, Toklo, when you fell down into the earth," Kallik commented uneasily, pausing at the mouth of the hole and craning her head inside to look around.

Yakone murmured agreement, touching Kallik's shoulder with his snout.

Though Toklo said nothing, he went cold at the memory of being trapped underground, struggling through the tunnels while surrounded by sharp rocks and choking earth. He could see a tunnel leading from the back of this hole, and he shuddered at the thought of forcing his paws to carry him down it.

But we don't have to go down there! he scolded himself. *We can stay in the entrance, and we'll be perfectly safe.*

"We're not on the island now," Toklo argued, bracing himself to take a step inside the hole. "There's nothing here: no wolves, no flat-faces, no hostile bears. And we won't find anywhere better to hide before dawn."

Reluctantly Kallik followed him inside, with Yakone bringing up the rear. They settled down close to the entrance. From the others' uneasy expressions, Toklo could see they shared his fear of being trapped if they went farther in.

As the day dawned Toklo dozed fitfully, knowing that he needed rest, but too anxious to let himself sleep deeply. He kept an eye on the slope leading up to their shelter, but nothing stirred under the hot sun. The day seemed to stretch on forever.

We must be close to the Longest Day, he thought. *And only the spirits know how far away we are from Great Bear Lake.* His paws itched with the need to be on the move again, though not for fear of missing the gathering. *Have we missed Lusa somehow? Where is she? Is she making her own way to Great Bear Lake?*

When he became aware of Kallik and Yakone shifting restlessly beside him, Toklo rose to his paws. "I know it's not dark yet," he said, "but I think we should get going. The nights are so short now, we're not making much progress."

"Okay," Yakone agreed with a glance at Kallik, who nodded as well. "We'll have to keep a sharp eye out for flat-faces, though."

Toklo's pelt tingled as he and the others left their refuge

and climbed to the top of the slope. Something was telling him he had to move, and move fast. He didn't understand his sudden urgency, but he knew he had to obey the inner voice.

"Which way?" Kallik asked as they left their shelter behind.

Toklo paused, feeling the breeze nudging his fur, and swung into the direction he sensed it wanted him to go. "Follow me," he said confidently.

Kallik gave him a bright, questioning look. "Do you know this place? Or is Ujurak guiding you?" she asked.

Toklo hardly dared to reply. "I think he is."

As they crested the ridge, a vast stretch of grassland unrolled in front of them. It seemed deserted; as they padded on they saw only a few flat-face dens, and a couple of narrow BlackPaths here and there. The air was clear, with only the faintest tang of flat-faces or firebeasts, and they could walk undisturbed. When darkness fell, the bright shape of Ursa blazed out ahead of them, confirming their course and beckoning them on.

In spite of the peaceful landscape, Toklo felt strangely anxious. His friends were clearly on edge, too, and all three of them jumped when a bird flew up unexpectedly from a clump of long grass. Even then, no bear commented on their strange mood. Instead, they picked up their pace into a steady lope, faster than they were used to traveling.

The ground rose gently to the crest of another hill. Beyond it, Toklo looked down onto a stretch of dense forest. Along the foot of the nearest trees he made out a dark, muddy swath of earth, as if the grass had been trampled by countless hooves.

Yes!

Toklo raced down the hill and spun around at the edge of the forest to wait for Kallik and Yakone, who galloped down after him. "Look!" he exclaimed. "Caribou tracks! We've found them again."

Kallik's eyes shone. "It's as if Ujurak wants us to know we're still going the right way."

The tracks followed the edge of the forest for a short distance, then swerved into the trees. Their unspoken urgency growing stronger, the bears plunged after them.

On and on they went, pushing between the trees, flattening undergrowth and leaving tufts of their fur on brambles. As they paused briefly in a starlit clearing, Toklo caught Yakone's gaze.

"This is it," he said. "I feel it now, more than ever. We're going the right way to find Lusa."

CHAPTER EIGHTEEN

Lusa

Lusa plodded along the caribou tracks, her head down and her paws aching. She had been traveling through the night, and her legs were feeling heavy. *I've traveled like this nearly all my life,* she told herself. *I can do it.*

But traveling was different on her own, without her friends to distract her when the horizon felt as far away as ever and her legs were heavy with weariness. *Is this what Ujurak meant? Will this trail really lead me to my friends?*

The ground here undulated almost like waves of the sea, and as she trekked to the top of each rise, Lusa peered into the distance to see if she could spot three familiar figures: two white and one brown. But each fold of the land only revealed more of the scrubby wasteland, dotted with occasional flat-face dens and crossed by narrow, almost deserted Black Paths.

At least I won't have much trouble from flat-faces or firebeasts, she thought, trying to cheer herself up. *And there's enough food. The roots of these bushes are quite juicy.*

As Lusa traveled on, her mind drifted back to the flat-face

den where she had been imprisoned. It had felt wrong, uncomfortable, and threatening there, compared with the wide-open spaces she had discovered on her journey.

I could hardly breathe, she thought, pausing to take a few deep gulps of the warm air around her. *But Taktuq is happy there . . . or at least, he's content.*

Lusa knew how difficult it would be for a blind bear to survive in the wild. She figured you might be able to find roots or berries with only your sense of smell to depend on, but it would be almost impossible to find shelter or escape from enemies. *It would even be hard to know where to walk safely!* She closed her eyes and tried to walk while sniffing the air, only to stub her paw on a large rock that was in her path.

"Ow!"

Cloud-brain! she scolded herself as she opened her eyes and licked her sore paw. *But that just proves how hard it would be.*

She started off again, skirting the rock, remembering how skillfully Taktuq had used his hearing to work out what was going on in the den. He had adapted to make the den his home in a way that Lusa knew she never could. Perhaps she'd have been able to once, long ago, but now even her life in the Bear Bowl felt so distant, and she couldn't remember how she had survived. She remembered her dream of growing glossy black wings and flying across the mountains in the wide-open sky. That was what her spirit had longed to do every day she was in the flat-face den with Taktuq.

Lusa slithered down a steep slope to the bank of a narrow stream where shallow water chattered over smooth, mossy stones. Dipping her snout, she drank thirstily, then padded forward to let the current cool her paws. The sun was high overhead, beating down on Lusa's fur. A little farther downstream she spotted a huge rock overhanging the water, and she waded down into the shade. Climbing out onto a sandy spit of land beneath the overhang, she settled down to rest with her nose on her paws. After a while, she drifted into a doze.

As she dreamed, Lusa became aware of caribou all around her; she was walking in the middle of the herd, swept forward by the unstoppable river of bodies. Bright stars shone down from the night sky. There were no other bears there, only the caribou surrounding her with their clicking feet. Lusa padded calmly with them, her paws fitting neatly into the hoofprints pressed into the earth. *I'm going to Great Bear Lake,* she thought, a feeling of peace enfolding her. *The Pathway Star is showing me the way.*

Lusa woke with a start. The sun had slipped a little farther down in the sky, and its position reminded her that following the caribou trail was actually taking her farther and farther *away* from Great Bear Lake. She let out a yelp of panic. She had made the decision to head back to the mountains for good reasons, but she was suddenly aware of what a huge risk she was taking, retracing her steps to look for her friends. *They could be long gone. They might even be at the lake already! Is it the Longest Day yet?* There was so much daylight now, and the nights were so short, that it was hard for Lusa to tell how much longer it would be to the gathering.

What if I end up back in the mountains alone? she asked herself.

Will I have to turn around and come back all this way? She knew that if she reached the mountains without finding the others, by the time she had retraced her steps it could be too late for the Longest Day Gathering. Lusa pictured herself arriving at Great Bear Lake to find it deserted, the gathered bears long gone and the lakeshore desolate. She let out a whimper of despair. *I might never see Miki and his family again.*

Then Lusa sat up, bracing herself. *I won't be alone, and I'm not alone now! Ujurak is always with me, even if I can't see him.*

Lusa reminded herself that she was going this way because it felt right. She couldn't question the signs now! She had found food and places to sleep ever since she'd left the flat-face den, and in her dream Ujurak had pointed her this way. She was certain that he was watching over her, and felt reassured.

And I trust myself to read the signs around me, just like Ujurak did. She pulled herself to her paws, took another drink from the stream, and set off again.

When Lusa reached the top of the next hill, she was confronted by a swath of dark forest unfurling away into the distance. She could just make out more open ground beyond it, but for a while she would be walking among dense trees. A worm of panic began gnawing at Lusa's belly, though she tried hard to ignore it. *It will be so easy to miss the others among the trees!*

But the tracks left by the caribou led straight into the forest, and Lusa's instinct tugged her forward. A bird piped somewhere ahead of her, as if it was urging her on.

She headed into the trees. As the thick branches cut off the sunlight, she felt like she was plunging into cool, green water.

Her paws stumbled on the hoof-marked ground, but Lusa kept going, even when a bush with bright-red berries seemed to reach out its branches to tempt her to stop.

A strange sense of urgency filled Lusa now. She felt like she was getting close to something huge, something almost within her grasp.

As Lusa pushed her way forward, the trees closed up behind her and she was enveloped in the whispering, rustling world of the forest. A gray-and-white bird swooped over her head, almost brushing her fur, and Lusa watched it disappear into the branches. *Is that Ujurak, keeping an eye on me?* The thought warmed her and gave more energy to her paws.

The forest fell eerily silent once the bird had vanished. Lusa picked up her pace, loping along faster and faster, until her paws skidded on a loose stone and she fell down a slope, landing hard in a bramble thicket at the bottom.

"Seal rot!" she spat.

When Lusa tried to struggle to her paws, the tendrils of bramble coiled around her, seeming to tug her deeper into the thicket. A fresh awareness of how alone she was surged over Lusa, and she barely stopped herself from whimpering.

Wrenching again at the brambles, Lusa only managed to tear her fur, but then she looked up and spotted a knot in a tree trunk above her head. As she stared, it took on the shape of a bear's face with warm, kind eyes and a soft, furry muzzle.

Lusa gasped with wonder. "It's a bear spirit, watching me!"

Looking around, she saw more bear faces emerging from

the trunks of the trees. *You are not alone,* they seemed to tell her. *We are with you.*

Urged on by their kind encouragement, Lusa calmed herself and withdrew little by little from the thicket, freeing herself from the clinging brambles with small, delicate movements. At last, scratched and missing several tufts of fur, she stood on open ground again.

"Thank you!" she exclaimed, bowing her head to the bear spirits. "Thank you for saving me. I have to go now, but I'll never forget you."

The caribou trail wound through the trees, and Lusa padded along it without stopping. She knew the bear spirits were still with her. She could feel their encouragement boosting her on, and a breeze whispered through the leaves like gentle voices.

"Lusa . . . Lusa . . . all will be well. . . ."

Thin shafts of reddening sunlight angled through the branches, telling Lusa that the sun was going down and the long day coming to an end. Though her legs ached with weariness, her paws still tingled impatiently; she didn't want to stop for the night. She emerged from the trees in a small clearing filled with soft green grass, and paused there, relishing how the cool grass soothed her paws.

I could lie down and sleep here—but I feel so close. . . .

At that moment Lusa heard heavy lumbering noises up ahead, as though some large animals were blundering through the forest.

More caribou? she wondered, her heart beginning to thump.

Lusa glanced around, trying to figure out which trees would be best if she had to climb to safety.

The noises grew closer, and now Lusa could see branches waving as the animals passed through the bushes. She crouched down behind a thick clump of ferns, hoping they would pass by without noticing her.

Then three faces appeared from the shadows on the opposite side of the clearing. Lusa stared at them: two white faces, one brown. For a moment she felt her heart stop. *Am I seeing things?*

"Kallik?" she whispered, springing to her paws. "Toklo? Yakone? Is it really you?"

"Lusa!" barked the tired-looking brown bear in the lead, and Lusa bounded forward, suddenly feeling as if she could run forever. She had found them!

Kallik, Yakone, and Toklo raced forward as well, and Lusa met them in the middle of the clearing. They pressed around her, covering her face with licks, pressing their muzzles into her shoulders until Lusa could hardly breathe. Delight pulsed through her; she wanted to leap up into the sky or sing like a bird, and even that wouldn't have been enough to express her happiness.

"I've found you!" she exclaimed. *Thank you, Ujurak. Thank you, caribou.*

Kallik hooked Lusa's paws out from under her, rolling her over on the soft grass and flopping down on top of her. Lusa wrestled joyfully with her old friend, feeling as if she was enveloped in a gentle white cloud. All her fear and weariness had evaporated like dew in sunlight.

"Where have you been?" Kallik demanded, lifting her head and looking down at her. "Oh, Lusa, we've been so worried. We thought you were with us when we escaped from the mules, but you'd simply disappeared. We followed your trail to the edge of the BlackPath, but it got lost among firebeast tracks."

"We thought you must have been captured by a firebeast," Toklo added. "Did that really happen?"

Lusa nodded. "I can't remember much about it," she told them. "I was kicked in the head by a mule, and the firebeast took me on its back to a den with a lot of other animals and birds."

Kallik looked puzzled. "Why would a firebeast do that?"

"There were flat-faces with it," Lusa explained. "Flat-faces who look after animals that are sick or injured. I met a blind bear there . . . a black bear like me. His name was Taktuq. He seemed to like living there, but all I could think about was getting back into the wild."

"So how did you escape?" Yakone asked, giving Lusa a friendly nudge.

"I made friends with a young flat-face," Lusa said. "I made her think I was cute, by acting funny for her. I felt like such a cloud-brain, but it worked! She took me out of my cage on a vine—"

"A vine?" Yakone looked confused.

Lusa shrugged. "Some sort of flat-face thing. But there was a coyote, and it got out of its pen, too, and I had to fight it."

Shock throbbed through her at the memory. *I don't know how I did that!*

"You fought a coyote?" Kallik looked appalled. "Are you hurt?" She began to sniff Lusa all over.

"No, I *beat* it. I wish you three had seen me! And then I ran and ran, and then I got lost in some corn. It was awful! Then finally I found the caribou trail. I'd had a dream about them, so I knew I had to follow their path. Thank the spirits Ujurak showed me which way to go! But what happened to you?" Lusa sprang to her paws again. "Tell me everything!"

"We looked for you," Toklo began, "and then Ujurak told us that we should find the caribou."

"And we figured out that meant we should follow them," Kallik added.

Lusa gave an excited little bounce. "Ujurak told me *not* to follow them!"

"We crossed a glacier." Yakone took up the story. "And Kallik fell down a crevasse."

Lusa stared at her friend in alarm. For a moment she felt as scared as if she had been there to see Kallik fall, even though Kallik was standing in front of her, alive and well.

"I've never been so afraid," Kallik said. "But Ujurak was with me, and he helped me to get out."

"We kept coming across flat-faces, so we started traveling at night," Toklo went on. "Even when we lost the caribou trail, Ujurak and Ursa showed us the way with their stars. We sheltered in a flat-face den and got trapped there. . . ."

"Stupid flat-faces," Yakone rumbled. "Why can't they make dens you can get out of without half killing yourself?"

"And then we followed the caribou tracks into this forest," Kallik concluded, nodding to the trees behind her. She glanced at Toklo and Yakone. "It was strange, because once we entered the trees we all felt this urge to go as fast as we could without stopping to hunt or rest, as if our paws just knew where we should be."

"I felt that, too!" Lusa squeaked.

"It must have been Ujurak again," Yakone said. "We would never have found each other without him."

The four bears huddled together. Lusa felt like she wanted to touch all their pelts at once. She never wanted to take her eyes off them ever again.

"We can't lose each other again," Kallik murmured, echoing Lusa's thoughts.

Toklo was the first to step back from their huddle. "It'll be dark soon," he pointed out. "I think we should spend the night here." As the others murmured agreement, he added, "Lusa, what's the land like beyond these trees?"

"Open and flat, with grass and scrubby bushes. I didn't see any flat-faces and only a couple of firebeasts, but I don't think there's much prey, either."

"Okay," Toklo decided. "We'll hunt now, and eat well. Lusa, do you want to come with us to hunt?"

Lusa nodded. "I'm not letting you out of my sight!"

The bears headed into the trees. Lusa was still too stunned

by joy to pay much attention to the hunt, but it wasn't long before Toklo spotted a grouse roosting in a clump of ferns.

Every hair on Lusa's pelt quivered with delight as she and her friends spread out into their familiar hunting pattern. When they had surrounded the grouse, Yakone let out a growl to drive it out of its nest. Lusa blocked it as it took off in her direction, making it swerve toward Kallik and Toklo. They both leaped toward it at the same time, though it was Kallik who straightened up with the bird in her jaws.

When they had carried their prey back to the clearing, Lusa accepted a small portion of the grouse, just for the fun of sharing, then satisfied her hunger with fern roots while her friends divided the rest of the bird. They all kept casting quick sidelong glances at one another as they ate, as if they couldn't believe they were all together again.

By the time they had finished eating, the sunlight had faded and shadows gathered under the trees. The bears settled down to sleep, curling up together in the soft grass.

"I was so scared I'd lost you," Toklo confided to Lusa as he folded his warm bulk around her. His voice quavered. "I promised to take you to Great Bear Lake, and I almost failed." He buried his snout in Lusa's fur as if he was too ashamed to look at her.

"But you didn't fail. And you're not responsible for me," Lusa told him gently. "Haven't I just proved that I can survive on my own?" She shuddered at the memory of escaping from the flat-face den and felt Toklo shift closer to her.

"You did well, Lusa."

"Besides, in spite of everything," Lusa continued, "we found each other again. This is *our* journey," she continued. "We will finish it together. Ujurak will make sure of that."

CHAPTER NINETEEN

Kallik

Kallik yawned and stretched, awakened by the early morning light. This was the second sunrise since they had been reunited with Lusa, and the others were still sound asleep in the grassy hollow where they had made a den for the night.

I feel like I've hardly had time to close my eyes, she grumbled to herself. *The nights are so short now.*

Rubbing a paw over her face to wake herself up, Kallik thought about the days ahead. *We found Lusa, just as Ujurak promised. Now we have to find Great Bear Lake. And maybe I'll see Taqqiq again and hear his news about the Melting Sea.*

Kallik's paws prickled with urgency. The days were so long, and the nights passed so quickly, that she knew they must be close to the Longest Day.

She was distracted from her thoughts by Toklo, who lumbered to his paws beside her and gave Yakone and Lusa a sharp prod. "Come on," he ordered. "It's time to go."

"I'm still sleepy . . ." Lusa mumbled.

Yakone stretched out his paws and let his jaws gape in a

massive yawn. "Me too," he said to Lusa. "But maybe walking will wake us up."

They set out across the swath of grassland that stretched empty and windswept ahead of them. Outcrops of no-claw dens were rare in this open landscape, and the bears skirted them without any trouble. The grass was soft underpaw, soothing their scraped pads, and in spite of Lusa's concerns they found just enough ground-nesting birds to keep them from going hungry. Water was more of a problem, though, and the bears learned to lick the dew off the blades of grass just before the sun rose and dried up all the moisture.

Now that they were heading for Great Bear Lake, they had veered away from the caribou trail. Toklo took the lead, regularly checking the angle of the sun and the direction of the mountain slopes, and at night, the position of the Pathway Star, leading them gently on.

We're lucky he remembers the way from the last time he traveled to the lake, Kallik thought. *We don't have time to get lost again.*

"Yakone's paw doesn't seem to be hurting him much," Kallik pointed out to Lusa, who was walking beside her. "He's hardly limping at all."

Lusa nodded, though there was a shadow of anxiety in her eyes. "I hope that means the infection has cleared up," she said. "I don't think I could find any herbs to treat him with out here."

Yakone glanced back over his shoulder. "Don't worry. I'm fine."

As the sun rose higher in the sky and the day grew hotter,

the bears paused for a short rest. Kallik sat down beside Yakone in a small patch of shade cast by a thornbush.

"I'll be glad when the gathering's over and we can go back to Star Island," she panted.

Yakone murmured agreement. "It'll be good to see my family again. Even Unalaq!"

Kallik wasn't sure that she was looking forward to meeting the troublemaking bear again, even if he was Yakone's brother. But she felt a stirring of excitement about their return to the island. *I can't wait to make a real home for myself after all this traveling. . . .*

"They'll be surprised to see us, that's for sure," Yakone continued.

Toklo gave him a friendly shove. "At least you won't have a black and a brown bear tagging along this time."

Kallik knew Toklo was just joking around, but sadness passed over her like the flicker of a black wing as she thought about how finding her home would mean leaving her friends, perhaps forever.

I'll never stop missing Lusa and Toklo!

Anxious to get to the lake, none of the bears wanted to rest for long, and soon they set out again, trudging up a long, shallow slope that led up to a ridge. When they reached the top, they halted.

"Wow, look at that!" Lusa exclaimed.

More wind-ruffled grassland unrolled in front of them, but this time three vast rivers sliced through it, with only narrow stretches of dry land between them.

"Toklo, did you cross these rivers last time?" Yakone asked.

Toklo looked puzzled. "I think we crossed one of them . . . but it must have been farther upstream."

Kallik felt a faint stir of worry that Toklo couldn't remember the rivers from before, but her concern was lost beneath the tempting thought of swimming in cool water.

"Come on!" she called. "Let's race!"

All four bears sped up as they galloped down the hill, pushed through the bushes that edged the first river and plunged into the cool, greenish-brown water. The river was broad, but the current was gentle, and Kallik felt no fear as she pushed out into the middle.

Yakone appeared in the water beside her, swimming strongly. "Let's fish!" he puffed.

The two white bears dove below the surface side by side. In the underwater dimness, Kallik could see silver flickers as fish darted past her. She lunged at one of them and snapped her jaws closed on it. Kallik kicked out with her hind legs and pushed herself back to the surface, keeping a firm grip on her fish. Shaking drops from her ears, she spotted Lusa and Toklo making their way across the placid water. They both looked like they were enjoying the cool water after the relentless heat of the sun.

Yakone's head broke the surface beside Kallik. He, too, had a flapping fish in his jaws. Together they made for the far shore, flicking water from their fur as they waded up the bank.

"That was easy!" Kallik exclaimed, dropping her fish in front of Toklo and Lusa.

Lusa's eyes gleamed. "You're great fish hunters!"

"And we're so clean now!" Kallik declared, looking down at her spotless, streaming fur.

Toklo wasn't so pleased. The white bears could now be seen from the far horizon, and his pelt prickled with anxiety.

The bears settled down to feast on the fish in the shade of some spindly trees. Fully fed and comfortable, Kallik felt herself drifting off to sleep.

She dreamed that she was surrounded by several white bears, padding along with them in a mist that obscured the landscape. Yakone was by her side. Kallik was happy to be with him, relieved that she had reached the end of her journey, and comfortable to be wreathed in the scents of the other white bears.

In her dream, Kallik stirred. *Wait . . . other bears?* Opening her eyes, she sat up and sniffed the air. *Other white bears have been here!*

Kallik gave Yakone's shoulder a nudge. "What is it?" he mumbled.

"Wake up!" Kallik urged him. "I can smell bears like us!"

Yakone scrambled to his paws, his muzzle raised to scent the air. "You're right. And they were here not long ago."

Leaving Toklo and Lusa to finish their nap, Kallik and Yakone began to scout around the tiny copse. Kallik came across the shallow scoop of a sleeping place.

"White fur," Yakone said, pointing to a tuft caught on a rough bit of tree trunk. "Wow!" he went on. "There are other white bears traveling this way!"

"They must be coming from the Melting Sea," Kallik guessed. She recalled her first lonely slog across the open land, with nothing but a fox for company. "These bears seem to be in a group," she said, concentrating on the smells around her. "I can pick out three or four different scents." *I wonder if one of them is Taqqiq,* she added to herself, hopeful but at the same time dismayed that she couldn't be sure of her brother's scent anymore.

By this time Toklo and Lusa were stretching and opening their eyes.

"What are you doing over there?" Toklo grunted.

Kallik padded across to him. "Other white bears have been here," she announced.

Toklo and Lusa shared a surprised glance. "That's great!" Lusa barked. "They must be on their way to Great Bear Lake, too. I wonder if we'll catch up to them. Maybe we should try."

Kallik saw that Toklo didn't share Lusa's enthusiasm. He had a wary look. "We'd better not," he responded to Lusa. "We don't know if they'd be friendly, and we don't want to be fighting over prey. Besides, a large group of bears are more likely to attract flat-faces."

"But there aren't many flat-faces around here," Lusa protested.

"It would be interesting to meet new bears," Yakone pointed out. "Surely none of them will want to stop and fight. The Longest Day is a time of peace, right?"

"It isn't the Longest Day yet," Toklo muttered, clearly not convinced.

Lusa looked up at the sky. "We hope," she said. "Come on, let's keep going."

"Okay," Yakone agreed as they set off again. "If we don't meet these bears, maybe we'll find some other white bears to travel home with after the gathering is over, Kallik."

At his words, Kallik felt a jolt of dismay that struck her like lightning out of a clear sky. *The final good-bye is too close. Oh, spirits, do we really want to reach the end of our shared journey?* She said nothing to the others, but inside she had a growing feeling of dread that dragged at her paws and made her breath feel tight in her chest. *We've been traveling to reach this moment for so long, but now I don't want it to come.*

Yakone let his shoulder brush against hers. "Are you okay?" he murmured. "You seem very quiet. You're not worried about meeting these other bears, are you?" He nudged her gently. "I'll look after you!"

Kallik huffed in protest. "I can look after myself, thanks!"

Yakone butted her with his head. "I know you can, cloud-brain. I was only teasing. Come on, don't fall behind."

The sun was sliding down the sky when the bears approached the next river, a faster current foaming over stones.

Yakone gave a bark of excitement. "Look! The white bears are here!"

Gazing ahead, Kallik made out four white shapes, two large and two small. They were just about to enter the water. It had been so long since she had seen other white bears that the distant figures seemed to leap out of the flat green landscape.

"Let's hurry up and join them," Yakone urged. "They might know the bears we met on the Melting Sea."

But Kallik felt her paws slowing down. "There's no hurry," she said. "We don't want to alarm them!" Yakone looked surprised, and she added hastily, "Don't forget that we're traveling with a black bear and a brown bear as well. We should let the white bears get safely across the river first."

Yakone looked puzzled, but Toklo gave a nod of agreement as he fell in beside Kallik. "I'm happy to wait before we catch up to them," he said.

Lusa trotted beside them, swallowing a leaf that she had picked from a bush. "We must be in time for the Longest Day," she pointed out, "since other bears are still traveling."

"Unless they've missed it, too," Toklo warned. "Look, they've started swimming. Let's hang back and let them cross without startling them. We can catch up to them tomorrow, after we've had a chance to rest and hunt."

To Kallik's relief, Yakone didn't argue, and as the sun went down they began to search for a place to camp, leaving the second river crossing for the next day. The other white bears had trekked onward without glancing back. *The wind is blowing toward us,* Kallik thought. *It's carrying their scent to us, but they don't know that we're following them.*

They found a sheltered spot in a hollow between two big boulders, where the sound of flowing water drifted faintly to their ears.

Toklo touched Kallik on the shoulder. "Let's hunt," he suggested. "Lusa looks tired, and Yakone should rest his paw."

"Sure."

Kallik tried to put her worries about meeting other bears out of her mind as she and Toklo headed back up the slope to look for prey. At first the land seemed to be deserted. Then she spotted a hare, almost invisible against the rocks in its brown burn-sky pelt. She pointed it out to Toklo with a nod in its direction.

Without a word, Toklo slipped into their well-practiced hunting pattern, circling around the hare in a wide arc until he could come upon it from behind. Kallik crouched low to the ground, taking advantage of the long grass for cover.

Toklo let out a roar. The hare sprang up, its eyes bulging in panic, and streaked off at an angle. Kallik raced to intercept it while Toklo bounded in pursuit.

Kallik reached the fleeing hare first. Toklo hung back at the last moment to let her make the catch. As she slammed her paw down on it, she asked herself, *How many more times will we do this together?*

CHAPTER TWENTY

Toklo

Toklo rose to his paws, gave his pelt a shake, and gazed across the flat land toward the river. Dawn light filled the sky, and there was a rosy glow on the horizon where the sun would rise.

There was no sign of the four white bears they had seen the day before. *They must have set out early,* he thought with a grunt of relief. He felt it was much better for him and his companions to walk on their own. *Two white bears, a brown bear and a black . . . I don't want to spend our last days answering questions about what brought us together.*

Toklo roused his friends, and they set out for the river. This one flowed more swiftly than the first one they'd crossed, but it wasn't as deep. Near the shore, the shallow water rippled and murmured as it rolled over tiny, smooth pebbles. Light from the rising sun danced on the surface.

Wading into the current, feeling the cold water tug at the fur on his belly, Toklo was plunged into a memory of learning to fish when he was a cub. He glanced around, half expecting to see other brown bears peering into the water. But he only saw Kallik and Yakone, swimming in the middle where the channel was deepest, splashing water at each other and diving like a couple of cubs.

Staring down into the water again, Toklo caught a flicker of movement. *Salmon!* He launched himself at it, recalling long-buried instincts, and his claws dug deep into the fish before he snatched it into the air.

"Nice work, Toklo!" cried Lusa, who was watching him from the bank.

Toklo tossed the salmon to her and pushed his way deeper into the river. His ears filled with whispers, the murmurings of long-dead bears as their spirits washed around him. Salmon flashed around his paws, but Toklo was transfixed by the bear spirits.

"Oka, are you there?" he called softly, pierced by a pang of longing for his lost family. "Tobi? If you are there, I hope you're free now. I hope you have endless fish to catch."

An image of Aiyanna came into Toklo's mind, and he imagined fishing with her in the broad rivers in the valleys of his territory.

Will I live there with her until our spirits wash away together in the river?

A shiver went through him at the thought of spending the rest of his life with one bear, but it was a good feeling, filling him with anticipation. Then Lusa splashed up to him, jerking Toklo back to the present.

"Are you okay to swim across?" Toklo asked.

Lusa nodded. "It's not far," she mumbled around his

salmon, which she carried in her jaws.

But Toklo felt strangely reluctant to cross the river. Reaching the other side would take them even closer to the lake where they would part forever. *Ujurak said it was important for me to get to the lake. I wonder what he meant.*

Pushing that thought from his mind and wanting to delay, he slapped his paw down on the surface of the water to splash Lusa, thinking of how much better it would be to stay here and play than continue with their trek.

Lusa backed away, snorting as the water spattered over her face. "Stop that!"

"All right, why don't you practice your fishing skills?" Toklo suggested.

Lusa stepped up to him and waved the salmon in his face. "We've got a fish, cloud-brain!" she said around it.

Toklo sighed. "Give me that," he said, taking the fish from her. "You'll manage better without it."

Lusa struck out, swimming strongly for the opposite bank, and Toklo followed, sheltering her from the current with his body.

When they had all reached the shore, the bears shared the salmon, then continued across another stretch of open ground until they finally reached the last of the three rivers. Toklo wrinkled his nose with disgust as he looked at it. The channel was narrow, and it would be no trouble to cross, but the water ran sluggishly, brown with silt. A foul stench rose from it, and when Toklo padded into it he could feel filth soaking into his pelt.

The water was so shallow that Toklo and the white bears could wade. Lusa was the only one who had to swim, with Kallik and Yakone on either side of her.

"This water is disgusting!" she yelped as her paws splashed busily. "I can't—"

A ripple splashed into Lusa's mouth and she choked noisily, flailing her paws until Yakone grabbed her by the scruff and held her up.

"Thanks!" she gasped as she recovered and began to swim once more.

"Keep your jaws shut this time, chatterbug," Toklo advised.

When Toklo emerged from the water his fur felt dirty and slippery, and he longed for clear, running water to wash off in.

"We didn't stay clean for long," Kallik remarked ruefully. She gave her chest a half-hearted lick, curling her lip at the taste of the dirty water.

The ground on the far side of the river sloped up steeply, and instead of soft grass, now the bears were trudging over loose stones and grit. As they clambered upward, they began to hear strange growling sounds from somewhere ahead, and the ground seemed to tremble under their paws.

"I don't like this," Toklo muttered. "What's happening on the other side of this hill?"

"Don't you remember?" Kallik asked. "Or you, Lusa? You've been this way before."

Toklo shook his head. "Not exactly this way. I don't remember all those rivers, and I don't recognize this place at all."

"Me either," added Lusa.

Panting and scrabbling on the rough soil, the bears reached the top of the slope. They paused to catch their breath and stared in horrified silence at the scene below them. A dizzying precipice fell away in front of their paws, revealing a huge, flat-face-made canyon gouged out of the earth. Enormous roaring firebeasts moved slowly across it, leaving deep tracks in the dust. The sides of the canyon were sheer cliffs, crisscrossed by scars, and gigantic holes gaped in the rock. The growling the bears heard as they climbed the hill was so loud now they could hardly hear one another speak.

"We can't go this way!" Lusa squeaked.

Yakone let out a low growl. "This is a route for bears. Flat-faces have no right to carve it up."

Toklo's nostrils flared, and his grubby fur stood on end. "We'll have to go around," he decided, trying to sound confident.

Lusa looked up to study the sky. "I'm trying to remember where the Pathway Star is," she said. "I wonder how far out of our way we'll have to go."

"We'll be okay," Kallik told her. "All the bears who're coming this way will have to change direction, just like us."

Lusa nodded, though she still looked worried and went on gazing up into the sky, as if she could make out the stars beyond the blue.

"I think we should wait here on the cliff until it gets dark," Toklo said. "It'll be safer to travel then."

"But we're losing time!" Lusa protested.

"We've made good progress up until now," Toklo pointed

out. "And in the meantime we can go back down to the river and hunt in the undergrowth. It doesn't look like we'll find anything to eat up here."

Lusa shrugged miserably.

"I'll go with you to hunt," Yakone offered. "Kallik, you stay here with Lusa and try to get some rest."

Kallik nodded and gave Lusa a gentle push into the shade of a nearby rock.

Toklo led the way as he and Yakone scrambled down the hill again to the bushes that bordered the river.

"We'll still get to Great Bear Lake, won't we?" Yakone asked quietly. "Even though we're on a different route from the one you took before?"

Toklo bristled at the question. "Of course we will! The stars are guiding us."

Yakone was silent for a moment as they approached the river and began scenting the air for prey. "Those other bears we saw . . ." he began. "Don't you think we should try to catch up to them and travel together for the last part of the journey?"

A flash of defensive anger rose up in Toklo, but he quickly calmed himself and said, "We might not be welcome to join their group. Besides," he added, "we're different. We've seen more, and traveled farther. Other bears won't understand that."

"But in the end we'll need to mingle with other bears, and go back to living with our own kind, won't we?" Yakone persisted. "That's the whole point of the journey. To find a home for each of us."

At that moment, Toklo picked up the scent of a goose somewhere in the foliage beside the river. Tracking it was a welcome distraction, and he didn't reply to Yakone's question.

By the time the bears had eaten, night had fallen. They set out along the edge of the chasm, casting glances down at the hordes of yellow-pelted flat-faces, who seemed to be churning up the ground with huge firebeasts and lifting stones out of it.

"Weird," Toklo muttered, but he had seen too much of the strange ways of flat-faces to pay them much attention now.

Harsh, unnatural lights illuminated the canyon, and massive firebeasts growled in and out. The bears had to slink along the flat, dusty ground at the top of the cliff, making the most of the scanty cover. Now and then a bright white glare lit them up. *How can the flat-faces not see us?* Toklo wondered uneasily.

They crouched down when they came to a BlackPath and waited until it was safe to scuttle across. At first Toklo thought this wouldn't be too difficult. The BlackPaths were narrow, and as they approached there hadn't been that many firebeasts passing by.

But then a harsh rumble filled the air. Gazing in the direction of the chasm, Toklo's heart began thumping as he saw a whole herd of firebeasts heading their way, one after the other, their glaring yellow eyes slicing through the darkness.

Lusa, who was standing beside him, caught her breath in terror. "We have to hide!"

Toklo glanced around, but there was no cover nearby, only a few rocks far too small for them to hide behind. The white bears' pelts stood out, pale against the dirty ground.

"Quick!" Toklo said to Kallik and Yakone as the leading firebeast roared up the BlackPath, closer with every passing moment. "Roll in the dust to hide your white fur!"

Kallik opened her jaws as if she was about to protest.

"Just do it!" Toklo growled, launching himself at Kallik and carrying her off her paws.

To his relief, Yakone flopped down beside Kallik and began to roll. Kallik did the same, until both their pelts were smeared with dirt. Then all four bears crouched behind the small rocks, just as the firebeast herd swept past.

"Oh, spirits, let them not see us!" Lusa breathed out.

Toklo peered out from behind his rock and watched the firebeasts growling past, their glaring eyes lighting up the devastated landscape. He breathed a sigh of relief as the last one vanished into the distance, leaving the bears in darkness once again.

"They're gone," he said, getting to his paws.

Kallik rose to stand beside him. "You were right, Toklo," she told him, "we blended in better covered in dust. But I've never felt so filthy!"

Toklo understood. They were all getting dirtier with every pawstep, and his own pelt itched from ears to tail.

"We can all wash our fur in the lake," Lusa puffed. "I can't wait!"

"We don't know how close we are," Toklo reminded her. "We could have a few more sunrises of traveling."

Lusa twitched her ears impatiently. "But we'll get there soon, won't we?"

"Yes," Toklo replied heavily. "We will."

CHAPTER TWENTY-ONE

Lusa

The bears kept on walking after the short night had passed and the sun had risen over the ruined expanse of land. They all wanted to put as much space as they could between themselves and the unnatural chasm in the earth. Lusa could still feel the ground rumbling beneath her paws, and her heart beat faster whenever she pictured the massive line of firebeasts roaring past them while they were trying to hide.

Ahead the landscape was flat and barren, with no promising spots to hunt or forage. Lusa tried digging around a couple of straggly bushes, but the roots there were dry and brittle.

"Yuck!" she exclaimed, coughing on the tough fibers. "That's horrible!"

The other bears didn't talk much, just slogged on with their heads down, lost in their own thoughts.

At last a small copse of pine trees appeared on the horizon, growing larger as the bears trekked toward them.

"Why don't we rest there for a bit?" Lusa suggested. "We've been traveling since nightfall."

The others agreed, and they headed for the clump of pines, where they lay down in the shade on a thick covering of pine needles. But although Lusa was tired to her toes, her belly was growling too much for her to sleep. The others were shifting restlessly, and she thought hunger was keeping them awake, too.

After a while, Toklo rose to his paws and went to peer out at the flat land from the other side of the cluster of trees. "There's no prey around here—there's not enough cover," he reported over his shoulder. "But I can see a flat-face area. Just a few dens. We might be able to find food there."

"*You* want to look for food near flat-face dens?" Lusa asked, surprised.

"You should have seen us steal chickens right out from under some flat-face noses, Lusa. You would have been proud!" replied Toklo.

Maybe, thought Lusa. *But that's not how wild bears are meant to do things.*

Lusa's pelt prickled as they set off again. Although in daylight she couldn't see the Pathway Star, she knew that by heading for the flat-face dens they were turning away from their route to Great Bear Lake. *We don't have time for any more detours. We might miss the gathering! How could our journey have become so twisting and difficult so close to the end?*

At the edge of the flat-face dens, Lusa crouched with the others behind a row of wooden slats. Farther along she could hear dogs snuffling, and she picked up their rank scent.

"I'll create a diversion," Toklo whispered to her, "while you see if you can find anything to eat."

Lusa knew he meant that she should look in the shiny silver containers where flat-faces sometimes kept food. Every hair on her pelt was bristling from being so close to a denning place again. Even though her belly was still growling, she felt a spurt of rebellion rising up inside her.

"Why am I always the one to get flat-face food?" she demanded.

"We'll keep you safe," Toklo assured her, touching her shoulder with his snout.

Lusa shrugged him off. "That's not the point! I'm a wild bear now! I forage for roots and berries like a real black bear."

The others stared at her in astonishment.

"Of course you're a wild bear," Kallik told her. "I've never thought of you any other way. But you're the best at this, and we need your help."

Her soothing words didn't impress Lusa. "We're so close to the end of our journey," she said, "and we're never going to live with flat-faces again. We can't rely on their food." Turning back to Toklo, she added, "I'm not doing it, and that's that."

Though Lusa tried to sound determined, she was also fighting back a sense of rising panic. Images of being trapped in her cage next to the angry coyote flooded into her mind. Crushed by the fear of cage bars surrounding her again, she felt desperate to run anywhere, in any direction except toward the flat-face dens.

"Come on, Lusa," Yakone coaxed. "It'll be okay. Sure, we're wild bears, but that doesn't mean we can't steal from flat-faces now and then."

Lusa glared at him. "I said no, and I meant it."

"We can't force her," Toklo said, shrugging.

He looked closely at Lusa, and she wondered if he had any idea what she was feeling. It wasn't just the certainty that she was a wild bear now, a long way from the bear she used to be who was comfortable around flat-faces and happy to eat their cast-off food. Memories of being captured were too fresh in her mind, and she could feel herself freezing with terror being this close to flat-faces again. *I can't let them catch me again. I might never make it to Great Bear Lake.*

"Okay," Kallik said at last. "Let's go."

Lusa's belly was rumbling as they headed into the open again, away from the flat-face dens. She knew her friends must be just as hungry, and guilt crept up on her.

We're wild bears; we'll find our own food! And I can't take the risk of being caught again. They don't understand what that feels like.

Gradually the barren scrub gave way to grassland again, and Lusa hoped they had returned to the right path. Her nose twitched at prey-scents in the air.

Toklo picked them up, too, and paused, snuffling happily. "This is better," he growled. "We'll find some prey here."

As the bears waded into deeper grass, suddenly Kallik darted to one side. There was a scuffle, and a moment later she returned with a ptarmigan in her jaws.

"Excellent!" Yakone huffed.

The bears stopped to eat, hungrily gulping down the prey. Some of Lusa's guilt eased along with her hunger.

"Was that wild enough for you?" Toklo asked gruffly,

giving her an affectionate cuff around her ear.

"Absolutely," Lusa responded. A warm feeling spread through her, and the rest of her guilt disappeared as she realized Toklo had forgiven her.

The prey gave the bears fresh energy, and they traveled on briskly until they reached the crest of the next hill. Stopping for a quick rest, Lusa gazed down on a shallow, rocky valley and tried to remember if she and Toklo had passed this way on their previous trip to Great Bear Lake.

"I don't recognize this, do you?" she asked him.

Toklo shook his head thoughtfully. "Maybe not . . . but see that mountain over there, the one shaped like a fish head? I think we traveled on the other side of it."

"You could be right," said Lusa, reassured that they had returned to the right path.

Searching the landscape for more familiar features, she spotted two brown bears in the distance, walking side by side.

"Look down there," she barked. "More bears! Why don't we join them?"

She noticed that Yakone was looking closely at Toklo, as though his reply was immensely important.

"No," Toklo replied. "Let them travel alone."

Kallik gave a firm nod. "I agree."

"But they must be going to Great Bear Lake!" Lusa protested. "We should at least follow them."

"What if they're not friendly?" Toklo asked. "We've had trouble with grizzlies before, remember?" He pointed in a slightly different direction from the one the brown bears were taking. "We'll go that way."

"Good idea," Kallik said. "We don't want any trouble so close to arriving at the lake."

"Going that direction will take us off course again." Lusa looked at her friends, scanning each of their faces. "Any bear would think you don't want to get to Great Bear Lake," she said. Then a horrible thought struck her. "Wait . . . is that it? You don't *want* to arrive?" Her frustration surged up inside her and spilled over. "Toklo, you have Aiyanna waiting for you. Kallik and Yakone, you have each other. But what about me? Once our journey ends, I'll be all alone unless I can find some other bears to settle in with. And our journey *will* end. We can't keep on walking forever!"

For a moment her friends were silent, looking guiltily at one another, and Lusa's heart beat faster. "This could be my only chance of finding other black bears," she said quietly. "How many have we met since . . . since Chenoa? I can't make a home on my own; that's not how black bears live. You have all found someone, a bear of your own kind, *and* a territory to call home. But I haven't, and I can't miss this chance."

Toklo was the first to speak. "I'm sorry, Lusa. You're right. Maybe we have been dragging our paws. But I promised I'd get you to Great Bear Lake in time for the Longest Day, and I'll keep my promise."

"I'm sorry, too," Kallik added. "It's just that I know we'll be splitting up when we get to the lake, and I'm not looking forward to it."

"Me either," Yakone agreed. "Not one bit. But we know

what the gathering means to you, Lusa, and we'll get you there."

Lusa drew a long breath. "Thank you," she said. She felt a wave of sadness well up inside her as she gazed at her friends. She understood why they had been delaying. *I don't want to say good-bye, either.* "Maybe we should let those other bears go on ahead," she added, understanding how precious their remaining time together was for everyone.

Continuing their trek, the bears crossed the shallow valley, heading farther away from the other two brown bears. At the opposite side of the valley they began climbing up to the next ridge, though boulders and patches of loose scree drove them away from the direct route.

Toklo halted, panting, after a particularly hard scramble. "How much longer are we going to be stuck on this spirit-cursed hill?" he demanded to no bear in particular.

I wonder if the brown bears found an easier route, Lusa thought. *Maybe we should have followed them after all.* But she didn't dare say that to Toklo.

At last they struggled up to the ridge and found that they were looking across a stretch of barren ground to a lake. Bushes and a few scrubby trees surrounded it. Islands rose from the water here and there, dark against the glimmering surface, and the far shore was just visible through a haze.

Lusa stared down at it. She hadn't expected to come to the end of their journey quite so soon.

"Is this it?" Yakone asked.

"I think so," Toklo said hesitantly. "It's big enough, and

there are islands dotted all over it."

"There are bear scents everywhere, too," Kallik added, sniffing the air. "But I can't see any bears. Where are they all?"

"Maybe they haven't arrived yet," Yakone suggested.

"Lusa, what do you think?" asked Toklo.

"It's not quite how I remember it," she began, "but it probably looks a little different because we're coming at it from a different direction. Right, Toklo?"

Toklo just grunted and led the way down the slope toward the shore. Lusa's mind whirled as she followed. They had arrived! And yet she didn't feel triumphant or excited or relieved. She felt scared. *What if the other black bears don't want me around? Will I ever find friends as good as Toklo, Kallik, and Yakone?*

The bears crunched over small, sharp stones as they neared the water. The lake was almost completely still, barely rippled by the warm breeze. Suddenly Kallik and Yakone bounded forward and flung themselves into the water. In a spume of white foam, they dove under the surface and vanished for several long moments, emerging farther into the lake with a toss of their heads. Their fur already looked several shades whiter.

Toklo waded into the shallows, head tilted down as he searched for fish swimming around his paws. Lusa watched him for a little while, then splashed into the lake until the water was deep enough for her to swim. Cool water soaked into her fur, and she relished the feeling of dirt washing out of it. She had almost forgotten what it felt like to be clean.

But even though she was enjoying her swim, Lusa began

to feel more and more uneasy. *Something's wrong.* When they had all returned to shore, she could see that the others were troubled, too. Kallik's ears were flat, and Yakone's eyes looked serious.

"Why are there no other bears here?" Kallik asked again.

Forcing the fur on her neck to lie flat, Lusa gazed up and down the shoreline. It was empty in both directions, apart from a few birds pecking near the edge of the waves.

"Maybe they're just not in this part," Toklo said. "We should check farther along."

Lusa took the lead as they padded along the water's edge. Her pawsteps grew more and more urgent as she looked around the lake and searched among the trees for bears and other recognizable signs of Great Bear Lake. But nothing was familiar to her. Lusa couldn't see the stretch of woodland where she had met Miki and the other black bears, and she didn't recognize the pattern of islands. And though she could pick up bear scents, they were all stale, as if bears had paused here briefly and were now long gone. She stared across the lake, letting her ear fur blow in the wind. Whichever direction she looked, nothing fit her memories from the previous Longest Day.

At last she turned to the others. Toklo raised his head, reading the look on Lusa's face. "There's no denying it," he growled. "This is the wrong lake."

CHAPTER TWENTY-TWO

Kallik

Kallik braced herself to keep walking. It was a shock to find they had still more traveling to do. But inwardly she couldn't deny a pang of relief that they hadn't arrived at Great Bear Lake yet.

I'm not ready to say good-bye.

When they set out, Yakone drew up alongside her and leaned close to murmur in her ear. "You'll have to say good-bye soon."

"I know," Kallik responded, grateful that Yakone understood her so well. "But not yet."

"Lots of bears have clearly passed this way," Toklo announced, giving the air a good sniff. "Great Bear Lake must be close."

"If we were birds," Lusa said, sounding discouraged. "Look at the size of this lake! We can't even see the ends of it. And look, Toklo—those hills on the other side . . . didn't we cross them last time to get to Great Bear Lake?"

Toklo squinted into the distance. "You could be right," he grunted. "I didn't notice them before."

"So we need to get to the other side of the lake?" Yakone asked.

Kallik nodded. "It looks like it. But there's nothing to tell us which direction is best to go," she added. "The scents don't help."

"Then let's look for tracks," Lusa suggested. "The bears who passed through here might have known the route better than we do."

All four of the bears walked alongside the lake, spread out from the water's edge to the bottom of the ridge they had crossed earlier. But tracks didn't show up on the pebbly shore and the short, tough grass. The slight traces of other bears they found didn't tell them anything useful.

"This is hopeless," Toklo said, halting at last. "What do we do?"

"Maybe if we wait for dark we can follow the Pathway Star," Yakone suggested.

Kallik dug her claws into the ground in frustration. "But the days are so long!" she objected. "Think of all the time we'll waste."

"I think I remember the Pathway Star is in that direction," Lusa said, pointing with her snout.

Toklo let out a grunt. "Not even close! Look, the sun's over there, and that means the Pathway Star would be . . ." He let his voice trail off, staring up at the sky.

"You're not sure, are you?" Lusa challenged him.

"How about wind direction?" Yakone asked, facing into the breeze that blew off the lake. "Does that help?"

Kallik shook her head. "We've just got to choose a direction and go."

"What if we pick the wrong one?" Toklo snapped.

"Well, there's one way that is definitely the shortest," Kallik retorted, stung. "Across. We can swim."

Lusa's eyes flew wide open in alarm. "It's so far!" she protested.

"It is. But we don't have much time," Toklo reminded her. "The nights are so short now that the Longest Day must be close. Kallik's idea might be best."

"I know it's a long way," Kallik said, hoping to reassure Lusa. "But there are islands all the way across where we can stop and rest. And I'll help you," she added. "We promised to get you to Great Bear Lake, and we *will*."

Lusa nodded glumly. The four bears headed for the shoreline and stood there with the lake water lapping at their paws.

"Look over there," Toklo said, angling his head at the nearest island. "See that rock shaped like a crow's beak? It's easy to spot, so that's where we'll head first."

"Okay," Kallik agreed, newly energized now that they had a plan. "Don't forget that there will be currents. If you feel like you're being swept away, then swim across the flow."

Yakone nodded. "And don't let the cold water bother you," he added. "It'll be colder farther from shore, but it's not cold enough to be dangerous."

Lusa let out a little snort, half-amused and half-frightened. "So says the ice bear!"

Kallik touched Lusa's shoulder with her muzzle. "Swim

close to me," she said. "And if you get tired, tell me right away so I can help you."

"Thanks," Lusa responded.

Kallik took a deep breath, aware that her friends were doing the same. They exchanged determined glances.

"We can do this," Toklo said.

"Sure we can." Yakone nodded confidently.

Together the bears waded into the water and began to swim. The sun was so hot that Kallik reveled in the cool touch of the water slicing through her fur as she headed for the crow's beak rock jutting up from the nearest island. She swam beside Lusa, but the black bear was paddling strongly and didn't need any help.

Just as Yakone said, the water grew colder as they swam farther out, and Kallik felt the tug of a current, but she kept the crow's beak rock in sight, swimming strongly toward it. Glancing back over her shoulder, she saw the shore was already fading behind them.

The waves were growing choppier, and Kallik noticed Lusa spluttering, as if she was tiring. Kallik swam closer to her, but Lusa battled on, churning her legs and holding her muzzle above the water.

"I'm fine!" she gasped.

"It's not far now," Kallik encouraged her, seeing the crow's beak rock looming above her head.

A moment later she felt her paws strike stones. Managing to stand, she gave Lusa a shove forward, until both of them could wade up the island shore, their fur dripping.

"You made it, Lusa!" Kallik exclaimed.

Lusa nodded, too out of breath to speak.

Toklo and Yakone had come ashore together, a few bear-lengths away on the far side of the rock, and they padded over to join Kallik and Lusa.

The island was tiny, with a pebbly shoreline and smooth, grassy slopes leading up to a clump of bushes in the center. There were no tracks, no scents of other bears, and Kallik realized they must be the only ones who'd taken this route.

I hope we made the right decision, she thought with a faint prickle of anxiety.

Toklo shook the last of the water out of his pelt. "I don't know if there's any prey," he panted, "but I'm going to take a look."

"I'll come with you," said Yakone.

The two male bears headed away along the waterline, disappearing after a few moments around a shoulder of the hill. Meanwhile Kallik and Lusa found a sheltered spot underneath the beak-shaped rock.

Lusa's jaws gaped in a massive yawn. "I think I'll take a nap while we wait."

She had barely closed her eyes when Toklo and Yakone reappeared, each carrying a duck.

"They were swimming in an inlet just around that bend," Toklo reported as he dropped his catch. "They had no idea we were creeping up on them."

"That's right," Yakone agreed. "In fact, they hardly had a chance to even know they'd been caught!"

"Nice work," Kallik commented, her jaws beginning to water as Toklo divided up the prey.

Once the bears had eaten, they settled down to sleep for a while. When they awoke, the sun was close to the horizon, casting scarlet light across the surface of the lake.

"We'd better cross to the next island before it gets dark," Toklo warned.

He took the lead as they trekked up the slope, past the clump of bushes in the center of the island and down a steeper incline to the opposite shore. A narrow channel separated their island from the next one.

"That doesn't look too bad," Toklo commented, as he gazed out at the low-lying stretch of land. "It should be an easy swim before night falls."

"There isn't a good landmark to aim for, though," Yakone pointed out. "Do we really want to do this now?"

Kallik gave Lusa a concerned glance.

"I'm fine," Lusa said determinedly, clearly aware of Kallik's anxiety. "I want to keep going."

"Let's go, then," Toklo said, wading out into the water.

As soon as Kallik launched herself into the water, she felt the stronger current. She struck out forcefully, keeping her eyes on Lusa and resisting the pull of the water that threatened to sweep her down the length of the lake.

When she looked back toward the island, cold fear seized her. All she could see was tossing water: the low-lying island had vanished altogether. She couldn't see where she needed to go.

"Kallik! Lusa!"

Yakone's voice rang out across the water. Turning her head, Kallik spotted him and Toklo, their heads close together among the waves.

"This way!" Toklo roared.

Kallik nudged Lusa into the lee of her body, trying to protect her from the current. "Stay close to me," she said, then churned her paws to battle the current and haul herself back in the right direction. But Lusa was struggling. Her strokes were feebler, and Kallik saw her head dip briefly under the water. When she reappeared, she was coughing as if she'd swallowed a chestful of lake.

"Yakone!" Kallik called out. "Lusa needs help!"

Instantly Yakone powered over, speeded by the current, and reached Lusa, who was floundering desperately to keep afloat, her eyes wide with terror. After coming up on the other side of Lusa, he and Kallik supported her with their shoulders as she bobbed in the waves.

"Thanks!" Lusa gasped.

"You'll be fine," Yakone reassured her. "We're almost there."

Kallik wasn't sure that was true because she still couldn't see the island, but Yakone seemed to know which way to go, and Kallik was content to let him lead.

"This way!" Toklo roared again.

Looking up, Kallik realized that the brown bear wasn't swimming anymore, but standing in water up to his shoulders. She and Yakone headed for him, with Lusa between them, and at last Kallik felt her paws scrape against the lake bottom.

She was massively relieved to feel solid ground beneath her paws, though her legs gave way when she first tried to stand up. She took a deep breath and forced herself through the belly-deep water.

Still supporting Lusa between them, Kallik and Yakone waded out of the water and let the little black bear flop onto the shore, where she crouched with her flanks heaving.

Toklo was waiting for them, his fur slick and dark. "Are you okay?" he asked Lusa.

"Fine," Lusa croaked, coughing up a mouthful of water.

By now the sun had sunk out of sight, and the last streaks of red were disappearing as clouds massed on the horizon. The island they'd landed on was nothing more than a narrow spit of gravel, only a paw's width above the waterline. Nothing grew there. To make matters worse, black clouds were gathering around the edges of the sky, and a cold wind had blown up, slapping the water against the pebbly shore. The sharp, bitter taste of rain filled the air.

We can't stay here, Kallik thought. *If a storm blows up, we could be swept away. We need to find shelter.*

"We should keep going," Toklo said, as though he had read her thoughts. He pointed with his snout across a choppy, white-flecked stretch of water to where a far bigger island rose out of the lake. A few trees grew there, surrounded by thick shrubbery. "It's not far to the next island, and we still have a bit of light."

"It looks like a good spot for prey," Yakone remarked,

taking in the island in the distance.

Kallik agreed. "What do you think?" she asked Lusa. "Can you make it that far?"

Lusa staggered to her paws and peered across the water to the other island. "I think so," she said. "I don't want to stay here."

"Come on, then," Toklo urged them, bounding across the strip of land and wading into the water once more. "We should move quickly."

Kallik exchanged a glance with Yakone. She knew she didn't need to tell him to keep a careful eye on Lusa as they followed Toklo and headed toward the next island.

Far from being a relief from the heat of the day, the water felt cold and unwelcoming now. But the shore of the next island was steadily growing nearer.

Then Kallik realized that the ominous black clouds had grown. The waves were growing bigger, too, slapping her in the face. The wind picked up, buffeting her around her head and driving the clouds across the sky. A flash of lightning split the gloom, and thunder bellowed overhead. Before Kallik could call a warning to Lusa, the skies opened and rain lashed down so hard the air seemed full of water.

As the waves rose, Kallik lost sight of the island. Fighting down panic, she caught only fleeting glimpses of her friends as the waves swelled up between them.

"Lusa! Lusa!" she shouted, terrified that the black bear wouldn't be able to cope in the storm-lashed lake. She kept losing sight of her in the chop.

Oh, spirits, help me keep Lusa safe!

She spotted Toklo for a moment, his paws flailing, and Yakone a bearlength away from him, rushing to help. In the next moment a wave crashed down over both of them, and they disappeared.

Kallik let out a roar of panic and anger. Leaving Lusa momentarily, she struggled toward the place where she had last seen them, just as their heads bobbed up again. Toklo was spluttering and cursing, but Yakone was swimming strongly, and in a couple of strokes he was alongside the brown bear, boosting him up.

Kallik immediately turned back to Lusa, but she couldn't see her through the waves. To make matters worse, a swell lifted Kallik, and to her horror she saw that the island they had been heading for was much farther away than when they started. The storm was sweeping them into the center of the lake. Paddling furiously, she reached Yakone's side. "Help me find Lusa!" she bellowed over the shrieking of the wind.

Before Yakone could reply, Kallik caught sight of a huge fish, swimming close to the surface and encircling her, Yakone, and Toklo. *Is it hunting us?* she wondered, fighting back panic. *Is it waiting for us to give up?*

Then a wave brought the fish closer to Kallik, and she saw that its eyes weren't the cold eyes of a fish, but those of a scared brown bear. Its gaze was fixed on them, full of distress.

"Ujurak?" Kallik choked out.

The fish kept on circling, and Ujurak's voice echoed in Kallik's mind. *You shouldn't have tried to swim across the lake!*

With a fresh onset of fear, Kallik realized that it really was the star-bear, but in fish shape he was helpless to rescue them.

"Ujurak, where's Lusa?" Kallik cried. "Please, find—"

Her words were cut off as another wave arched above her head and crashed down on top of her, driving her down into the lake. Kallik thrashed her legs, not sure where the surface was.

I'm drowning. . . .

Something soft and pale bumped up against Kallik, and she realized that Yakone was beside her. Teeth fastened in her shoulder and dragged her upward. Her head broke the surface, and she gulped painfully at the air.

Then she caught sight of the Ujurak-fish again, pushing a small, dark shape through the water toward her. She spotted a single black paw flailing above the surface.

Lusa!

Kallik plunged forward and stretched to grab Lusa by the scruff of her neck. Using all her strength, she heaved the black bear back to the surface of the water. Lusa coughed and choked as she struggled to breathe. Kallik bumped into Yakone, who was supporting Toklo while the terrified brown bear caught his breath.

Great spirits!

The storm raged on. Clouds hid the stars, and the lake water surged around them, black and hungry.

Is this the end? Kallik wondered. *Have we come so far only to die in the wrong lake, so close to the end of our journey?*

CHAPTER TWENTY-THREE

Toklo

Toklo battled to stay afloat, hearing bear spirits screaming all around him. *Or is it only the howling wind and crashing thunder?* He thought he could see Oka and Tobi swimming toward him, but as he struck out to join them, they were lost in the waves. The sky exploded above him, another lightning flash splitting the darkness.

I'm going to drown!

Toklo's limbs ached with exhaustion, and he could hardly summon the strength to keep moving them. Thank goodness for Yakone in the waves beside him, the white bear shoving him upward with his strong shoulder.

"Hang on to me," Yakone rasped to Lusa as Kallik pulled the black bear over to him as well.

Lusa seemed almost helpless to obey, so Kallik hoisted her onto Yakone's back, but the extra weight almost sank him. "Yakone, you can't—" Kallik shrieked.

"I can!" Yakone insisted, the words gasped out. "I'm fine!"

All four bears huddled together, fighting for their lives

against the tumult of wind and water. Toklo had no idea where they were anymore, only that the island they had tried to reach was lost forever in the storm.

Then, to his amazement, a dark shape loomed up ahead amid the towering waves and torrential rain, blacker than the night.

"Another island!" Kallik exclaimed.

But as she spoke, a flash of lightning crackled across the sky. It lit up the vast shape beside them, and they saw that it was not an island, but a swimming firebeast, wallowing to and fro as the waves tossed it. As the lightning faded away, the firebeast lurched toward the bears. Toklo let out a howl of terror, afraid it was attacking them. Suddenly Yakone's shoulder slipped from under Toklo, and he felt the water beneath him start to drag him down, as if a massive fish was trying to suck him in.

The firebeast loomed closer, and from the way it listed sideways in the water, Toklo realized it was drifting aimlessly, pushed by the current of the lake and the wind. It bobbed beside the bears, apparently unaware they were there. Perhaps it wasn't attacking them after all.

Instinctively Toklo fought his way upward through the churning water with all the strength he could muster. Something slapped against his head, and he hit out blindly and found his claws snagged in some kind of vine dangling over the side of the firebeast. Gulping in air, he found that he could grab onto it with his front paws and hang out of reach of the hungry waves.

Toklo saw his friends struggling in the angry water a bear-length away. "Over here!" he called to them. "Come and hold on! I don't think this firebeast wants to hurt us!"

With Kallik and Yakone supporting Lusa between them now, the other bears floundered their way to the side of the firebeast. They crowded around the dangling vine, and Kallik and Yakone managed to grab it with one paw each and still hold on to Lusa, who was limp with exhaustion.

For a few moments they clung there together. Now and again the firebeast would lurch and waves would wash over them, or ram them against the side of the beast, but at least they could breathe and they didn't have to keep fighting the waves.

Toklo was grateful for the respite, but he didn't know how long they could hold on. He was getting colder and colder, more and more exhausted.

An idea flickered in his mind like a star in the black night. "Wouldn't we be safer if we could climb up onto this firebeast?"

Kallik blinked at him through the water streaming down her face. "What if the firebeast realizes we're here? And what about no-claws? There might be some inside its belly."

"We'll drown if we stay here for much longer," Toklo retorted. "It's our only hope."

Yakone nodded. "Toklo's right. We have to risk it."

"I'll go first and check it out," Toklo said.

Not waiting for a reply, he began to climb up the vine. It was tough and strong and the strands were woven together in loops, so he had somewhere to put his paws. He was half-way up when the firebeast lurched, swinging him out over the tossing waves. Toklo heard Kallik cry out from below. He felt his paws slipping and grabbed the vine with his teeth for extra security until the firebeast righted itself, flinging Toklo back against its side with a thump that drove the breath out of his body.

"Seal rot!" Toklo muttered, starting to haul himself upward again.

By the time the next wave came, he was almost at the top of the vine. As the wave crashed over Toklo, he managed to dig in his claws and grip the vine with his teeth again. Now he was able to scramble up onto the firebeast's back. Glancing side to side, he found himself alone, pitching up and down with the firebeast amid the raging water.

Toklo peered over the edge to where his friends were still clinging to the vine. They looked very small and distant among the swollen waves.

"Okay, climb!" he shouted over the noise of the storm. "I don't see any flat-faces!"

Lusa came first. Toklo wondered where she found the strength to heave herself upward, then noticed Kallik right behind her, boosting her up. As the firebeast dove and plunged, he leaned over the side and managed to get a grip on Lusa's scruff, tugging hard to help her up the last bearlength. She was almost a dead weight, too sodden and cold to speak, and barely able to put one paw in front of another. As the next wave hit the firebeast, Toklo nearly lost his grip on her.

No! I will not lose her now!

Then the firebeast steadied itself, Lusa scrabbled with her hindpaws, and Toklo heaved until Lusa collapsed beside him on the firebeast's flat, slippery back. She rolled to one of the firebeast's flanks and lay there unmoving.

"You can't kill us!" Toklo bellowed into the wind and driving rain. Looking down again, he saw Kallik was nearly at the top of the vine herself, and he leaned down again as far as he dared to help her. "If the firebeast tilts, just hang on," he called out to her.

Kallik had more strength left than Lusa, and she scrambled up the vine without much trouble. But another wave struck just as she reached the top, and her claws slipped on the water-logged surface. Toklo lunged for her, sinking his claws into both her shoulders. A horrible vision of her being carried far away from the firebeast by the receding wave flashed through his mind.

"No!" he howled to the water. "You can't have her!"

Kallik's eyes were wide with fear. "I can't hold on!" she panted.

Toklo kept his grip on her, but her weight was dragging at him, and he realized with a pang of pure terror that they were both in danger of plummeting into the ravenous waves. But he didn't let go.

At the last moment the firebeast lurched the other way and, still clinging together, Toklo and Kallik slid away from the edge until they banged against the structure where Lusa was lying.

"Thanks, Toklo," Kallik gasped, then tried to stagger to her paws. "We've got to help Yakone!"

She scrambled to the edge of the firebeast and looked down. Joining her, Toklo saw that Yakone had already begun to climb. But he was in trouble because his injured forepaw couldn't grip the vine tightly, and he kept slipping back down.

"I have to go help him," Kallik panted.

"No!" Toklo grabbed for her, but she was out of reach.

Before Kallik could lower herself down the vine, the firebeast tilted wildly to one side. Lusa began to slide toward the water, and Toklo lurched after her and grabbed her shoulder in his jaws. Then he and Kallik hooked their paws over the edge to stop themselves from falling backward, while the side of the firebeast where Yakone was trying to climb was suddenly almost flat.

"Now, Yakone! Hurry!" Toklo roared.

Paws skidding, Yakone tottered up the side of the firebeast. He reached Toklo and Kallik just in time, before the firebeast rocked back the other way. They gripped him by the shoulders and pulled him to safety.

Yakone flopped down on top of the firebeast and choked up a huge amount of lake water. His injured paw was scarlet with blood, and there was a patch of missing fur on his flank where he had been thrown against the side and it had torn on something.

But at least he's alive, Toklo thought. *We're all alive. There don't seem to be any flat-faces here, and the firebeast hasn't tried to eat us—yet.*

Now that they were up there, being on the firebeast hardly

seemed safer than being in the water. Rain and wind still lashed them, the thunder boomed around them like massive rocks thrown around the sky, and lightning ripped from one horizon to the other. The firebeast lurched and heaved, its back slick with water. Toklo and the others had to cling to whatever they could. Lusa was dazed, barely conscious, and Toklo held her scruff in his teeth, terrified that she wouldn't be able to hold on herself. Every wave that crashed over them dragged them to the edge, threatening to sweep them back into the storm-tossed lake. Toklo was terrified that sooner or later one of them would be swept away and never seen again.

Is this how our journey will end?

The sky grew lighter as the short night passed, but the storm kept on, as fierce as ever. All around them was a waste of gray water. Sometimes Toklo thought he could glimpse a darker gray blur of land in the distance, but he couldn't be sure, and even if it was land, it was too far away for them to swim.

Then he heard another sound, a harsh screaming that seemed to come from the depths of the firebeast itself. To his horror he saw a gap suddenly zigzag across the top of the firebeast, a dark line stretching from one side to the other.

Yakone saw it, too. "It's breaking up!" he barked.

Toklo briefly let go of Lusa and pulled Kallik and Yakone close, desperate for all of them to stay together. But when he reached for Lusa again, she had slid onto the other side of the slowly widening gap.

"Lusa!" he roared.

The black bear looked up, blinking, but she obviously had no idea what was going on. Toklo had a vision of her tossed away, lost to them, as the firebeast broke into pieces. With the screams of the dying firebeast battering his ears, he leaped across the gap and staggered through the lashing rain to Lusa's side.

"Get up!" he ordered her, shoving her to her paws. "You have to move. We need to be over there with Kallik and Yakone."

"Lusa!" yelled Kallik. "Come to us!"

"We'll help you!" Yakone roared.

Numb but obedient, Lusa scrabbled across the slanting top of the firebeast. She let out a squeal of panic when she saw the gaping crack between her and her friends. Toklo gave her a boost from behind while Kallik and Yakone reached for her, gripping her with claws and teeth to help her across. Once he was sure she was safely on the other side, Toklo followed, bracing himself for a massive leap over the yawning gap. He landed well clear of the edge, colliding with Yakone as the firebeast tilted again.

The bears clung together, overwhelmed with horror and deafened by the screeching of the firebeast as the two halves of it pulled slowly, hideously apart.

"No!" Toklo howled.

Water surged up to meet them, and Toklo found himself struggling to swim again. The bones of the firebeast splintered around him before scattering in all directions, tossed on the white-crested waves. Toklo looked frantically around for his friends, but they had vanished. The tumult of sky and water surrounded him, pitching him this way and that until he sank down and down, and knew nothing more.

CHAPTER TWENTY-FOUR

Lusa

Lusa opened her eyes, blinking in the sunlight. Gentle waves rippled around her, rolling pieces of wood onto the sandy shore. The storm had passed, and a weak sun shone overhead through a thin covering of cloud.

I didn't drown . . . Lusa thought muzzily. *I can't believe it. . . . Was it all a dream?* She remembered the storm, the lashing waves, and how they clambered onto the firebeast to save themselves. *Oh, spirits, then the firebeast broke up! Where are the others?*

Lusa scrambled up, every muscle in her body shrieking in protest, and coughed up several mouthfuls of water. She felt battered and too exhausted to take a single pawstep, but she knew she had to find her friends. Gazing around her, Lusa saw that the lake lay eerily peaceful, perfectly blue in the sun. It was hard to believe in the fury of the night before. The shore was littered with branches and scraps of flat-face stuff that Lusa guessed had come from the shattered firebeast. Apart from the soft waves, nothing moved as far as she could see.

Fear swelling inside her, Lusa limped along the shore,

pushing aside lumps of broken wood and sniffing through churned-up weeds from the bottom of the lake. As the moments dragged by, her search became more desperate.

"Toklo! Kallik! Yakone!" she called desperately, but there was no answer.

I can't be the only one who survived . . . I can't be!

Then Lusa spotted what looked like a brown-and-white boulder lying on the beach at the water's edge. As she drew closer, she realized it was Toklo and Yakone, slumped together in a heap of two-colored fur. Neither of them moved.

"Toklo! Yakone!" Lusa shrieked, racing up to them and prodding them frantically with her snout. "Wake up!"

Relief crashed over her as Toklo began to stir. He let out a confused grunt, then wriggled out from underneath Yakone.

"Lusa," he rasped. "You're okay?"

"I feel like a firebeast ran over me," Lusa choked, almost overcome with emotion. "But I'm all right."

By this time Yakone was rousing, too. He blundered to his paws with a yelp of pain.

"Where's Kallik?" he barked, looking around.

As if in answer, a faint cry sounded from farther along the beach. Lusa spun around to spot Kallik tottering toward them.

"There she is!" Lusa shouted. "We made it—all of us!"

As Kallik joined them, the bears pressed themselves together, nuzzling with heads and noses as if they couldn't believe that they were all together again. Lusa couldn't get close enough to her friends. Even though she was bruised, exhausted, and waterlogged, she didn't think she had ever felt happier or more relieved. She could see the same joy shining in the others' eyes.

"I've never been so scared in my life," Kallik said quietly, stepping back to look at her friends.

"Me either," Toklo agreed. "And where was Ujurak when we needed him?"

"He was there!" Kallik protested, her eyes widening. "I saw him in the shape of a fish. He pushed Lusa over to me when I couldn't find her."

Lusa nodded as the memory returned, the flash of silver scales in the darkness. "I saw him, too."

"There was so much pain in his eyes," Kallik added. "Pain that he couldn't save us. It was terrible for Ujurak, too. But now it's over."

"That's not all," Toklo added. He took a pace back to check the position of the sun. "Look where we are. We're on the far side of the lake, right where we wanted to be."

"Thank the spirits!" Lusa exclaimed. "I couldn't go through all that again."

A strong fishy smell surged into her nostrils. Following the scent around a rock, Lusa noticed that this part of the shoreline was strewn with fish that had been pushed into a narrow inlet and washed up in the storm. "Look at this!" she called to the others. "Food!"

Lusa and Kallik collected some of the fish, while Toklo and Yakone scouted around and found a sheltered spot in a grassy hollow above the beach.

There was more than enough fish for all of them, and

Lusa's belly was stuffed full for the first time in days. "Do we have to leave yet?" she asked drowsily.

"No, we all need to rest." Toklo gave a massive yawn. "We'll get going again when we're ready."

"If you're sure there's time," Yakone said. "We don't know how close we are to the Longest Day."

"Ujurak was with us in the storm," Kallik reminded him. "He's still helping us to reach Great Bear Lake in time."

"You're right." Yakone flopped down beside her. "Let's sleep."

Lusa woke at twilight and saw Arcturus right above her, shining more brightly than any other star. Joy thrilled through her from snout to paws. *We're almost there!*

Unable to contain her excitement, she roused her sleeping companions with sharp prods in the ribs. They staggered drowsily to their paws, becoming quickly more alert as Lusa pointed up at the stars. Ujurak's star-shape sparkled down at them, and it felt like he was reassuring them that he would be with them until the very last pawstep.

Lusa thought again how Ujurak had helped her when she was struggling in the lake. "Thank you, Ujurak," she whispered. "I know you're watching over us."

The bears ate more of the stranded fish, then set off again, traveling through the brief night. It was never fully dark; there was a glow on the horizon the entire time, as if the sun had only just barely dipped below it. The ground had been washed clean by the rain and was squishy underpaw with little streams gurgling through it, which made for easy walking. The air was cool and clean, soothing Lusa's aching muscles.

As dawn approached, Lusa began to hear voices from somewhere in the distance. At first she thought she was imagining things, but when the daylight strengthened she was able to make out a group of black bears—two adults and three cubs—traveling a little way ahead.

"Look!" she whispered. "Black bears!"

She glanced at Toklo, who gave her a nod. "We're nearly there, Lusa. It's time to join the other bears."

Lusa hesitated, glancing uncertainly at Kallik and Yakone. Yakone gave her a friendly nod, while Kallik prodded her gently in the shoulder and said, "Go for it!"

Breaking into a run, Lusa caught up to the group of black bears. As she galloped up, they stopped and turned toward her. Lusa didn't recognize any of them from the gathering the suncircle before, and for a moment she was daunted by the sight of so many bears who looked just like her. *They seem so small!* she thought, then reminded herself that they were the same size as her, just much smaller than the companions she was used to.

"Hi!" said Lusa.

"Hello," the male bear said.

"I'm Lusa. I'm on my way to Great Bear Lake."

"So are we," the male bear told her. He sounded friendly, though there was surprise in his voice as he added, "You're not traveling alone, are you?"

"Oh, no, I'm with my friends," Lusa told him, pointing with

her snout to where Toklo, Kallik, and Yakone were making their way toward them.

Exclamations of shock came from the black bears, and the cubs huddled together, gazing warily at the white and brown bears.

"Those are white bears and a grizzly," the male bear said, his eyes narrowing in suspicion. "Why are you traveling with them? Where did you meet?"

"They aren't dangerous!" Lusa retorted, annoyed by the male bear's abrupt questions. "I came to the last Longest Day Gathering with two of them." Dipping her head to the cubs, she added more gently, "There's nothing to be scared of."

As she spoke, the cubs peeped out from behind their mother. The youngest gave an excited little bounce. "Oh, wow, you've been to Great Bear Lake before? That's so cool! Tell me about it."

A slightly bigger male bear let out an exaggerated sigh. "Why can't you wait till we get there?" He rolled his eyes at Lusa. "Ignore her. She's always pestering us."

"Right," said a third cub. "She never stops talking!"

Lusa felt a moment of sympathy for the young she-cub. "Well," she began, speaking to the little one, "there are lots and lots of bears there, black, and white, and brown, as many bears as there are trees in the forest."

"Really?" the little cub squeaked. "I didn't think there were that many bears in the whole world."

"You'll see them soon," Lusa promised. Turning to the adult bears, she asked, "When you were there before, did you meet a black bear cub named Miki, or his family?"

The adult bears shook their heads.

"I don't know that name," the mother bear replied. "But like you say, there are so many bears there."

Lusa knew it was a long shot, but still, she felt a stab of disappointment. *I don't even know if Miki will be there this time.*

The black bears started to walk again and Lusa walked with them, while the cubs plied her with more questions about the gathering. Kallik, Yakone, and Toklo followed a few bearlengths behind. Lusa knew they wanted to give her some time alone with the other bears. As the sun rose higher in the sky, a small copse appeared on the horizon. Drawing closer, Lusa could see thick undergrowth beneath the trees, and welcoming shade from the worst of the heat.

"We always stop here on our way to Great Bear Lake," the male bear told Lusa. "There's just one more sunrise of walking to get there, so this is our last chance to rest peacefully."

"I see berry bushes!" one of the older cubs announced. He and his brother raced for the trees, with their sister scurrying behind them.

"You're welcome to come eat berries with us," the mother bear invited.

Lusa glanced back at her friends, who were watching from a respectful distance, giving her some space. *If we're so close to our journey's end, then I want to spend the rest of the time with them.* "No, thank you," she replied. "I'm not hungry right now. Maybe I'll see you at the gathering!"

"Yes, I hope so," answered the mother bear.

Lusa watched as the black bears disappeared into the shade of the trees, making faint grunts of pleasure as they found the berry bushes. Lusa turned and padded over to her friends. Kallik dipped her head to give Lusa a gentle lick around the ears, while Toklo nudged her shoulder. Yakone gave her a friendly nuzzle on top of her head.

Lusa closed her eyes with a mixture of relief and sadness. This was where she belonged for now. Tomorrow they would reach the end of their journey. *And I'll arrive at Great Bear Lake with the bears who have traveled with me from the beginning.*

CHAPTER TWENTY-FIVE

Kallik

Will Taqqiq be at the lake? Kallik asked herself. Excitement built up inside her as she and her friends continued their trek, leaving the black bears behind. More trees and bushes appeared as they padded on, and now—with the sun at its highest point—every leaf and twig glistened from the recent rain.

Kallik knew that if she and Yakone continued to Star Island, she would end up very far away from her brother. *Whatever else has happened, Taqqiq and I are still bonded through Nisa. I hope I can see him one more time before I start my new life.*

Kallik was pulled from her thoughts as Toklo, who had been leading the way, stopped and looked back.

"Let's hunt," he barked. "There's a group of trees over there that looks promising."

Kallik saw a large clump of trees growing closely together, the ground beneath them filled with dense undergrowth. Her belly growled as she headed toward it, and her jaws started to water at the thought of prey.

"Can I hunt with you?" Lusa asked as they drew closer to the trees.

"Of course," Kallik replied. She was surprised that Lusa wanted to hunt when there were berry bushes beneath the trees, red berries shining temptingly among the leaves. Then Kallik realized this might be their last hunt together before they reached Great Bear Lake.

Of course Lusa wants to share it with us.

The bears plunged into the copse, trying to tread silently through the clumps of ferns and bramble thickets. Kallik was the first to spot prey, a grouse squatting in the shadows of a juniper bush. She crept over to it with Lusa stalking quietly up from another direction, in case the grouse tried to break out that way. But it was Kallik who reached it first and leaped on top of the bird as it tried to fly off. She snapped its neck cleanly with one paw.

Picking up the grouse, Kallik padded over to Toklo and laid it down at his paws. "This is for you," she said, dipping her head solemnly, feeling the need to give him the first catch from their last shared hunt. *We've looked out for each other for so long. . . .*

Seeming to understand, Toklo dipped his head in return and kicked fallen leaves over the grouse until they were ready to carry it away. As they headed farther into the trees, Toklo stopped to sniff the air, his ears pricked alertly. Kallik heard a scuffling sound from the debris underneath a tree and picked up the scent of a ground squirrel.

Toklo slunk forward, crouching close to the ground, while

Kallik and the others spread out silently in a wide circle. The ground squirrel must have sensed them, for it popped up into view, darting frightened glances all around. Yakone let out a low growl, and the squirrel fled away from him, right into Toklo's paws. Toklo sank his claws into it, and the creature let out a thin shriek that was cut off as it went limp.

This time Toklo picked up his prey and carried it over to Kallik and Yakone. "This is for you," he told them, repeating Kallik's words with the same solemn bow of his head.

Yakone looked around, his ears pricked. There was a bush not far away with scarlet berries hanging from the branches. Yakone padded over, broke off a laden twig, and carried it in his mouth to Lusa. He laid it at her paws, the berries looking like drops of blood on the dusty ground. "This is for you," he murmured.

Kallik's throat felt too choked up to reply. The exchange of prey had proven how much they cared about one another, and the debt that they owed one another for their survival on this long and often terrifying journey.

Lusa clearly felt it, too, her dark eyes bright with emotion. "Thank you, Yakone," she whispered.

But all this will end soon, Kallik thought, fighting with sadness.

Dusk was falling, and the bears found a comfortable spot in a hollow between two trees where they settled down to share their prey. The Pathway Star glimmered above them, pointing them toward the very end of their journey.

As they ate in the silver-gray light of evening, Kallik noticed some movement just beyond the hollow. Turning her head, she saw a shadowy brown bear pad up to join them. It sat just outside the circle, silent and barely there, but sharing with them the last day of their journey.

"Ujurak!" Kallik exclaimed.

Toklo caught her eye and nodded, while Lusa let out a murmur of delight.

Yakone leaned closer to Kallik. "I see him, too!" he whispered. "He deserves to be here. I wish I'd known him before . . . before he left."

Kallik blinked lovingly at the white bear. She couldn't put into words how much it meant to her that Yakone believed in the star-bear's friendship. "We will never forget him," she promised.

Kallik woke in a warm huddle of bears: brown, white, and black. Dawn light trickled through the trees and traced a shifting pattern on their pelts. Kallik could spot patches of blue sky among the branches, but the day was cool, with a fresh breeze whispering through the leaves.

Her three friends were asleep. Kallik lay still for a moment, listening to their soft breathing, trying to capture the whirl of emotions that swept through her.

This could be the last time we wake up together. . . .

Memories flickered through her mind of all the places they had been, and all the adventures they had shared. *Rescuing Ujurak from the healing den . . . stampeding the caribou to save the wild . . . watching the spirits dance in the sky.* She remembered their grief when Ujurak died, and their wonder when he turned into blazing stars and rose into the sky beside his mother. *Riding the firesnake . . . chasing the wolves away . . . and now we're here, and it's almost over.*

But Kallik didn't only look back. She was full of wild hopes for the future, too. Hopes of meeting Taqqiq again at Great Bear Lake, of finding a home where she could spend the rest of her life with Yakone. Above everything, she felt an immeasurably deep gratitude for the three bears who had been her best friends, her family, her guiding stars, for so long. And for Ujurak, who had saved them more times than she could count, and who had never let them down.

The light was brighter by the time the other bears stirred and rose to their paws. The distant sound of bear voices reached them on the breeze. Toklo pricked his ears, his gaze traveling around the other bears. Anticipation and dread mingled in his glance. "Ujurak, I guess I'll find out what you meant soon," he muttered.

Kallik didn't understand what he was talking about, but she suspected she wasn't supposed to have heard. Ignoring the puzzling words, she gave Toklo a nod. There was no need to say anything. *We all know this is it.*

Toklo took the lead as the bears set off, but when they emerged from the trees, they walked a little more closely than usual, their pelts brushing, their paces matched evenly. The land in front of them rose in a smooth, gentle slope. The bears padded in silence until they reached the top of the hill. Kallik caught her breath when she saw what lay beyond.

Great Bear Lake spread out in front of them, a silver

expanse that seemed to stretch on forever, dotted with the dark shapes of islands. There were bears everywhere, black, white, and brown, clustering close to the water's edge or shuffling through the surrounding woodland or among the rocks. The vast stretch of water glittered in the sunlight, with bears of all colors splashing at the edges. Beyond the lake, the horizon burned with the heat of the lengthening days.

Kallik let out a deep sigh. "We made it!"

Warriors: The New Prophecy

Follow the next generation of heroic cats as they set off
on a quest to save the Clans from destruction.

Warriors: Power of Three

Firestar's grandchildren begin their training as warrior cats.
Prophecy foretells that they will hold more power than any cats before them.

Warriors: Omen of the Stars

Which ThunderClan apprentice will complete the prophecy that
foretells that three Clanmates hold the future of the Clans in their paws?

Warrior Cats Come to Life in Manga!